A BLACK HEARTS STILL BEAT STORY

RIOT

l. a. cotton

USA TODAY AND WALL STREET JOURNAL BESTSELLING AUTHOR

RIOT

A Black Hearts Still Beat Story

L A COTTON

Published by Delesty Books

RIOT
A Black Heart Still Beats Story

Edited by Andie M Long Editing Services
Cover by Opulent Design

CHAPTER ONE

MOLLY

"Okay, this is your ID badge." Letty Panem handed me a lanyard. "Keep it on you at all times."

"Got it." I slipped it over my head and took a deep, calming breath.

"You good? she asked.

"Fine." The fake smile I wore was a total contradiction to my words, but I didn't want her sympathy.

Or her questions.

This—going on tour with one of the world's hottest rock bands—was my chance at a fresh start.

One I desperately needed.

Besides, it meant I got to tour Europe with my best friend in the whole world.

Who wouldn't leap at the chance to do that?

Evangeline Star Walker was my ride or die. My best friend since we were just little kids. We'd grown up in the small town of Lyme, Tennessee, and I didn't have a single good memory that didn't include her.

But Eva wasn't small town anymore. She was America's newest country music sweetheart. And I was proud of her. So damn proud.

When I'd entered her into the Jamesboro Talent Showdown almost a year ago, I'd never imagined that we would be here now; about to embark on a world tour with Black Hearts Still Beat, her boyfriend's band.

That's right. My best friend hadn't only found herself, she'd found love. The once in a lifetime kind. The kind of love people told stories about.

I was happy for her, so freaking happy.

Even if it hurt.

Even if it was a constant reminder that I would never find what she had. Because I was tainted.

Damaged.

I was broken and I wasn't sure I would ever heal.

———

"Hi, Mom," I clutched the cell phone in my hand, forcing myself to take a deep breath.

I did that a lot lately.

Breathed deep, as if every day was a battle.

"Molly, oh, thank goodness, sweetheart. I've been worried sick."

Dread curled into my stomach as I said, "Sorry, I... I just needed some time."

"I know, baby. I know. Breakups are hard. And Carson,

he was such a nice guy. It's such a shame. I really thought—"

"Don't." A violent shudder rolled through me as I swallowed over the giant lump in my throat. "I... I can't—"

"When are you comin' home, Mol. I need you."

"Listen, Mom, I need some time—"

"Time? What the hell is that supposed to mean? You've been gone almost two weeks. I thought—"

"I'm not comin' home, Mom." I blurted out the words that I'd been putting off for days. "They offered me a job, and I said yes. I leave with Eva and the band tomorrow."

"What do you mean, you're not comin' home?" she shrieked down the phone. "You can't just leave. What will I do? The twins... what will I tell them?"

Guilt rose inside me, crashing over me like a tidal wave. Silas and Timmy were everything to me.

Everything.

I'd helped raise them, after all. But things were different now.

I was different.

And I couldn't go back to Lyme, I just couldn't.

Not yet.

"I'm sorry. I am, Mom. But this is somethin' I need to do. Tell them I love them, and I'll see them soon, okay?"

"See them when, Mol? You can't just decide to take off. I need you. They need you."

Her words should have comforted me, made me feel all warm and fuzzy inside. But my mom meant she needed me to be there to watch the boys and pick up her slack.

The tears I'd fought so hard to contain burst free and rolled down my cheeks. "I'm sorry. I just... I can't..."

"Molly Ann Steinberg, you listen to me and listen good. I know it hurts. I know breakups are hard. But you have responsibilities, young lady. You can't just abandon them. Abandon me. Not when I need..."

Blood roared between my ears, drowning out her tirade of how selfish I was.

She didn't understand...

She didn't *know*.

And I could never tell her. I could never do that to her. To myself.

We were at an impasse. A standoff that might well be the final crack in our relationship. But I could live with her hating me, dubbing me a childish, selfish person. What I couldn't live with was ruining her—ruining us.

Mom would find a way to muddle through... and me? Well, I hoped to find my way back to myself.

The girl I used to be *before*.

———

"Hey you." Eva joined me at the window overlooking one of the runways at Hartsfield-Jackson. The band and their management team were sequestered away in the VIP lounge, waiting to board our flight to Paris.

It should have been one of the most exciting times of my life, but the sparkle inside me had all but flickered out in the aftermath of Carson Dutton. Now I was going through the motions.

Eva laced her arm through mine and laid her head on

my shoulder. "I know you don't want to talk about it, but I just want you to know that when you're ready, I'm here. I'll always be here."

"I'm fine."

"Please, stop sayin' that." She let out an exasperated breath. "You're not fine. Not by a long shot. And that's okay. Whatever you're goin' through—"

"Stop." I pulled my arm free, stepping away slightly. "Please, babe, just stop." Tears burned the backs of my eyes, but I refused to let them fall.

The sympathy in Eva's concerned gaze was almost too much to bear.

"I need this job, Eva. I need a fresh start. But you need to stop lookin' at me like I'm one second away from a breakdown. I'm fine. I'll be fine." Glancing away, I inhaled a shuddering breath.

"Okay," she whispered. "I'm sorry. I won't push."

When I met her gaze again, a bright smile was pasted on her face. "Are you excited about the trip?"

"Who wouldn't be?" I returned it the best I could, even if it did feel fake and all wrong.

"Paris, Mol. It's Paris." She beamed. "I hope we get some time to explore."

"Don't get your hopes up." Letty had shared the schedule with me and it was intense. A new city every other day. But that was a good thing. If I was busy, if I kept moving, I didn't have time to think.

"Yeah, it's goin' to be a lot. But we'll find some free time. We have to. It's the trip of a lifetime."

"What are you two ladies talking about?" Eva's

boyfriend Rafe slid his arms around her waist and dropped his chin to her shoulder.

"Eva's hopin' to see some of Paris," I said.

"We'll find time." He kissed her cheek. "How you holding up?" he asked me, and I frowned.

"I'm fine."

"Have you talked to Hudson?"

That name clanged through me like a physical blow to my body.

"No. Why would I?"

Rafe shrugged. "After Long Island, I just thought…"

"Nothing happened." The defensive edge to my words made Eva flinch and she quietly warned Rafe to leave it.

"The next few weeks should be fun," he murmured, but I pretended not to hear him.

Then *he* walked into the lounge.

Hudson Ryker, drummer for Black Hearts Still Beat, and the band's resident heartbreaker.

Our eyes collided and I saw the hundred silent questions written all over his expression.

Was I okay?

Did I need anything?

Why had I pushed him away?

Before he saw the answers in my eyes, I dropped my eyes, breaking the connection.

Since that night two weeks ago when I'd turned up outside the club where Eva and the band were celebrating, Hudson hadn't let me out of his sight.

· · ·

"My name is Molly Steinberg. I'm Eva Walker's best friend. If you'd just go inside and ask—"

The big, muscly doorman shot me a toothy grin. "And I'm Levi Hunter's best bud, sweetheart."

"Seriously." I let out an exasperated sigh, digging my wallet out of my overnight bag. "Here, see. Photos, of me and Eva." I opened it to the clear pocket and thrust the damn thing in his face. "I've known her my whole life."

"Not my problem, sweetheart. Party is invite only and your name isn't on the list."

"Sonofa—" He waved me off, giving me his back. I pulled up Eva's name and hit call again. "Answer. Come on, Eva, pick up."

When she didn't answer, I tried her assistant Letty again. But she wasn't answering either.

Goddamn it.

I had to get inside.

I'd come all this way. I just needed... I really needed my best friend.

Panic swelled inside me, making my pulse speed up. What if they didn't let me inside and I missed them leave? Where would I go? What the hell would I do?

Tears streaked down my face. When I'd fled Lyme, I hadn't anticipated... this. I hadn't really been thinking much at all except forgetting away from there. Of course they wouldn't just let me in. Eva was a big star now. She had security and an entourage and fans.

And I had...

"Oh my God, there he is," someone yelled. "Hudson, Hudson over here. I love you, oh my God! Hudson, I love you."

The commotion behind me drew my attention and I turned to find a group of scantily clad girls all screaming and pointing at...

Hudson Ryker, one fourth of Black Hearts Still Beat, and the guy I'd spent many a night fantasizing about.

Shit. I swiped at my eyes, trying to dry them quickly. This was so not how I wanted to see him again. He was one of Eva's boyfriend's best friends. A rock star. A freaking world famous idol.

And for a brief moment in time, he had been mine.

I inched backward, suddenly regretting coming here. I needed Eva, God, I needed her more than anything. But I'd underestimated what seeing Hudson again would do to me.

I turned to leave, to get a cab and hightail it back to some shitty motel. I could call and connect with Eva tomorrow. Yeah, that seemed—

"Molly?"

My heart stopped dead.

"Mol?"

Sniffling, I turned slowly and met Hudson's clouded expression.

"What are you—" His whole demeanor changed, his eyes narrowing. "What the fuck happened?"

"I-I..." I stammered. "I..." The emotional storm raging inside me spilled over and an ugly sob escaped my lips.

Hudson shoved past his bodyguards and dropped to his knees before me. "Molly, what is it? What's—"

"Mol?" Eva appeared, barging through the crush to reach me. "What happened? What are you doin' here?"

Tears slid down my cheeks as sheer relief filled me. She was here.

Eva was here.

"I-I... I got here and then security wouldn't let me in. I-I... I waited."

Out of the corner of my eye, I saw Hudson leap up and lunge for the doorman, knocking his big body into the wall. "You wouldn't let her in? Are you a fucking idiot? That's Molly… It's—"

"Hud." His bandmates Rafe and Damon yanked him back, directing him to one of the cars, and Letty jumped into action, checking the man over.

"Molly?" Eva touched my arm, bringing my attention back to her. "What is it? What's wrong?"

And then I said eight little words I never thought I'd ever say.

"Can I stay with you for a while?"

SHAKING the memory out of my head, I risked peeking back over to where Hudson was standing with Damon and Levi at the bar. He didn't look back at me. Not that I blamed him.

For the last two weeks, he'd shielded me from the world, from the questions everyone had about my sudden arrival.

But the band's vacation was over. The first leg of their *Blood Runs Thicker* world tour started today and if I was going to be a part of it; if I was going to leave Lyme behind and chase a fresh start, I couldn't hide behind Hudson Ryker anymore.

CHAPTER TWO

HUDSON

"THIS BEATS the tour bus any day of the week." Damon grinned as he stretched out in his first-class seat.

We'd boarded the plane twenty minutes ago. Next stop, Paris.

There were days when I still couldn't believe this was my life. The sold-out arenas. Hit records. The fans. Fuck, the fans were something else. Life with the band had been nothing but one big party for the last two years.

But this—the world tour we were about to embark on —was something else.

So why the fuck didn't I feel excited about it?

I scanned the cabin, rolling my eyes at Levi and his girl Phoebe whispering sweet nothings like they weren't surrounded by the rest of us. But I guess I needed to cut him some slack. They'd had it rough, and for a minute there, none of us were sure the two of them would work things out. Life with a rock star was hard. But life with a rock star with a serious substance abuse issue and enough emotional baggage to fill the plane we were sitting on... well, that required the love of a strong woman.

I was happy for them. The same way I was happy for Rafe and Eva. But watching them was a double-edged sword. One that often felt impaled through my chest. Right through my fucking heart.

I didn't want to fall in love. Love made you weak. It made you fucking crazy. Besides, touring, never staying in one place for more than a couple of nights, it made it too easy to take what the groupies were offering, and too damn difficult to put down roots.

Rafe and Levi got lucky.

I wasn't about to pin my hopes on the same fortune.

"So, what's going on there?" Damon flicked his eyes to the front of the cabin where Letty and Molly sat, poring over our schedule for the next six months.

"Nothing." I let out a heavy sigh and flagged down a stewardess. "Whiskey on the rocks. And keep 'em coming."

"Of course, Mr. Ryker." A knowing smile played on her lips, and I internally groaned.

She was a fan.

Of course she fucking was.

"But in Long Island the two of you—"

"Leave it, yeah, D." I groaned, reclining my seat.

"So you're not—"

I shot him a cold glare and he held up his hands. "Fine. Shutting up."

"Here you go, Mr. Ryker. If you need anything else,"

she said, flashing me a seductive smile, "don't hesitate to ask."

"Jesus," Damon mumbled. "She might as well have offered to sink to her knees and blow you right here."

"Jealous?" I quipped, because that was me. The joker. The sarcastic one. The one who hid behind innuendo and indifference.

"Have at her." He shrugged. "Although, I'm not sure Mol—"

"There's nothing going on between me and Molly, so drop the fucking subject." I drained my glass and closed my eyes. Pushing all thoughts of Molly Steinberg out of my head.

It was going to be a long fucking tour.

MY EYES FLICKERED OPEN, my skull pounding from all the whiskey I'd drank. The quiet cabin was bathed in a blue-tinged luminescent glow, everyone sleeping as the plane glided through the inky sky outside.

I glanced at Damon, smirking at his sleeping form. He'd always been the dad of the group. The one who kept us all in check. A constant voice of reason, even when me and Levi were too fucked up to listen.

Not anymore, I thought to myself. Levi was a changed man. Sure, he was still our tortured, formidable front man, but since he and Phoebe had figured out their shit, he was a lot calmer.

I raked a hand over my face, exhaling a steady breath.

Everyone was asleep. Even Letty, which was a surprise

given how hard she worked for us and the label. Everyone probably knew this would be the last proper rest we got before the roller coaster started again.

The arena tour across the US had been nonstop. But a world stadium tour... I still couldn't wrap my head around it.

Here we were, barely twenty years old, about to embark on a world fucking tour. It was a life guys like me could usually only dream of.

"N-no," someone murmured upfront. "No... please, no."

Ice trickled through my veins as I realized who was dreaming. Quietly, I slipped out of my seat and made my way down the aisle toward Letty and Molly.

She murmured something again, her expression drawn as she ran from whatever monsters chased her in her dreams.

"Mol," I whispered. "Wake up."

"No... please." The pain coating her words made my stomach drop.

She began thrashing in her big leather seat, fighting some invisible monster.

"Molly girl, you're dreaming. It's just a dream." I touched her arm, and her eyes flew open.

"H-Hudson?" Her eyes immediately dropped to where I was touching her, and I snatched my hand away.

"You were dreaming," I said flatly, trying to calm myself the fuck down.

I'd witnessed this before, while we were in Long Island.

When I'd walked out of The Riff Bar that night and

seen Molly standing there, tears streaking down her face, I knew... I knew something bad had happened. She'd always been this firecracker: a sassy, no-holds-barred kind of girl who wasn't afraid to say what she was thinking. But that night, she was... lost.

We had history. Not the kind of history Eva and Rafe had before they finally gave in to their connection. They were made for each other. But Molly Steinberg and me were two magnets who rubbed the wrong way.

We'd hooked up during the talent contest where the band had first met Eva. And there had been a handful of times since. But Molly knew the score. She knew I wasn't looking to settle, and she had responsibilities back home.

The sex was good, better than good; it was fucking fire. But I wasn't Rafe. I didn't have a heart to hand over to anyone. I couldn't offer her... *that*. And I'd never given her the impression I could.

Something had changed between us in Long Island. She was skittish, quiet and withdrawn. It didn't take a fucking genius to work out whatever had gone down with Carson—the guy she'd been dating back in Lyme—was bad, but she wouldn't talk about it. And I knew all about wanting to keep your secrets, so I didn't push.

"I was?" The blood drained from her face. "I... what did I say?"

My brow arched at that. "Want to talk about it?"

"N-no. I'm fine."

My teeth ground together. She wasn't fine. She was beyond being not fucking fine, but she'd made it perfectly clear that she didn't want mine or anyone else's help.

"I need to use the bathroom. Excuse me." She stared up at me with those big brown eyes.

"Uh, yeah. Sure." I backed up, giving her space. Unable to do anything but watch as she slipped out of her seat and hurried toward the bathroom nestled away behind the curtain.

"Hud?" another voice said, and I glanced back to find Eva frowning. "What's wrong?"

"She was dreaming."

From the look on Eva's face, I knew she understood I didn't mean a good dream.

"I'll go check on her." She pushed the thin blanket off her shoulders. Rafe stirred, but quickly settled when she leaned over and kissed his brow, whispering something to him.

A sharp tug pulled at my chest. I wasn't cut out for what they had, but it didn't stop me from wondering sometimes.

"Try and get some rest." She squeezed my arm as she passed me.

"Yeah."

But as I went back to my seat, I knew sleep wouldn't find me again. Not without something stronger to push me into oblivion. And the last thing the band needed was another self-medicating asshole to contend with.

———

BY THE TIME we touched down in Paris, I was as cranky as fuck. My head still hurt from all the whiskey, my neck ached from sleeping funny, and I couldn't get the sound of Molly crying out in her sleep out of my fucking head.

"Paris, can you believe it?" Letty grinned at me as we were ushered off the plane and into the connecting bridge. Our security detail stuck close by, herding us like animals as we headed for customs.

"Holy shit, this is insane," Levi drawled, nudging my arm. Phoebe smiled up at him, snagging his attention and the two of them moved on ahead of me.

I muttered under my breath.

I liked Phoebe, and I loved Eva like a sister, but this new dynamic was going to take some getting used to.

Between Letty, Eva, Phoebe, and Molly, we were almost outnumbered. Thankfully, Damon had not shown any interest in girls of late—groupies or otherwise—so I didn't anticipate him abandoning me anytime soon for the wifed up life.

But shit wasn't the same anymore.

Maybe it was better this way. All the partying and girls and living life on the edge... it was fucking exhausting. Even I was man enough to admit that.

My cell phone vibrated in my pocket, and I dug it out, frowning.

"You have reception?" Damon asked, coming up beside me.

"Yeah, I guess it auto-switched to a local carrier." I frowned at the unknown number before bringing the cell phone to my ear. "Hello?"

"Hi, baby."

"Mom?" I whisper-hissed, slowing down to put some

distance between me and the guys. "I thought I told you not to call me for a while. I have the tour."

"The tour, right. Right." The words were slow, every syllable elongated. I clenched my jaw. "I'm so proud of you, baby. So proud..."

"Mom, you sound—"

"No. Noooo, Hudson. I'm fine, baby. Better than fine, I'm perfect. Everything is perfect."

Shit. I couldn't do this. Not now. Not when I was about to embark on the biggest tour of my career so far.

"You should call Kenny, Mom." Just saying his name made my spine go rigid. The guy was a Class-A asshole, but she was his problem. Not mine. "I'm sure he can—"

"Kenny, he... uh, he ended things." She sniffled.

"He ends things all the time, Mom. But you always figure it out. I can't do this now. I have to go."

"Wait, wait, please, Hud, baby. I miss you. I just... I'm sorry, my sweet boy. I'm really sorry."

"Yeah, Mom. Me too." I hung up, cutting her off.

Damon, along with Stalter, one of our security detail, hung back for me. "You good?" Damon asked as I reached him.

"Nothing new." I pocketed my cell phone and tried to shake off the guilt churning in my stomach.

"Hey, look, man, if you need—"

"I'm fine."

Fuck. I hated those words. I hated every time Molly said them and I hated hearing them come out of my own goddamn mouth. But I couldn't worry about my mom right now. She'd made her bed—she would have to fucking lie in it.

Maybe that made me an asshole, but I'd spent my whole life listening to her bullshit. Watching her self-destruct time and time again. Only to pick herself up and promise me that next time would be different.

It was never different.

It was never going to be different.

But I couldn't cut her off. No matter how many times she let me down, how many times she ended up right back at square one, I couldn't do it.

Because she was the only mom I had.

And that had to count for something.

Didn't it?

CHAPTER THREE

MOLLY

THE HOTEL ROYALE PLAZA was like nothing I've ever seen and under any other circumstances, I would have been unable to contain my excitement as I took in the opulent foyer with its huge hanging crystal chandelier and the splashes of gold and deep red everywhere. But the truth was, I was numb.

Ever since I woke up on that plane with Hudson staring down at me, I'd been on edge. His heavy gaze had followed me all day and I felt like I couldn't breathe with him watching me. Questioning me. Silently begging me to give him something.

It was exhausting.

And it had to stop.

"Okay, we're all checked in," Letty said, approaching us. "Let's go find our rooms." She motioned for me to follow her. "We have the entire top floor. Penthouse suite and the two adjoining suites. Me and you will take one suite. Security will be set up in the second, and the guys, Eva, and Phoebe get the penthouse."

"Got it," I said as if I had a clue about any of this.

Part of me still didn't understand why they'd brought me along, but I wasn't about to look a gift horse in the mouth. I needed this. I needed to be as far away from Lyme as possible.

It didn't get much further than four-and-a-half thousand miles across the ocean.

Guilt began to swarm inside of me, but I pushed it down, smothering it. Locking it away tightly where it couldn't touch me. I'd given everything to my mom, to my twin brothers. I'd sacrificed my social life, my hopes and dreams, my future, all to be there for them. But now I needed to put myself first.

For once, I needed to save myself.

"Molly?" Letty frowned at me, and I blinked.

"Sorry, I'm here. What do you need from me?"

"Once everyone's situated, we'll go through the arrangements for later again. We need to be at sound check for three. The guys will want to eat, so maybe research local takeouts and ask what they'd like or we can check out the room service menu. I have to make some calls, make sure Duke is making good time."

"Right, got it."

Duke was the band's tour bus driver and was due to arrive with the tour bus tomorrow morning. When I'd asked why the guys wouldn't fly from venue to venue, Letty had explained they actually preferred the bus. They got more downtime that way and spent less time dodging the paparazzi.

Eva had told me all about what it was like traveling on the road with them and there had been a time when the thought of it sounded like one big adventure. The stuff dreams were made of. But that was before.

Now I wasn't sure how I would fare sleeping in close confines with other people. But thankfully, Letty had already explained we would be on the second bus with a couple other members of the team.

At least, I wouldn't have to survive Hudson's questioning gaze at every turn. Although, I was pretty certain once the tour started, he'd be too distracted by the hordes of adoring fangirls to think about the last couple of weeks.

THE SOUND of laughter filtered in through the windows. Everyone was in the pool, splashing and fooling around. But I couldn't stop crying. Even though I had no tears left to fall, I still sobbed, the force of each shuddering breath physically wrecking me.

Eva had tried countless times to coax me to join them. But I couldn't do it. I couldn't be around them and pretend. Not yet.

So I hugged my pillow tighter and closed my eyes, hoping I would fall into a deep, deep forgiving sleep. The kind where you didn't dream and monsters couldn't reach you.

But sleep didn't find me because every time I closed my eyes, I saw him.

Footsteps outside my room startled me and I pushed up on my elbows, half expecting to see Eva peek inside. But it wasn't Eva at all.

"Hudson," I breathed.

"I just wanted to see how you're doing?" He ran a hand over his dark hair and down the back of his neck. "Do you need anything?"

"I... no, thank you."

"You've been crying."

A statement, not a question.

He stepped further into the room, taking the air with him.

Hudson Ryker was devastatingly gorgeous. The epitome of a sexy, bad boy rock star.

And boy oh boy, did he know it.

He wore his confidence like a second skin, turning on his easy charm and flashing that playful smirk. It was hardly any wonder girls dropped their panties for him in droves. Or that there was a trail of broken hearts across the country.

Hudson f'in Ryker was that guy. The guy you knew you should stay away from, but the guy who was worth the hurt.

I knew firsthand how good it felt. For those few nights that I'd been the center of his attention, I hadn't cared about the consequences or the fact he would never offer more than a night of hot, sweaty, downright sinful sex.

But this Hudson... the one who had dropped to his knees outside that club at the sight of me. Well, I didn't know what to do with that Hudson.

"Did he hurt you?" There was a softness to his voice that made my heart ache.

"I... I can't talk about it."

"Molly girl, look at me." The words were a plea. A tight, frustrated breath that matched the expression he wore.

"I..."

"Look. At. Me." The bed dipped and he was there. Right

freaking there. But I still couldn't look. I still couldn't meet his heavy gaze.

"Molly." He sighed, brushing the damp hair from my face.

"Please, Hudson. Don't do this. I just want to be left alone."

"Not gonna happen," he said thickly. "Scooch over."

"W-what?"

"You heard me, Steinberg." He nudged me gently and I finally met his eyes.

"There she is." He smiled and it was blinding. "Now scooch over and stop hogging the covers."

"Hudson..."

But he didn't listen, nudging me some more until he could slip in beside me. He pulled me into his strong arms and tucked me close. He was shirtless, in a pair of board shorts that rode low on his hips. But he didn't seem in the least bit bothered about his state of undress.

Silence enveloped us as he held me, my heart careening in my chest. I didn't understand, it was all very confusing. Especially when things had been weird between us recently. After the last time we'd hooked up he'd made it pretty clear it couldn't happen again... so I'd gone back to being alone, determined to move on and forget all about Hudson f'in Ryker.

But now he was here, holding me, and although I would never admit it out loud, I felt safer in his arms than I had in a long time.

WE PILED INTO THE ELEVATOR, and I was unable to escape my reflection. Unable to shake off the lingering memories of that hazy two weeks in Long Island. The plan had been to stay for a week, but then I showed up and everyone sacrificed their plans to stay until the tour started.

They stayed for me and now I was here, trying to figure out how to navigate this new life.

How could I do that when I didn't even look like me anymore? The sparkle in my brown eyes was gone, dimmed by circumstance, and my skin looked pale. I glanced down, not wanting to see the evidence of just how broken I was.

A hand curled around mine and I lifted my gaze, my heart beating in my chest.

For a second, I thought it might be Hudson. It was Eva though, and I didn't know whether to be relieved... or bitterly disappointed.

"I could eat a small cow," Hunter grumbled, and Letty shot me a knowing look.

"We're on it," she said. "Get settled, showered, all that stuff, and we'll order in. Sound check is at three. Security is doing a dummy run ride to the stadium to make sure we don't hit any snags."

"Paris," Rafe said, still slightly awed.

"Fucking A," Hudson whooped. "Hey, do you think they'll sing back to us in French or English?"

"English, asshole." Levi snorted.

"What? It was a valid question."

Everyone chuckled.

Everyone except me.

"Okay," Letty said as the elevator came to a stop. "Here we are. And please for the love of God and my sanity, don't trash the place."

"Don't worry, Let." The doors pinged open, and the

guys began filing out once security gave them the go ahead. "We're all grown up and shit now." Hudson ruffled her hair and winked. But before he stepped out, he glanced back at me.

Time stopped.

My heart stopped.

Please, don't say it. I silently pleaded with him to leave it.

To leave me alone.

His lips parted, the air charged around us. But at the last second, he swallowed whatever he'd been about to say and slipped out of the elevator without another word.

I slumped against the wall, letting out a soft sigh.

"Want to talk about it?" Letty asked me.

Offering her a sad smile, I shook my head and said, "There's nothing to talk about."

Maybe if I said the words enough, they would eventually come true.

———

"Where are you putting it all?" Eva asked Levi as we all watched him hoover down another slice of pizza.

"I'm a growing boy." He grinned around a mouthful of food and Phoebe rolled her eyes.

"Babe, you're a pig."

"But I'm your pig." He dove for her, pinning her to the couch and smothering her in greasy kisses while the rest of us watched on.

"Fuck this." Hudson shot up and stormed into his bedroom, slamming the door.

"What crawled up his ass and died?" Levi asked, finally coming up for air.

Everyone looked at me and I wanted nothing more than to disappear into the big armchair I was sitting in.

"Guys." Letty shook her head, offering me a sympathetic smile. "We need to leave soon. Maybe one of you should go check on him?"

"I'll go." The words were out before I could stop them.

"Mol, I'm not sure—"

"It's okay, I got this." We needed to clear the air anyway.

Before I could talk myself out of it, I crossed the room and knocked on Hudson's door. He didn't answer, but it wasn't locked, so I let myself inside.

"Fuck—*Molly?*" He gawked at me.

"We should probably talk. Look, I'm sorry if I—"

"Not everything is about you, you know," he spat the words.

They hit me like a physical blow, and I reared back. "Excuse me?"

"You heard me."

"Hudson, I..."

"You can go." He folded his arms beneath his head and focused on the ceiling, refusing to look at me.

I didn't blame him.

I'd shut him out. He'd been nothing but understanding. He'd held me every single night we were in Long Island. He'd waited for me to tell him... to open up and explain what had happened to send me running to Atlanta that night.

But I couldn't.

When it had come down to it, I hadn't been able to do it.

"Hey." Hudson slipped into my room. Or I suppose it was our room since he spent every night in here with me.

Everyone suspected we were sleeping together, but they were wrong. Hudson held me while I slept. I couldn't explain it, but his touch kept the monsters at bay, giving me some respite. I still tossed and turned, but he was there every time I bolted upright or cried out.

"Hey," I said, weary all the way down to my bones.

"So, it's the last night..." he said, searching my face for answers I didn't have.

"Yeah. Eva said she's going to talk to Letty."

Hudson stripped down to his boxers without a second thought. There had been a time when I would have salivated at the sight of his lean, cut body. The tan skin pulled taut over his rippling muscles, and the intricate ink swirled over his chest. But that was then... before.

Pulling back the sheet, he waited for me to nestle into his body and wrapped an arm around me. "You know, Molly girl, you're going to have to talk to someone eventually."

"I... I know."

"I'm here, I'm right here."

"I know," I whispered again, my chest tightening at the unspoken plea in his words.

But I couldn't do it. I couldn't tell him.

Part of me suspected he knew—that they all knew. I was

changed. Withdrawn and skittish. Scared. But no one pushed. Not even Eva.

Then he whispered back, "I'm sorry, Mol. I'm so fucking sorry."

He knew.

Hudson knew and he was still here, holding me.

I didn't know what to make of it.

What to make of him.

But I knew whatever had once existed between us was gone.

Because the girl who had once hoped to tame the Black Hearts drummer...

She was gone.

CHAPTER FOUR

HUDSON

THE STADE DE FRANCE wasn't all that dissimilar to the venues we were used to playing back home. It was bigger, sure, but it was the lilt of French accents echoing through the vast space as the roadies and stagehands got everything into place, that really stood out.

"I'm here, I'm here." Alistair Portman, our manager, appeared, looking more than a little flustered.

"Ali boy." Levi leaped down off the edge of the stage and greeted him. "You're looking... sweaty."

We all snorted, and Alistair fumed. "Yes, well there was a mix-up at airport security." He loosened his tie. Dude always insisted on looking the part even in the eighty-five-degree heat.

He hadn't been able to fly out with us. There was some big meeting he'd needed to attend back at Razorsharp Records HQ in Atlanta.

"But I'm here now. What did I miss?"

"We're running behind." Letty approached, running her eyes over the set list. "There was an issue with lighting, but it's sorted now."

"Good. I need a drink and then you can get me up to speed. Everything good here?" He motioned between the four of us. Five, including Eva.

"Everything's fine." She smiled, but Alistair didn't look convinced, searching out our newest recruit.

"And that situation?" he asked, scrubbing his jaw.

"Ali." Eva sighed. "I thought you were okay with this."

He held up his hands. "I am. I just... well, it's my job to make sure we don't have any distractions." His concerned gaze flickered to me. "We have a lot riding on this tour."

He didn't need to tell us twice. We all knew the deal.

We'd scored a big endorsement with Masterpiece a while back, but it had been touch and go for a minute when Levi slipped off the sobriety wagons and relapsed. We couldn't afford another screw up.

I glanced over to where Molly was handing out bottles of water to some of the roadies. She wore a smile, but I knew it was fake. I knew because she had the kind of smile —real smile—that was hard to forget. The kind of smile that imprinted itself on your mind, on your fucking soul.

So yeah, the smile she wore was as fake and as forced as they came. But it wasn't my problem. She'd made that as clear as a fucking day.

Even if I'd had to remind her earlier in the hotel suite.

Guilt snaked through me, but I ignored it. I didn't owe her anything, just like she didn't owe me a damn thing. But she'd caught me off guard coming to check in on me. I hadn't wanted to talk about it, so I did the only thing I was good at.

I lashed out.

Fuck.

Her being here, us being around each other twenty-four-seven. I was beginning to think it was a disaster waiting to happen.

But it was too fucking late now.

She was here.

I was here.

And neither of us were escaping anytime soon.

———

"Go again," Levi demanded, wiping the sweat from his brow.

"Dude, we already played it twice."

"Yeah, and it was off key both fucking times."

"It was not—"

"I swear to God, Ryker. Just do your goddamn job."

"Okay, okay," Damon intervened, as usual. Just like he did whenever tempers were frayed. And right now, I was two seconds away from driving my drumstick up Levi Hunter's fucking ass.

"It wasn't off key. It was near damn perfect. He's just being—"

"Hudson, leave it." Damon silently implored. "Go get a drink or something. We'll take five and when we come back, we'll run it again."

"Whatever," I grumbled, climbing out from behind my kit and stretching my legs.

I loved performing. Loved that moment right before the lights came up and the opening beat dropped—usually by my own fucking hand—and the anticipation crackled in the air, rising above the hum of the crowd.

But rehearsals... sometimes, like right now, rehearsals sucked ass.

"You sounded good out there," Letty said, handing me a bottle of water as I climbed off stage.

"Yeah, tell that to Levi."

"He's just feeling the pressure. You know as well as I do, the opening show sets the tone for the tour. He just wants it to be—"

"Perfect, yeah, I know." I ran a hand through my hair and glanced over to where Phoebe was rubbing Levi's shoulders, whispering words of reassurance and encouragement into his ear no doubt.

She'd only been with us a few months, but she had slotted in with ease. I liked her; we all did. She calmed Levi. Settled the storm inside him. She was his anchor.

His person.

"Hud?"

"Yeah... what?" I barked a little too harshly.

Letty frowned. "You sure you're good?"

"Jesus, Panem, get off my ass already. I'm fine. It's all fine."

"You know one day, I'm going to crack that tough shell of yours wide open." A playful smirk tugged at her mouth.

"Nah. You don't want to know what I'm hiding under

all this." I swept a hand down myself, giving her a Hudson Ryker trademark smirk.

She saw right through it but didn't say anything. Likely because she knew it wouldn't get her anywhere.

I didn't want to talk. I didn't want to stand around sharing feelings or any of that shit. I wanted to throw myself into the tour, into performing and do the one thing—the only fucking thing—I was actually good at.

When I sat behind my drum kit, sticks in hand, foot poised on the bass drum pedal, I wasn't Hudson Ryker, high school dropout and good for nothing, I was something.

Somebody.

I was a motherfucking rock star.

I didn't need anything except a heavy beat and a hungry crowd.

That's all I would ever need.

The rest was just white noise, a way to kill the time and forget all the other shit. The parties and girls and all that stuff, it was fun, sure. But it didn't matter. It didn't fill the void.

This... *this* filled the void.

This made me come alive.

It made me feel worth something.

"You're a good guy, Hud." Letty went on. "One of the best. Don't sell yourself short. You know, now Rafe and Levi have found their—"

"Don't even go there, Let. This rock star isn't looking to settle down. Too much pussy in the ocean for that shit."

Letty chuckled, but her expression quickly dropped as

something caught her eye over my shoulder. I didn't need to turn around to know what—or who—had her attention.

I felt her.

Molly.

Fuck.

I glanced back and our eyes collided, hurt written all over her face.

"I... I was just... getting more refreshments."

"You don't have to do that, you know. The venue has people—"

"I don't mind." She focused on Letty, refusing to meet my eyes.

I didn't blame her.

Me and my big fucking mouth.

But it was better like this, better if the line was redrawn between us. I wasn't like Rafe and Levi. I didn't have the emotional capacity to let somebody in. Even if for a second, I'd wondered...

Wondered what it might be like.

"I'll just..." She thumbed in the opposite direction and took off as if the devil himself was nipping at her heels.

"I see things are—"

"Do me a favor, yeah, Let?" I said, and she gave me a small nod.

"Anything."

"Look out for her."

Because I couldn't do it.

I couldn't be that person for her.

Not now.

Not ever.

"So what's the plan?" I asked as we all piled into the black SUV.

"I don't know about anyone else, but I could eat a horse."

"Seriously, Hunter. At this rate, Phoebe will have to put you on a diet."

"Don't look at me." She chuckled, laying her head on Levi's shoulder.

"You do realize he's probably replacing one addiction with another." My brow lifted.

"Hud, don't be an asshole." Damon glowered.

"What? It's true. He's clean, sure. But he's constantly eating. He's got—"

"Do you know what, fucker? I don't even care. I'm sober. I'm happy. If I start getting a muffin top, I'll have to get some stretchy pants. Isn't that right, Bee?" He hooked his arm around Phoebe's neck and dropped a kiss to her head.

She let out a big yawn and Levi frowned. "What's wrong?"

"Nothing's wrong, babe. I'm tired. Must be jet lag."

"We can get an early night."

"Like hell we can," I said. "It's our last night of freedom for a while, we're going out."

A chorus of groans filled the car. Letty looked up from her cell phone, finally joining the conversation. "It's too late to organize—"

"We have security. We can be incognito." I didn't want to go back to the hotel and sit around watching

Rafe with Eva, and Levi with Phoebe, it was fucking depressing.

"So... who's in?"

Molly didn't even acknowledge me, staring out the tinted windows watching the city roll by. She'd avoided me since overhearing my conversation with Letty. I didn't try to apologize. What was the point? I needed to focus on the tour, on ignoring the constant texts from my mom, and Molly needed to do whatever the hell it was she needed to do.

"Seriously, no one wants to get out and see the sights? Damon?"

He shrugged. "I'll go with the majority."

"Fuck that. It's Paris. *Paris*. We can't just sit in the hotel and—"

"Fine." He let out a heavy sigh. "I'm in."

"Right choice. Rafe? Eva?" They shared a look and I murmured under my breath. "This is supposed to be the best time of our lives. We're living the fucking dream and you four are too wrapped up in each other to care."

"You're just jealous you haven't got pussy on tap," Levi shot back.

"Leviathan Hunter." Phoebe gasped, flushing from the tips of her ears to the curve of her neck.

"Honeybee, it's cute you're embarrassed but there's no hiding the way I make you scream."

Levi brought his mouth down on hers, kissing her hard, giving zero fucks we were all crammed into the SUV.

"You coming or what?" I turned my attention back on Rafe.

"I think we'll pass tonight."

Of course they fucking would.

"Just you and me then, Donnelley. Hope you're ready to paint the town red."

"Hud," Letty started. "Alistair—"

"Ali boy can go fuck himself. I need a drink."

And I needed not to be surrounded by all the puke-inducing PDA.

———

"This wasn't quite what I had in mind." I glanced around the hole-in-the-wall dive bar Stalter and Johnson had brought us to. Letty had wanted to call ahead and make proper arrangements, but we'd reassured her we could be discreet. And Stalter said he knew a place where we wouldn't be accosted.

There was discreet... and then there was this.

"Yeah, well, just be thankful I'm even here," Damon grumbled.

"What the fuck is your problem?"

"My problem?" His brow arched.

I drained my beer and slammed it down on the bar. The old man who served us, clearly not recognizing us from Adam, glanced our way. "Sorry," I mumbled, mouthing, "Another."

He nodded and got me a fresh beer.

"Merci beaucoup," Damon said.

"*Merci beaucoup*," I mocked. "Who the fuck are you right now?"

"You're a dick."

"At least I use my dick. When's the last time you dipped your end in something other than your fist?" I leaned back against the bar, rubbing my eyes over the handful of other people drinking. All old balding men. Not a woman in sight.

Where the fuck had Stalter brought us?

"You'd do it, wouldn't you?"

Damon's question caught me off guard and I asked, "Do what?"

"Pick up some French hottie and *dip your end in her?*" Sarcasm dripped from his words.

"French women are hot."

"You think all women are hot."

"Touché."

"You didn't answer my question..."

Turning back around, I dropped my forearms on the bar and lowered my head. "Why do I feel like you're trying to make a point?"

"What are you doing, Hud? With Molly?"

"Nothing. I'm not doing a goddamn thing."

"But in Long Island—"

"She needed a shoulder. I was happy to oblige."

"A shoulder?" He barked out a disbelieving laugh. "Yeah, keep telling yourself that."

"Look, what do you want me to say? It's better this way. I can't give her more than I have to give."

He laid his hand on my shoulder and let out a heavy sigh. "Maybe what you have to give her is enough."

I clicked my tongue, bringing the beer bottle to my lips. "I'm not cut out for that life. Never have been, never will be."

I'd seen what love could do to a person. How it could seep right down into their soul and poison them, rotting them from the inside out.

"You know what happened to your mom—"

"Don't." It came out a harsh breath.

"She's sick, Hud. She's always been sick."

But she wasn't sick.

She was heartbroken.

Ruined.

And she would never recover.

CHAPTER FIVE

MOLLY

"Mornin'." Eva gave me a warm smile as I joined her at the breakfast counter in their suite. "Sleep well?"

"Okay, I guess. You?"

She flushed, dipping her head and I managed a small chuckle. "That good, huh?"

"Rafe is—"

"Rafe is what?" The guy in question appeared wearing dark gray sweats and a fitted black tee. I didn't think I'd ever seen the Black Hearts bassist look so casual before.

"Your girl was just telling me how well she slept," I teased, ignoring the pit in my stomach.

"Was she now?" He cupped the back of Eva's neck and kissed her. "Morning, Starshine."

They were so freaking cute, and no one deserved happiness more than Eva.

But watching them hurt.

It hurt because I knew I would never have that.

Not now.

Not after everything.

Bile washed in my stomach, churning like a laundromat.

"Molly?" Eva's voice held a note of concern.

"I'm fine."

"Any sign of Hudson yet?" Rafe asked no one in particular.

"He's still sleeping." Damon wandered out of their room, looking a little worse for wear.

"Late night?"

"Don't ask." He gave Rafe a strange look, his gaze moving to me.

"Anyone for more coffee?" I rushed out, needing to keep myself busy.

"I wouldn't say no."

"Rafe? Eva?"

"Sure." She pushed her mug toward me, and I set out making a fresh pot.

Levi and Phoebe joined us next, Letty and Alistair too. Until the only person missing was Hudson.

"Do I even want to know?" Alistair asked, leaning back against the counter.

"He'll be fine," Damon said. "Let him sleep it off."

"He gets another thirty minutes, then I want him up and ready. The first interview is at noon."

"Don't remind me," Levi muttered.

"You, play nice." Alistair pinned him with a hard look. "You know the deal."

"Yeah, yeah, keep your hair on, Ali boy."

"How are you feeling about tonight? Ready?"

"Born ready." Levi's grin was every bit as cocky as the one he'd worn on stage the few times I'd seen them perform.

The Black Hearts front man had something to prove. Not only to the world, to their fans and the fat cat music execs at Razorsharp Records, but to himself.

And that grin plastered on his face was the epitome of determination.

"That's what I like to hear. I have a good feeling about this tour, guys. A real good feeling."

The doorbell rang and I used it as an opportunity to sneak away from their conversation. "I'll get it," I called, practically jogging to the door.

"Room service," the guy announced in a thick French accent.

"Thank you." I stepped back to let him wheel the trolley inside, the sweet scent of buttery croissants and waffles filling the hall.

"If you need anything else, don't hesitate to call." He gave me a blinding smile, lingering in the doorway.

"Uh, thanks."

I gripped the trolley and started backing up, feeling uncomfortable under his intense gaze.

"Molly?" Letty rounded the corner and stalled the second she saw the attendant.

"Is there a problem?" she asked him.

"No, no, I was just, how you say, admiring your pretty friend."

Sweet baby Jesus.

My cheeks burned as I dipped my head, finding the swirled pattern in the carpet suddenly very interesting.

"Okay, well, thank you. I think we can handle it from here." Letty dismissed him, and the door clicked shut. "He was cute," she said, and my head whipped up.

"I..."

"Molly?" Pity crept into her expression. "If he overstepped—"

"No, it's fine. He... he didn't. I just... I'm fine."

"You know, you can't keep it all locked up inside forever. Talking might help. It might—"

"Where's the food?" Levi shouted.

"Jesus, he's a pig. Come on, before he turns into a rabid dog."

We headed back into the suite. Letty had barely begun to lay out the plates of food when the guys descended.

"What's that smell?" Hudson appeared, bleary eyed, and still wearing last night's jeans. His dark hair stuck up in all directions as he scratched at the tattoo on his chest, drawing my eye to the dips and planes of his perfect body.

I immediately looked away, a strange feeling snaking through me. My brain knew he was attractive, my body remembered how good he felt pressed up against me, but it was like there was this icy wall of fear there now.

Not because I was scared of him, never. But I was scared.

And I hated it.

I hated that Carson had turned me into this jittery, skittish, weak, emotional girl.

"When in France," Eva said, snagging a croissant off the tray.

"I'll pass."

"Feeling a little rough, Ryker?" Levi taunted.

"Fuck off," he grumbled, moving toward the coffee maker.

"Where'd you two end up anyway?"

My heart beat erratically in my chest as I listened with baited breath.

"Just some dive bar."

He didn't so much as look at me as he said the words.

"You find some unsuspecting French girl to—"

"Levi," Eva hissed, shooting me an apologetic smile.

"What? It's Ryker. He always finds fresh pussy to—"

Without a word, I hurried toward the bathroom and slipped inside, right as I heard Rafe say, "Way to be an insensitive asshole, asshole."

"What, I didn't..." Their voices drowned out as I locked the door and turned on the faucets.

It didn't matter what—*or who*—Hudson was doing last night.

There was a reason I'd pushed him away. It was for the best. He needed to focus on the tour, and I needed to try and move on with my life.

Letty had given me a wonderful opportunity letting me come on board as her apprentice assistant. I needed to focus on that. I was safe here. The band had round the clock security for Pete's sake. Not to mention the fact we were over four thousand miles from home.

Nothing could hurt me here.

But as I joined everyone for breakfast, picking at a croissant as I sat quietly listening to them talk about tonight's opening concert, my eyes found Hudson across the breakfast counter.

And I knew I was lying to myself.

———

"Letty, we've got a problem," Phoebe came up to us, keeping her voice low enough as to not disturb the interview happening right in front of us.

"What now?"

It had been a stressful morning. We'd hit traffic on the ride over, then one of the guys had a wardrobe malfunction, and to top it off, we got to the hotel only to find out the original host was sick.

I swore Letty had turned gray in the last two hours.

"Someone leaked the location, and we're drawing a crowd."

"When you say crowd..."

"It's bad. The Die Hearts are circling."

"Shit." She blew out a thin breath. "Okay, talk to Travis or Stalter, see if we need to make a plan B to get the guys out of here. We cannot be late to the next interview; it'll have a domino effect if we are. And Levi is already irritated about the last-minute change. Fuck," she whispered.

"Is there anything I can do?" I asked, needing to keep busy. It was fine when we were on the move, riding in the SUV, or arriving at venues and being swept up in the chaos. But right now, when all there was to do was watch, I felt... antsy. Like a thousand spiders were crawling under my skin.

"No, it's fine. Phoebe can handle it. I want you here, learning the ropes. I'll make a PA of you yet." She winked, throwing me a bone.

She knew how much I needed this. Even if she didn't know the whole story, she knew enough.

They all did.

And it was becoming more and more apparent with the lingering stares and concerned expressions.

I was hoping once the first show got underway tonight, everyone would be too busy riding the high to notice little old me and my fake smile.

"Should we be worried about the fangirls?" I asked.

I'd heard the stories about them. The rabid, thirsty groupies that followed the band wherever they went, all hoping to catch a glimpse of the object of their obsessions.

"We'll handle it," Letty said, but I didn't miss the tight expression she wore.

A tall, slender woman with a thick French accent beckoned Letty over and she grasped my arm. "I need to go speak to her. You good here?"

"I'm fine, go."

She left and I turned my attention back to the interview. The host: a young woman with jet black hair and bewitching eyes was laughing and joking with Eva and the guys, but her gaze lingered on Hudson the most. It didn't surprise me. There was something about him. Call it charisma, or swagger, or straight up hot-guy genes, but Hudson Ryker had it in spades. The ability to make a room laugh, to make a young woman's heart flutter so wildly in her chest she felt breathless, to make her feel like she was the only woman on the planet.

But it was all a lie.

Temporary.

Impermanent.

Because although Hudson gave everything to the people around him—his smiles, his humor, his loyalty, and talent—he would never ever give them the thing that mattered most.

His heart.

No, that was locked away, guarded by his overconfidence and cocky swagger.

As if he felt me watching, he looked up and our eyes collided. Because that's how it felt every time he looked at me, a physical blow to my heart.

Goddamn Hudson f'in Ryker.

Why did he have to be so sweet in Long Island? Why did he have to hold me every night, whispering soothing words in my ear?

Now I couldn't look at him without seeing my savior. My knight-in-ripped-jean and t-shirts.

But he wasn't mine.

"So, Hudson, Damon. Tell me, how does it feel to be back on tour, especially now that Levi has announced his relationship to the world?"

"Nothing's changed," Damon offered. "We're here to play music."

The host chuckled, a flirty sound that grated on my nerves. "But it must be strange, no? For two of you to be so happy and how do you say, in love?"

Levi looked murderous while Rafe shifted uncomfortably beside Eva.

"How about we stick to—"

"Look, Mariella," Hudson said smoothly. "Can I call you Mariella?"

There was that smirk, the one you felt all the way down to your stomach when it was turned your way.

"Oui." She batted her eyes.

Batted. Her. Freaking. Eyes.

"The way I see it now that Rafe and Levi are off the market... is less competition for me. What do you say, Damon?"

Damon shot Hudson an incredulous look, earning him another chuckle from Mariella.

"You'll have to excuse Hudson," Rafe added, slinging his arm around Hudson's neck. "He doesn't have the best manners."

"I'm sure our viewers will be more than happy to hear that he's still on the market."

Please.

On the market for what?

It wasn't like he was ever going to pluck a girl out of the hordes of fangirls and hand over his heart.

They didn't want his heart anyway, not really. They wanted their five minutes of fame. Their night in the spotlight with a rock star.

I knew. I'd been that girl once, after all.

Letty stormed back over toward me. "She'd better wrap this shit up before Levi does something stupid."

"W-what do you mean?"

"We briefed everyone for the interviews. His relationship with Phoebe is off-limits. But she just had to go there. Stupid rookie trying to score with the ratings."

"Levi, can I ask—"

"No, bitch. Don't fucking go there," Letty gritted out.

"You recently announced your relationship with Razorsharp Records employee Phoebe—"

"We're done here." He shot up, tore off his mic and stormed off stage, sending the room into disarray.

"Shit, *shit*!" Letty thrust her clipboard and took off in his direction.

"What happened?" Phoebe came back into the room and rushed up to me. "Where's Levi?"

"Uh, you might want to go find him."

"What happened?"

"Mariella went off-script."

"Shit." She paled.

"Yeah, shit."

"Okay, I'll go find him."

I nodded. "Letty already went after him."

Phoebe hurried off and I was left standing there, watching Eva and the remaining guys talk to Mariella and the producer. It looked tense, but the mood completely changed when Letty joined the fray.

"Save it," she yelled. "You knew it was off-limits, and you went there anyway."

Mariella didn't have the sense to look apologetic, offering a small shrug.

"You need to get your rookie hosts under control," Letty barked at the producer who tried his best to placate her.

Eventually, Eva wandered over. "It isn't always like this, you know," she said around a tentative smile.

"Rather Mariella than me."

"True. Letty is fiercely protective of the band, I'm glad they have her."

"Yeah. She's something all right." I glanced back to find them all heading in our direction.

"Fenton and Johnson have Phoebe and Levi, we're leaving. But we have a small problem."

"Plan B?" I asked, and she nodded.

"Plan B."

CHAPTER SIX

HUDSON

Plan B was a fucking shitshow. By the time security got us to the back entrance of the hotel, the sidewalks were crawling with paparazzi and Die Hearts.

Letty had warned us that this might happen, but we had laughed it off. It was our first time in Europe. We knew our music was making waves globally but knowing it and experiencing it were two different things.

"We're going to have to make a run for it," Letty said as she scanned the growing crowd. Fenton and Johnson fought to keep the raucous crowd contained, but we needed to move and move fast if we had any hopes of the SUV making it out of here.

"This is crazy," Molly breathed.

She wasn't really talking to me, but we'd ended up standing together after being herded down the delivery access to the back entrance.

"Welcome to their world," Phoebe said, rolling her eyes.

She knew firsthand how crazy shit could get where the fangirls were concerned. Levi pulled her tighter into his side, anger still etched into his expression.

He was pissed that the interview host went off-script. It happened from time to time and usually we batted the questions away, but as far as Levi was concerned, Phoebe was off-limits, and it wouldn't have surprised me if heads rolled at the TV station for Mariella's screw up.

But we'd learned a long time ago that scandal and intrigue sold records and pulled in ratings.

"Okay, we're all set," Travis said, muttering something into his wrist mic.

"The girls go first," Levi said, ushering Phoebe forward.

"You too." She grabbed hold of him.

"Both of you, go." Letty gave the order and security swooped in, escorting them through the chaos and safely into the SUV.

Eva and Rafe went next, followed by Damon. "Hud, let's go," Letty reached for me, the shrill of our names deafening.

"Wait, what about Molly?" I asked, suddenly realizing she was no longer beside me.

"She's—shit."

Molly was frozen in place, fear shining in her eyes, the blood drained from her face.

"We need to go," Letty urged. "Before we lose—"

"Go. I'll get her." Without thinking, I closed the short

distance to Molly and cupped her face. "Steinberg, eyes on me."

Shit. Her entire body was trembling.

"Molly girl, we need to go, now."

"I-I... I can't—"

Dipping my head, I looked right in her eyes. "Yes, you can. Come on." Taking her hand in mine, I tugged gently but she'd really dug her heels in. "Shit, Molly," I said. "We need to leave."

"I..." Her gaze darted around the place, wild and skittish. She was locked in some memory somewhere, triggered into this state of fear.

"Fuck this." I bent down and scooped her up, cradling her body to mine and heading straight for the door.

Stalter arched his brow at me as I approached and I grunted, "Shield her." The last thing I wanted was for her to end up on the front of some tabloid. It wouldn't be good for her—or us. Not that I cared about that at this moment in time.

Rafe was there ready to help me get Molly in the SUV. She seemed to jolt back into herself the second she was inside. I climbed in and security slammed the door shut.

"Mol—"

"Fine, I'm fine," she breathed, refusing to meet my gaze. "It just caught me off guard."

The lie rolled off her tongue. I didn't doubt the crowd was overwhelming. But it wasn't enough to send her into a panic attack like that.

I sank back into the seat opposite her and tried to catch her eye, but she wouldn't look at me. And it pissed me the hell off.

She pissed me off.

The car rumbled to life and slowly made its way out of the alley, leaving behind the flashing cameras and screaming women.

"I'd heard the French were a passionate people," Damon said drolly.

"I'd forgotten how much this part sucked," Levi let out a weary sigh, squeezing Phoebe's hand. He always had to be touching her, reminding himself that she was there.

Letty and Levi launched into a heated debate about reminding the interviewers that his relationship was not up for discussion. But I tuned them out, resting my head back against the cool leather seats.

I was already exhausted, and we hadn't even started the shows yet. But my cell phone was burning a hole in my pocket. Mom had called twice again this morning, barely coherent. I hated hearing her so... so broken. But we'd danced this dance enough times for me to know I couldn't fix her.

My eyes shuttered as I soaked up the few minutes of rest.

"Are you sure you're going to be okay?" Eva asked Molly.

"I said I'm fine."

"Okay, but if you aren't..."

"Eva," she snapped, and the air turned thick with tension.

Letty's cell phone chose that exact moment to ring, giving us all a reprieve from the awkward atmosphere. Usually, I'd crack a joke or say something highly inappropriate, but I had nothing.

Between Mom and Molly, I was off my fucking game.

And this was just the beginning.

––––––

"WHERE'S MOLLY?" Phoebe asked as we all crammed into the elevator ready to head to the stadium.

The second interview went better. The host stuck to the script and Levi was more relaxed. They'd even laid out food and drinks for us afterward, so we hung around for a bit. Then we'd headed back to the hotel to get ready for the final sound check before tonight's show.

"She's not feeling so good. She's going to stay here," Letty said.

"What?" Eva paled as the doors closed. "But she didn't tell me."

"She didn't want you to worry. She's going to get some rest before we roll out tomorrow. I'm sure she'll be fine."

"Yeah."

Eva's expression said otherwise but I didn't call her out on it. Maybe it was better that Molly wasn't here. She'd freaked out pretty badly earlier.

"Has she... said anything about what happened yet?" Phoebe asked.

"No. I've tried to talk to her, but I don't want to keep pushing."

"Come on, Angel," Levi scoffed. "We all know what happened with that fucker."

"We don't know that, not for sure."

"You saw how she was when she turned up in Atlanta."

"I know." Eva let out a heavy sigh. "But I can't believe... she said he was a nice guy."

"And so are hundreds of other rapists out there."

"Levi!" Phoebe glowered at him.

"Shit, sorry, Bee. I didn't... I just think it's pretty obvious what happened. She won't talk about it. She spent the entire time in Long Island locked up in her room." He locked eyes on me and frowned. "Did she confide in you?"

"No, and if she had, I wouldn't tell you. That's her business," I snapped, a little too defensively.

"Hud." Damon gripped my shoulder. "Levi knows that. He's just worried. We all are."

"Yeah, well, maybe bringing her with us was a bad idea." The words were out before I could stop them.

Everyone looked at me like I'd grown a second head, but I simply shrugged.

"You really are a cold-hearted bastard sometimes," Rafe murmured. "But you're not fooling anyone."

"What the fuck is that supposed to mean?"

"You know exactly what it means. You barely let her out of your sight in Long Island and now you're—"

"Enough." Letty stepped in between us, pinning each of us with a harsh look. "We haven't come halfway around the world for you to fall out on the first night of the tour. Molly is grown enough to make her own decisions. I'll check in with her later. But for now, focus on the show. Because that's what matters. Got it?"

"Yeah," Rafe said sheepishly.

"Hudson?" she pushed.

"Yeah, whatever."

"Jesus, you're like a bunch of little girls sometimes. I

don't know whether to put you in time out or give you all a hug and tell you everything will be okay."

"Please don't," Levi snorted. "With the hugging, I mean."

"Asshole." Letty grinned.

"Never claimed to be anything else. But admit it, Panem, you still love us."

"I'll love you a lot more when you get out there tonight and do your goddamn job."

"Relax, we know the score."

"Good." She gave Levi a small nod. "Then we don't have anything to worry about, do we?"

———

"Hey, you," Eva strolled up to me as we waited backstage. We were due to go on in less than twenty minutes, so I'd taken myself off to a quiet corner to collect my thoughts.

Mom had been blowing up my cell again. It had gotten to be so much, I'd turned the damn thing off, not wanting to deal with her bullshit. Not tonight, when we were about to play one of the biggest shows of our lives.

Playing on home soil was one thing. We'd become a household name in the US. The hottest rock band of the last two years. Even if people didn't appreciate our sound, the music we made, they knew us. It was hard to escape when we'd dominated the charts for the last eighteen months.

But performing to an international audience, earning

their screams and applause, their fucking tears, that would be something else.

"How come you're hidin' back here?" She smiled up at me, perching on a stack of pallets.

"Not hiding, just catching my breath."

"Nervous?"

"Nope. You?"

"Dreadfully so."

"You'll be fine," I said.

It was the truth. Eva had grown into herself these last few months. Her faith in her talent, her on-stage presence and confidence. She deserved to be here.

"Thanks. I'm just hoping Levi won't do anythin' stupid and go off-script. I've made him promise me there'll be no surprises."

"This is Levi we're talking about."

"Yeah, you're right. I'm doomed." Soft laughter bubbled in her chest. "I spoke to Molly earlier."

"Yeah?"

"She's okay."

"Good." I scrubbed my jaw. "That's good."

"Do you think Levi is right? I mean, I've thought it. But I can't believe she wouldn't tell me if... if Carson had done that to her."

Just hearing his name made me feel murderous. If I ever met him... well, let's just say, I hoped we'd never cross paths.

"Something bad happened, Eva."

"I know, God, I know. I just..."

"You hoped it wasn't that bad."

She nodded, guilt shining in her eyes. "Does that make me a terrible person?"

"Of course it doesn't. And we can't be certain that did happen. But she's gone, Eva. The girl she was before... she's gone."

Admitting that hurt more than I expected.

The Molly I'd met last summer had been a breath of fresh air. Confident, unapologetic, and sassy. She'd made it clear from the start she wanted me and who was I to turn down a pretty girl?

But I'd underestimated the mark she would leave.

"She's still in there, Hud. She's just a little broken right now. But she needs us. All of us."

I didn't miss the unspoken meaning in her words.

Eva thought Molly needed me. But what she didn't know was, I couldn't be that guy. Even if I wanted to—and yeah, maybe part of me did want to be that guy—I wasn't wired that way.

And in the end, I'd only end up bringing Molly more pain and hurt.

CHAPTER SEVEN

MOLLY

IT WAS A MISTAKE STAYING BEHIND.

I knew that the second I watched my friends disappear into the elevator and the doors pinged closed.

But I couldn't call them back. Eva and the guys had one of the biggest shows of their lives to prepare for.

And I'd missed it.

Guilt sat heavy in my chest, but it wasn't the only emotion plaguing my thoughts.

Earlier, when Hudson had scooped me up as if I weighed nothing more than a feather, something fragile inside of me had broken a little more.

He could be so kind, so warm and attentive. When he'd picked me up and cradled me against his chest, I'd felt safe.

I'd felt... cherished.

But it was all an illusion. Hudson Ryker didn't get

close to anyone. And I knew if I gave in now, I would only end up more hurt than I already was.

I couldn't risk that, not when I was barely hanging on by a thread.

I checked my cell again, waiting for another update from Phoebe and Letty. They had kindly recorded Eva during her performance so I could at least see my best friend shine like the star I always knew she was.

But nothing came through. No text or video call. Nothing but the sound of deafening silence. And there was still at least an hour to go before the show was over, and then they had to schmooze with the VIP ticket holders before they would make it back to the hotel.

"Crap, this was a bad idea," I mumbled to myself.

The sudden vibration of my cell phone almost gave me a heart attack. I sat up, opening it with renewed anticipation, only for it to be dashed when I saw Mom's name.

MOM: The boys miss you. When are you coming home?

ATTACHED WAS a photo of the two of them grinning at the camera. Another pang of guilt went through me. But this one was worse, because she was right, I had abandoned them.

I couldn't stay in Lyme though. Not while... while he was there. I had to get away, I had to try to figure things out.

. . .

ME: I don't know, Mom. I need to figure some things out.

MOM: Just tell me what's going on. I'm worried. We all are. Derek said whatever happened between the two of you, he can help. Carson isn't handling it well, sweetheart. Just please, call me. Love you. xo

I DROPPED my cell phone like it was on fire. Just the mention of his name made my heart race.

You're safe, you're safe here. I forced myself to inhale and exhale slowly, refusing to give credence to the fear coursing through my veins. I was halfway around the world; he couldn't touch me here.

Yet wasn't he doing just that?

Physically, I might have been safe, I might have been out of reach. But I'd fled. I'd left the only home I'd ever known. And now I was in a strange country, trying to hold it together.

There might have been thousands of miles between us, but Carson's hold on me was as strong as ever.

Mom's text message proved that.

Derek said whatever happened between the two of you, he can help.

I highly doubted that, but I couldn't tell them the truth. They would never believe me. Derek adored his nephew. Everyone did.

Restless, I leaped up and went over to the mini bar. I needed a drink, something to calm my nerves. Shit, I didn't want everyone knowing though and wouldn't it show up on the room bill.

Glancing around, I decided to grab my purse and head down to the bar. No one knew me here. For all I knew, I was just another tourist enjoying the sights and sounds of the city.

But the second I entered the bar attached to the hotel, I realized my second mistake of the night. Not checking my reflection before I left the hotel suite.

I looked like crap.

Trying to tame my unruly hair, I ignored the glances of disapproval turned in my direction as I made a beeline for the bar.

"Bonjour," the bartender said. "Que voulez-vous boire?"

"Ah, Anglais... English?"

"Oui, of course. To drink?"

"Wine?" I paused, he seemed familiar. "Have we met?"

A knowing smile spread over his face. "I delivered your room service earlier."

Crap. He knew I was here with the band. Panic must have filled my features because he quickly added. "Your secret is safe." He patted his chest and went about pouring my drink.

"For the pretty lady." He pushed the glass toward me.

"Thank you." I dipped my head in thanks. Once upon a time, his words would have given me cause to smile or even blush, but I was too numb to care.

He hovered, watching me as I looked at my glass of

wine. I doubted one glass would even touch the anxiety clawing in my stomach. And I couldn't afford to screw up with Letty and the label.

I scooted back off the stool, so quickly that it almost toppled. "Crap," I murmured. "This was a bad idea."

"Wait, please," the guy rushed out, reaching across the bar as if he might try to grab me. "My name is Philippe. Stay. Talk. Drink." His eyes went to the untouched glass of wine. "You look like you need it."

His accent was rich, the letters rolling off his tongue. I'd always thought the French accent to be quite abrasive, but it was really quite charming.

"Please," he added. "A pretty girl like you shouldn't... how you say it... be sad and alone."

Sad and alone.

Sweet baby Jesus. Even Philippe could see what a mess I was.

But he had a point. If I returned to the room now, I might do something stupid like drain the mini bar dry and embarrass myself when everyone got back.

At least here, no one knew me.

Well, no one except Philippe.

LAUGHTER FLOATED OUT OF ME. It felt good to laugh. To feel like my old self. Philippe was good company, funny and charming, and that heavy French accent didn't hurt either.

The bar had remained quiet, the odd customer coming and going, but whenever he did have to tend to customers, I was happy to sit quietly, sipping my glass of wine.

I'd stopped at three, feeling a slight buzz in my veins. I didn't need to bury my pain with liquor, not when Philippe had taken it upon himself to pull me out of my stupor.

Until he asked me, "So, Molly Steinberg, what is home like for you?"

Home.

Just the thought of it clanged through me, and I suppressed a shudder.

"Ah." His expression fell. "I sense a story there."

Dropping my gaze, I murmured, "I'd rather not talk about it."

"Of course. No pressure. I'm happy to talk about my life some more." He winked, a playful smirk tugging at his mouth.

Philippe was handsome, with his dark, casually styled hair and flawless white shirt and black dress pants. But it was his personality that shone the most.

"You know, I really appreciate you talking to me tonight."

He probably did this all the time, taking pity on the lonely women that frequented the hotel bar. But it didn't matter.

I'd needed someone tonight, and I'd found it here, perched at the polished chrome bar.

"It has been my privilege, Miss Molly. You know, I finish here soon, we could talk some more."

"Oh, I'm not sure. My friends... they will be back soon." It was almost eleven thirty. I really needed to get back to the room soon.

"Very well. Will I see you tomorrow?"

"We leave tomorrow."

Disappointment flickered in his eyes. "That is a shame."

"Yeah." The air turned thick, and I didn't like it. I didn't like the way he was suddenly looking at me.

I knew Philippe was harmless. But gone was the easy relaxed atmosphere we'd shared all night, replaced by something thicker and less comforting.

"I should probably go, it's getting late. Thanks again for the conversation." I stood, offering him a small wave.

"Goodbye, Molly," he said. "Maybe we meet again."

With a small nod, I hurried out of there, making a beeline for the elevator. I'd almost reached it when he called after me, jogging toward me with a napkin in his hand.

"Wait," he said, reaching me. "I cannot let you go without at least giving you this."

"What is it?" I stared down at it.

"My number. Maybe you will return to Paris one day and we can—"

A commotion over by reception drew my attention and my eyes went wide.

"Molly?" Eva said, making her way over to me, her bodyguard Travis hot on her heels. "What are you doin'?"

"I... uh, this is Philippe."

"Hey." Her brows pinched as she glanced between us, at the napkin in my hand. "What are—"

"Philippe works in the bar. I went for a drink and he... uh..."

"Is there a problem here?"

I flinched at the warning in Hudson's voice.

"Steinberg?"

"I... no, no problem. Philippe was just saying good night." I pinned him with a desperate look.

"Yes, I was saying good night. Miss Molly." He inclined his head.

Just go, I silently implored, crushing the napkin in my fist and dropping my hand.

But of course, he had to go and say, "I hope to hear from you soon."

Philippe bounced away without a second glance, leaving Eva and Hudson glaring at me as if I'd committed some cardinal sin.

"What?" I snapped defensively.

"Who the fuck was that?" Hudson broke the tension swirling between us.

"Who, Philippe? No one." I shrugged.

"*Philippe*," he mocked. "So let me get this straight. You couldn't come to our opening show, you couldn't support your best friend on one of the biggest nights of her life because you were having some kind of emotional breakdown... Yet, you managed to venture to the bar and pick up a guy—"

"Hud." Eva shook her head gently, offering me an apologetic smile.

Tears burned the backs of my eyes. "That's not what happened. I..."

"Come on," Eva said, taking my hand. "Let's not do this here. Let's go up to the suite."

Everyone was watching. Our friends. The reception

staff. Even our security detail were failing to be discreet as they watched the three of us.

"Yeah, whatever. At least we know where her priorities lie." Hudson barged past us toward the elevator.

"Maybe I should—"

"Leave him be. He's got some stuff going on..."

That had my attention. "What stuff?"

"It's not my story to tell." She let out a weary sigh, glancing over my shoulder to where Hudson disappeared. "He's just—"

"It's fine. I shouldn't have left the room."

"Mol, you're not a prisoner. But we thought... I guess we didn't expect to find you down here."

"He's just the bartender," I said. "We talked, that's all."

"And if you'd found Hudson just talking to some girl, her number scrawled on the napkin in his hand?"

"We're not together, Eva." I reminded her.

"No, but you are somethin' and until you figure it out..."

"Starshine." Rafe slid his arms around Eva and entered the conversation. "We really need to take this upstairs."

"Yeah, I know. Okay?" she asked me, and I nodded.

Because what else was there to say?

I'd messed up tonight.

Eva was right. Regardless of what was or wasn't happening between us, I would have been hurt to arrive back at the hotel to find Hudson talking to some girl.

At the very least, I needed to explain myself.

But when we followed the rest of our group to the elevator, Hudson was already gone.

CHAPTER EIGHT

HUDSON

THE TOUR BUS felt like home.

What did that say about me? That being holed up with three other guys and Eva felt more like home than any other place I'd ever lived.

The low rumble of the engine of the gigantic Van Hool soothed me as I lay on my bunk, arms folded behind my head.

I'd escaped last night, fled back to the suite before anyone could catch me. I didn't want to talk. Not to the guys, not to Eva or Letty.

And definitely not to Molly.

Fuck. It had thrown me for a loop seeing her in the lobby, all up close and personal with that guy. Eva had tried to explain that he worked at the hotel, that he was just being friendly. But I didn't want to hear it.

Molly wasn't mine. I didn't want her. Not that way at least. But my stupid fucking heart clearly hadn't gotten the memo. Because seeing her with that French douchebag had sent jealousy coursing through my veins.

Molly kept her distance today, busy going over plans and routes with Letty. It was going to be a long old ride to Madrid. But after the voicemail I'd gotten last night during the show, I was relieved to have some downtime.

Everyone left me alone. Knew to give me space. Just how I liked it—how I needed it.

Snatching up my cell phone, I dialed the voicemail and listened to it again. Self-torture at its finest.

"BABY, Hudson... my sweet, sweet boy. It's me, your mama. I need you, baby. I can't do this... I can't... God, Hudson, sweetheart. I have regrets, so many regrets. I just wish I could go back in time and take it all back. I'd do things differently, so differently, baby. You believe me, don't you? You know how much I love you. You have to know..." Her voice cracked, her words becoming inaudible through the sniffles and ugly sobs.

I HUNG up and inhaled a shuddering breath. She talked such a good fucking talk, but it was all bullshit. She didn't care, not really. If she had, I wouldn't have spent my childhood in and out of foster homes.

All because she loved my sperm donor to the breaking point while he loved no one but himself.

Fists clenched at my side, I breathed through the pain and anger lashing my insides. Usually, I pushed it all down. Locked it away in that airtight box where it couldn't touch me. It was easy when she wasn't hounding me, trying to right past mistakes.

A bitter laugh crawled up my throat, burning like shards of glass. There was no fixing the damage she'd done.

No fixing me.

Some days I wished she would just stop. But there was still a part of me, the small boy vying for scraps of his mom's attention, that clung to every text and call. And I hated it. I fucking hated that she still had some kind of hold over me.

Hated it to the point that I loathed myself for being so weak. For giving her even an inch to worm her way into my life.

I didn't need her. I had everything I could want, the world literally laid out at my feet. More money than I knew what to do with, a stream of girls ready and willing to be mine for the night, brands lining up to offer me endorsements and photoshoots and commercials. And best of all, I got to do it all with my three best friends in the whole world.

We weren't only a band, we were family. And they were all I needed.

So why the fuck couldn't I cut her out of my life once and for all?

"Yo, Hud," Levi called from somewhere on the bus. "We're stopping for a break."

"Jesus, already," I grumbled.

He pulled back the curtain on my bunk. It afforded me some measure of privacy, acting more like a giant 'fuck off' than anything else.

"Seriously, dude, are you going to sulk all day?"

"We can't all be as happy as you, Hunter."

"What can I say, I'm a changed man." He smirked and I wanted nothing more than to knock it off his pretty little face.

"Go on, how much do you want to hit me right now?"

"On a scale of ten?" I arched a brow. "Eleven."

"Maybe we should get a punching bag on the bus. Work off some steam. Although I can think of better ways to burn off excess energy, if you know what I'm saying."

"You can leave now."

"No can do. Rafe and Damon sent me as the official spokesperson. We almost sent Eva, but she feels it's a conflict of interest given you and Mol—"

"There is no me and Molly."

"Yeah, well, you're stuck with me. So, we can either get off the bus and stretch our legs or we can hang out here while the rest of them go. It's up to you."

"Why are you doing this to me?"

"If you have to ask, Ryker, then we've got bigger problems than I realized." Levi smirked again, but I saw the sympathy in his eyes.

He got it; at least, part of it. Because we shared more than a love of music. We also shared the misfortune of having parents who shaped us into broken jagged pieces. Nearly all of Levi's issues—substance abuse, the ability to let people in, to trust people, his attachment issues—they all stemmed from his and Rafe's mom. She was gone now, thanks to an overdose.

It was morbid to think such a thing but at least she

couldn't hurt them anymore. At least she was a whisper of a ghost in their memories. Instead of a very real, very persistent voice that refused to stay quiet.

"Look," Levi exhaled a steady breath, scrubbing a hand down his face. "You didn't let me stay down, I'm not going to let you stay down. This is our time, Hud. Our moment. We've worked our fucking asses off to get to this point, do not let her ruin it for you."

He wasn't talking about Molly.

"You're right," I said with more conviction than I felt. "But every time she crawls out of her hole, I just…"

"I know, man. Trust me, I know. But you're not a kid anymore. You don't need her. Not when you have us and Eva and Letty and hell, even Alistair. We're your family now."

"Jesus, Hunter." I swung my legs off the bunk and pushed up. "If I'd have known you were going to go all girly on me, I would've just said yes." A weak smile traced my lips.

"Blame Bee. She's pussy whipped me, man. One hundred percent. Pussy. Whipped."

"I heard that," Phoebe called out, and Levi's mouth twisted into amusement.

"You were meant to," he replied, while shaking his head at me. "You sure you're good?"

"I'll be fine."

Because Levi was right.

I had everything I needed right here.

Even if it still felt like something was missing.

———

WE STOPPED at a rest area on the expressway. Letty and Phoebe went inside to get lunch while the rest of us took advantage of the decent sized bathrooms. Then we congregated around a couple of picnic benches on the edge of the huge parking lot. A few people glanced our way, probably intrigued by the sight of our Van Hool parked up in the distance, but nobody bothered us.

Stalter and his guys made sure of that.

"So, next stop Madrid," Rafe said, joining me.

"Yeah, should be a good show."

"Your enthusiasm is catching." He chuckled, nudging my shoulder gently. "Want to talk about it?"

"No, I really don't. Maybe if I ignore her, she'll go away."

"You're going to have to be a little clear here. Are we talking about your mom or Mol—"

"Rafe." I pinned him with a hard stare.

"Shit, sorry. I was just trying to lighten the mood. We're in France, Hud. In France en route to Spain. Part of me knows it's happening, but the other part can't wrap my head around how wild this is. Last night was..."

"Yeah."

It had been something else. Listening to forty-thousand French fans recite our lyrics back to us. You couldn't be unaffected by that, and I swear I spent most of the show playing with chills.

But it had been tainted by the women in my life.
Mom and Molly.

All night, I'd looked for her. And each time, when I'd remembered she hadn't come, it was like another blow to the stomach.

Our opening show and Molly hadn't even been there. She'd been too busy flirting with the bartender. Betrayal snaked through me. It was irrational, I knew that. She didn't owe me anything. But then, my thoughts and feelings weren't always rational.

As if he could hear my thoughts, Rafe said, "You know Eva said she only left the hotel room because she was going stir crazy."

"It doesn't matter."

"I think it does. It's okay to want her. To want something besides all the groupies and fangirls, and faceless, meaningless sex, Hud."

"I can't commit, you know that."

"And I would have said the same thing before I met Eva. Love doesn't care about the rules. It creeps up on you and catches you by surprise. And when it does, better to go with it than to fight it. Look at Levi."

I snorted at that.

"You deserve to be happy, Hud."

"I am happy. I have everything I could possibly want."

Rafe stared at me and said, "Do you?"

"We come bearing snacks," Letty's voice cut through the air, distracting me from my conversation with Rafe.

"We have crêpes, tartines, and of course, French fries." Phoebe laughed at her own joke earning her a chorus of groans from the rest of us.

My eyes flicked to where Molly hovered beside Eva, the two of them sharing a crêpe loaded with strawberries and chocolate sauce.

"I know that look," Rafe said with a teasing lilt, and I flipped him off.

He didn't know anything.

I wasn't some lovesick puppy. So I'd gotten a little jealous seeing Molly with that bartender. She was a free agent. She could call or do whoever she wanted.

Rafe's amused laughter grated on me, but I didn't want to give him the satisfaction of proving him right, so I sat there and ate my tartine, barely tasting it. Not looking at Molly, or him, or anyone for that matter.

But every now and again, I felt her. Felt her big eyes fixed in my direction, willing me to look up.

I couldn't do it though. I couldn't extend an olive branch or accept hers. Because for as much as things didn't feel right between us, it was for the best.

Molly deserved someone who could stand at her side without hesitation. Someone who could hold her when she was sad and pick her up when she fell down. Someone who shared her tenacity and inner strength.

Someone who hadn't been scarred by their abundance of emotional baggage.

And that someone wasn't me.

CHAPTER NINE

MOLLY

BY THE TIME we rolled into Madrid, it was late. Almost eleven. The show was tomorrow night, so the plan was to check into a hotel for the night because then the band had two back-to-back shows. One here, and one in Barcelona. After Barcelona we had the long ride to Italy for the shows in Milan and Rome.

It was only day three of the tour, and I was already exhausted.

"Okay, I'll get us checked in," Letty said as we gathered our overnight bags off the bus. "It's late so we'll order room service or just crash. Whatever everyone wants to do."

"I already feel like I could sleep for a week."

"Welcome to life on tour." She grinned. "Ready?"

"As I'll ever be." I followed her off the bus and we met Eva, Phoebe, and the guys. Hudson didn't even look twice at me. It hurt, but I got it. Things were broken between us. And maybe this time, there was no fixing them.

The hotel wasn't as grand as the one back in Paris, but it was still nicer than anywhere I'd stayed before.

"Molly, with me." Letty beckoned me toward the reception desk. "Hola," she said. "Reservations for Razorsharp Rec—"

"Ah yes, of course." The woman smiled. "Let me get you checked in. It'll just take a moment."

The hotel reception was quiet. No swarms of fangirls or paparazzi. Maybe it would be different tomorrow morning when word got out, but for now, I was thankful for the lack of fanfare.

"You have our luxury suite located on the top floor. Inside you'll find key cards and our welcome brochure. If you need anything you can call me directly." She slid Letty a thick envelope.

"Thank you. We will probably want to order room service."

"Of course. Just let me know how I can assist you once you're settled. Enjoy your stay."

We headed for the band who looked less than conspicuous milling around by the elevators.

"The label really spared no expense, huh?" Levi glanced around.

"Don't get too comfortable. We have two long days ahead of us."

The elevator arrived and we all piled inside.

"Should we expect Alistair tomorrow?" Damon asked.

"He's dealing with a family emergency, but he assured me he'll make the show tomorrow night."

"Is everything okay?" Eva asked.

"Something to do with Ruby. He didn't give me specifics."

"Ruby?"

Letty glanced at me. "His sister."

"Oh." I think I knew that. I had vague memories of Eva mentioning her to me once.

"Well, I hope everything's okay." Eva glanced at Damon, wearing a strange look.

But I didn't have the energy to ask.

Everyone chatted among themselves until the elevator doors pinged open.

"This isn't the penthouse," Levi said, and Phoebe nudged him in the ribs.

"Remember where you came from, rock star," she teased.

"Bee, I don't care where I fucking sleep so long as you're right there with me." He wrestled her out of the elevator, their laughter filling the long hallway.

"I'm guessing we're down here." Letty pointed to the sign marked 'Suite de lujo.' "Anyone hungry?"

"Does a bear shit in the woods?" Levi called over his shoulder.

"Room service it is then."

"I think I'm going to call it a night," I said. "I'm wiped. Do you have our room key?"

"Just a second." She emptied out the contents of the envelope and frowned. "Wait, this doesn't look right."

"What?"

"There are only key cards for the suite. We're supposed to have a room next door too. I'll have to—"

"Call from the suite," Eva suggested. "It's probably just a mistake. They can send room service up with the other key."

Ugh. I didn't want to go into the suite with everyone. I wanted to escape to our room and sleep.

But Letty was already heading toward the door at the end of the hall. "Here." She passed the key to somebody and then we were filing inside.

"Nice." Damon snagged a bottle of water from the complimentary ice bucket and dropped down into one of the big chairs.

I hovered by the breakfast counter, hoping to get our room assignment sooner rather than later. Eva sat down beside Rafe and patted the seat next to her, but I shook my head.

I wasn't staying.

"I need a shower." Hudson disappeared down the hall to what I assumed was one of the bedrooms.

Letty was already on the phone to the front desk. From her grim expression the call wasn't working in our favor.

Crap.

When she hung up she cussed under her breath. "Looks like we're all in here tonight."

"All of us?" Damon asked. "How many bedrooms are there?"

"Three."

"Looks like you're shit out of luck, Donnelley." Levi chuckled.

"I don't mind taking the couch," he said. "Letty and Molly can take the third room."

"Hudson will love that," Levi murmured, his gaze flicking to mine. I quickly dropped my head.

"It's fine." Letty let out an exasperated sigh. "Me and Molly can take the sectional. That thing practically looks like a bed anyway."

She wasn't wrong, but I'd so wanted a night in a soft, spongy hotel bed tonight.

"Yeah, sure," I said.

"I know." Eva stood. "Why don't the guys double up and the girls can take the third bedroom. We can have a pajama party."

"Ooh, yeah." Phoebe clapped.

"No. No fucking way. We're going to spend the majority of the next few weeks crammed up on the tour bus. I want to sleep next to my girlfriend in a proper bed."

"Levi, don't make a—"

"No, Bee. No fucking way. Sorry, Mol," he said, "but I need some alone time with my girl."

"Dude, we had two whole nights in that hotel in France. Quit acting like you haven't—" Damon said.

"Damon, it's fine," I cut him off. "So long as I have somewhere to sleep, it's all good."

"Are you sure?" Eva's expression fell but I saw the anticipation in her eyes. Levi wasn't the only one looking forward to a night in a luxurious hotel bed with his love.

"It's fine." I waved her off, hiking my overnight bag up my shoulder and making my way over to the sectional in the back half of the room. It was darker here, the whole area bathed in shadows thanks to the lack of artificial lighting.

"You want anything to eat?" Letty asked, dumping her stuff on the opposite end of the huge U-shaped sectional.

"No, I'm going to clean up and try to get some sleep."

"Okay. You still have those earbuds I gave you?" I nodded and she smiled. "Use them. According to Sofia down at the front desk there are extra pillows and blankets in the cupboard next to the master bedroom.

"Okay."

Digging out my toiletry bag and pajamas, I hurried to find the bathroom, hardly paying any attention to the beautiful ornate marble counters or the gold trimmed mirror.

A year ago, I could only have dreamed of being in a hotel like this, of seeing the big wide world. But I never wanted it to happen like this. I couldn't enjoy it or soak it up. It felt... it felt wrong somehow. A curse rather than a blessing.

Washed and changed, I gathered my things and made my way back into the living area. Hudson was still nowhere to be seen, but I guessed that was a good thing. I couldn't deal with his cold shoulder tonight.

I found the cupboard with the extra pillows and blankets and set myself up on the couch.

"Hey," Eva said, perching on the edge. "Are you sure you're goin' to be okay out here?"

"I'll be fine. I just want to get some sleep. It's been a long day."

"There are plenty more where that came from." She smiled but it didn't reach her eyes. "You know, I haven't wanted to say anythin' or to push, but whenever you're ready to talk..."

"I know and thank you. I know I'm probably makin' things difficult just by being here."

"No, Molly. Don't do that. I want you here. We all do. But I also don't want you to be sufferin' in silence."

"I can't go back, Eva. Not yet."

"You know, I hate this. I feel like I should be doin' more... getting you to open up and tell me what happened."

"I can't talk about it." A faint tremor went through me.

"But if he hurt you—"

"Please, babe. Don't do this."

"Yeah." She let out a weary sigh. "Okay. Try to get some rest. I'll tell them to keep it down."

"It's fine," I said, pulling out a fresh pair of earbuds. "I have these."

"I see you've been taking tips from Letty. Okay, get some sleep."

Eva squeezed my arm before leaving me alone. I didn't even say good night to the rest of them. But no one seemed to care.

After all, I wasn't here because I belonged. I was here because I'd needed a way out and Letty and Eva had taken pity on me.

Closing my eyes, I tried to ignore the jumble of thoughts whizzing around in my head. Maybe it was foolish to think I could pull this off. My pain was too raw, too fresh. It was a wound that had barely healed. If it ever healed.

But I had nowhere else to go. Eva was my person, and she was here.

But I wasn't Eva's person anymore. She had Rafe and the band and the girls. She had this whole other life... and me being here was dragging that down.

Tears pricked the backs of my eyes, but I swallowed them down. It was too late now. I couldn't go home. Not until I sorted through my feelings on everything.

God, I was a mess.

But just as I was drifting off, thoughts of Hudson and Carson and the future swirling together, I could have sworn I heard a collective, 'Good night, Mol,' come from the other side of the room.

And I don't know why, but it made me smile.

———

I WOKE UP WITH A START. Ripped from a nightmare I couldn't remember. Sweat coated my skin, and my mouth felt parched. Reaching over, I swiped the bottle of water off the table, thankful someone had left it there for me.

Uncapping it, I took a big gulp and tried to catch my breath.

Damn dreams.

I didn't need to remember it, to know who the star attraction was. I could still feel the lingering imprint of his hand on my thigh. His bitter breath wafting over my face.

I rolled onto my back, placing a hand over my chest, silently willing myself to calm down. Letty was sound asleep, and I didn't want to wake her. But I couldn't control the nightmares. I could only fall asleep every night hoping and praying I escaped without one.

The hotel room was cloaked in shadows and bathed in silence, leaving nothing but the steady beat of my heart. I plucked my earbuds out and dropped them on the table, soaking up the quiet. Letty snored softly, something I'd noticed on the tour bus last night. It was strange, climbing into a tiny bunk, knowing she and two other people were right there.

But I guess I would have to get used to it if I stayed.

And I wanted to. Not just because I had nowhere else to go. But because I'd found joy in the band's music once. I'd found joy in watching my best friend grow into her talent and fame. I wanted to be that girl again.

A door clicked open somewhere inside the suite and I lay deathly still, listening. Footsteps sounded down the hall and there was a low hum of voices.

No, not voices.

One voice.

Hudson.

It was almost three in the morning. Who the hell was he calling at this time?

He slipped across the room and around to the balcony door. Sliding it open, he slipped outside.

Strange.

He obviously wanted privacy if he was going outside but he must not have realized there was a window open. A window that afforded me a front row seat to his fraught conversation.

"You can't keep calling me," he said, anger and frustration bleeding into his words. "Yeah, I know. But I'm on tour, I can't babysit you. No... no... I just... I can't fucking do this."

It was wrong to listen but if I moved, I would out myself. So I laid there, silent and still, hoping he wouldn't notice me eavesdropping.

Although it wasn't my fault, he didn't check the coast was clear before slipping out onto the balcony.

"No, just stop. Just fucking stop." His voice echoed through the room, piercing my heart.

There was so much torment in his voice. He sounded so hurt and lost, I wanted nothing more than to go out there and hold him.

But before I could throw off the blanket and sit up, he came back inside.

And saw me.

CHAPTER TEN

HUDSON

"Hudson, I—"

"Were you listening?" My voice wasn't my own as I glared at her.

"I... not intentionally. The window..." She glanced over to the wall of glass and sure enough, the heavy drapes blew gently in the breeze. The breeze from what I could only assume was an open fucking window.

"How much did you hear?"

"I..."

"I'd appreciate it if you can keep it to yourself." I stormed past her toward the hall.

It was a mistake coming out here but when my cell phone had pulled me from a restless sleep, I hadn't been able to ignore it.

"Hudson, wait," she whispered. "Do you want to talk about it?"

"No." The word clanged through the silence.

"O-okay. But whatever it is, whatever's going on, I'm sorry."

I wanted to ask what she could possibly have to be sorry about, but I didn't. Because a world where Molly intersected with my mom wasn't a world I could fucking deal with.

I kept walking but something compelled me to pause before I slipped down the hall. Glancing back, I was hardly surprised to find Molly sitting up, watching me. She gave me a tentative smile. "He was just the bartender," she said.

"It doesn't matter."

It didn't.

And yet...

I shut those thoughts down.

"It's only day three of the tour, Hud. We need to find a way to be around each other. How about we start over... as friends?"

Friends.

There was a loaded word if ever I heard one.

Me and Molly weren't friends.

We had never been friends.

But maybe she had a point. The tour had barely started and if she was going to be sticking around, we needed to find a way to be in each other's presence.

"Fine. I can do friends."

"Yeah?" Her whole face lit up, making me feel like a giant dick.

"Yeah. I mean. It's not like we can escape each other anyway."

Wrong thing to say.

Her expression fell, right as my stomach dropped.

I was a fucking idiot.

She was trying... and I was fucking everything up.

Because that's what you do, asshole.

"Yeah." Molly forced a weak smile. "Well, I guess we should try and get some sleep before the rest of them wake." She pulled the blanket up around her body and laid back down.

She looked lost there, nestled into the huge sectional. It teetered on the tip of my tongue to tell her she could have my bed. But I didn't do it. Because it might send the wrong message, and the guys were already giving me enough shit about her.

If we were all going to survive this tour, keeping our distance was the only option.

———

I WAS UP FIRST. After my call with Mom, and my run in with Molly, I struggled to go back to sleep. For hours, I lay there, staring up at the ceiling, listening to Damon's gentle snores.

Mom was as high as a kite on her call. Full of slurred apologies and teary explanations. It cut me up inside hearing her like that, but I didn't know what I felt more of. Red hot anger or sad frustration.

Then there was Molly.

Sweet, gorgeous Molly Steinberg.

It would have been so easy to bury myself in her, to forget everything else and crawl under her skin. But she was broken too. I saw it every time I looked at her. Only three days into the tour, and she was already struggling to keep up.

She needed to talk to someone. After Long Island, I'd assumed she would eventually talk to Eva. But I saw the way Eva watched her, silently pleading for her to open up. To explain what really happened that had sent her running from Lyme.

Padding into the living area, I made a beeline for the coffee maker. Letty was already up, her blankets folded into a neat pile. But she was nowhere to be seen. Probably already making calls or liaising with security.

She was a fucking angel in disguise, holding us together and getting us to where we needed to be.

My bleary gaze moved over to where Molly slept. She was rolled onto her side, her lips slightly parted as she still slept. Her dark hair spilled around her. There was something peaceful about watching her sleep, like an anchor on stormy seas.

I didn't understand it. Didn't understand the way she'd buried herself under my skin all those months ago. She was just a girl, and I had a never-ending line of those.

But she was in there. Burrowed inside my chest, wrapped around my black fucking heart.

In Long Island, away from the media storm surrounding our lives, away from all the fangirls and groupies and paparazzi, it had been different.

I'd been different.

But that was fantasy, and this, right here, this was real life. It was messy and hard, and it hurt like a motherfucker sometimes.

"Hudson?" Her voice washed over me like the sun on a summer's day.

"Hey," I said, adding cream and sugar to my coffee. "You want?"

"Sure, thanks." She sat up, tamed her hair away from her face and then stretched her arms.

"Listen, sorry about—"

"It's fine. Where is everyone?"

"Letty's off doing whatever Letty does at this time in the morning and the rest of them are still sleeping."

"Oh, okay." Her eyes darted around the room. "I need to go and clean up and then I can make some breakfast if you're hungry?"

"I'm always hungry." Quiet laughter rumbled in my chest. "But you don't have to cook, that's what room service is for. I'm not even sure we have any food." I yanked open the refrigerator door, unsurprised to find it filled with beer and water, but sure enough, not an egg in sight.

"I could go to the store," she suggested.

My brow went up, and her expression fell. "Room service it is then."

"You'll get used to it."

"I'm not sure I will," she murmured. "But it's okay." Molly hurried off to the bathroom before I could reply. Not that I knew what to say.

"Is that coffee I smell?" Rafe appeared, towel drying his damp hair.

"Help yourself." I perched on a stool.

"Was that Molly I saw disappear down the hall?" I rolled my eyes, and he added a very innocent, "What?"

"Nothing." I blew out an exasperated breath. "Nothing at all."

"Shit, Hud, I was joking."

"Forget it, it's fine. We're trying the whole friend thing."

"Friends, right. Because that worked out so well for me and Levi."

"It's not the same and you know it."

"No, what I know is, you two have a connection. You always have. Right since that very first night we spent with them. She's... different."

She was something all right.

"It doesn't matter, man. Whatever happened to her..." I swallowed over the giant fucking lump in my throat. "She's broken."

"Hud, we're all a little broken on the inside. You know, when we came out of that club back in Atlanta and I saw you on your knees in front of her, I don't think I've ever seen anyone look so relieved."

"What? I didn't—"

"Not you, asshole. Her."

"She didn't come for me, she came for Eva." Eva was her best friend, her person. The person she wanted in her moment of need.

"Maybe. But I don't think she's the only reason Molly turned up outside that club."

A strange sensation tugged in my chest, but I didn't acknowledge it, instead letting silence answer for me.

"Anyway, what's happening with your mom? She still calling you?"

"Yep." I clipped out, hating the way just the mention of her twisted me up inside.

"Is she getting help?"

"Fuck knows. She doesn't talk any sense. Just wants to rehash the past, beg for forgiveness, the usual bullshit."

"I'm sorry."

"What for? It's not your fault she's a fucking disaster."

"She's still your mom though, and you only get one." There was a trace of sadness in his voice. His and Levi's mom had died years ago, but scars like the ones she left didn't heal. They only faded.

"Rise and shine, lovers," Letty's voice filled the suite. "I come bearing breakfast."

"Did somebody say breakfast?" Damon poked his head around the wall.

"There's tostados, breakfast tortilla, and some pastries, dig in." She dropped two brown bags on the counter, the scent of eggs and something sweet wafting out.

"You're perky this morning," I said.

"It's a good day to be alive." She beeped my nose.

I swatted her away. "Jesus, you're annoying."

"You won't be saying that when I tell you the news."

"What news?" Rafe asked, digging into a sugary-topped pastry.

"Where's Levi?"

"He's trying to fucking sleep." Levi appeared, looking more than a little disheveled.

"Do we even want to know?" Damon snickered.

"Not unless you want to hear all about how Bee—"

"Okay, you." She slid her arms around him and covered his mouth with her hand. "Morning everyone."

"If you're hungry, I'd hurry before these pigs eat it all."

"Good advice." Phoebe moved around Levi to grab herself a tostado, but he grabbed her hips and settled back against the counter, taking her with him.

"You two are so fucking—"

"Cute? Adorable?" He smirked at me, and I flipped him off.

"Mornin'," Eva finally joined us, and she wasn't alone.

"Hey." Molly offered everyone a small wave. She'd changed out of her pajamas into some skintight jeans and a pale pink sweater that hung off one shoulder. She looked... fuck, she looked gorgeous.

"Ooh, there's breakfast." Eva headed straight for the counter. "Molly?"

"I'm okay, thanks." She lingered on the periphery of the group.

"Letty has news."

"You do?" Eva asked.

"I just got off the phone with Ali. He wanted to be the one to tell y'all but since he isn't here, and I am... I get to do the honors."

"You're killing us here." Levi arched his brow.

"As of this morning, you are officially a platinum selling band."

"You're serious?" Rafe said.

"As a heart attack." Her grin widened. "You're platinum, baby."

"Holy shit... holy fucking shit," Rafe slung his arm

around Damon and shook him. "We're platinum. We're fucking platinum."

The three of them grabbed me, pulling me into a hug. "Fucking platinum, Ryker, you hear that shit?" Levi was smiling so hard it looked unnatural.

"This is a big deal, guys. Huge." Letty commanded our attention. "So, I was thinking we could go out tonight and celebrate."

"Fuck yes," I said.

Because suddenly I had all this pent-up energy zipping through me.

A platinum selling album was the thing dreams were made of, so why didn't I feel the excitement the rest of the guys felt?

"Awesome, I'll get on it. There's this club that contacted us about a VIP event. I'll call them."

"Or we could go for a low-key dinner," Eva suggested.

"No. No fucking way. We're celebrating, Angel, and we're celebrating big. Set it up." Levi nodded toward Letty.

"Tonight," he added, "we party Madrid style."

Maybe this was what I needed. A big blow out. Liquor, music, and girls. But as I looked over at Molly, that strange sensation slammed into me again.

And I didn't know what the fuck to feel anymore.

CHAPTER ELEVEN

MOLLY

THE ARENA WAS ELECTRIC, the constant noise of the crowd thrumming through my veins.

I'd forgotten how it was, watching the band and Eva perform. The crowd lapped up their set, their applause and frantic screams of adoration growing louder with every song.

It was a special thing to witness. The hum of anticipation in the air, a living, breathing thing. It crackled around me, making the hair along the back of my neck and arms stand on end. You couldn't be here, listening to this, watching this, and not be affected.

"Hey," Letty flounced over to me, dressed up more than usual. "How are you holding up?"

"I can't believe I missed the opening show." My body moved of its own volition as Levi caressed the mic with his gravelly voice. He was born to sing; to bless the world with his tortured lyrics and bewitching sound.

It wasn't any surprise that Black Hearts had catapulted to stardom as one of the biggest bands in the world. They had it. Talent, the look, the sex appeal. Even with everything else going on with me, everything I hadn't yet dealt with, I couldn't help but feel it. The charge in the air, the hum of anticipation.

It was impossible *not* to be affected.

Letty nudged my shoulder. "Don't sweat it, there are plenty more shows ahead of us."

There was an unspoken question in her words, but I ignored it.

I wasn't ready to address that yet.

"Yeah." I looked back to the stage. Levi was on his knees in front of Eva as they sang about love and loss and heartache. It was their hit song *Drown*. It had been Levi's song, but Letty and the label talked him into letting Eva in on it and it had exploded. The blend of Eva's silky country lilt and Levi's rough seductive tone shouldn't have worked, but it did.

So freaking much.

But my eyes quickly skated past them to the hidden figure behind the impressive drum kit. Hudson was on a raised platform, the head of his bass drum proudly displaying the band's logo.

Hudson played the drums like they were an extension of him, an extra limb he commanded with utter perfection. I'd never seen anything like it, the way his hands wielded the sticks and struck the cymbals and tom toms as if he was born to do it.

I was in awe. The fact he looked like a total sex god

didn't hurt either. His black shirt was open, revealing his hard chest, the piercing through his nipple, the intricate grim reaper tattoo right over his heart. There was a story there, but I'd never had the guts to ask before. Because Hudson kept a wall up. Even when you were lying in the dark in his arms, he kept his secrets—his heart—guarded.

Completely transfixed on his shadowy figure, I didn't realize the song had ended until Eva came off stage. "These fans are wild." She beamed.

Literally beamed as if she was floating on cloud nine.

"You were so amazing." I hugged her.

"I can't believe Levi got on his knees. He's such a goofball."

"He just likes to find new ways to embarrass you," Phoebe said. "Anyway, go get showered and changed. I'm ready to get out of here and hit the bar."

The bar was some swanky place that had reached out to Letty via the label. Apparently, it claimed to have the most exclusive guest list in Madrid, not to mention the open-air rooftop bar with the best views of the city. Everyone was excited.

Everyone excluding me.

I didn't want to get dressed up and go to a bar. I wanted to go back to the hotel and bury myself under the blankets. But Eva and Letty insisted I join them. Tonight was a celebration and everyone had to be there.

Even Alistair was joining us. Although he looked about as happy as I was at the prospect of staying up late to party with the band.

"Yeah, okay. You want to come, Mol, or—"

"I'll wait here." I folded my arms around myself and gazed back out at the stage.

For a moment, losing myself in the music, the lyrics, and the atmosphere.

But most of all, losing myself in him.

———

CELESTIAL WAS EXACTLY as I imagined when Letty had described it to me. Excessively lavish, decadent, and full of pretentious people in their designer labels and couture outfits.

A year ago, I would have loved it. I would have soaked up every second as we were ushered past the gold rope and escorted to the rooftop terrace.

Tonight though, I felt dreadfully out of place.

Everyone had dressed up. Eva in her black shapely dress, Letty and Phoebe in their edgy skirt and cropped top ensembles. But I couldn't do it. I couldn't bring myself to wear a skirt or a dress, to have my legs on display. So I'd opted for skintight glossy leggings and a thin sweater dress that hit mid-thigh, and paired it with some heeled boots. It wasn't half as sexy or sophisticated as some of the women in this place, but it was as good as it got. My hair hung over one shoulder, shielding the left side of my face as we were directed to a roped-off area on the terrace.

"Paola will be your server," the host said in a rich Spanish accent. Letty thanked him and we all got comfortable. The guys were already turning heads, although I wondered if it was their identity or the fact that they cleaned up well.

Too freaking well.

"This is... holy crap, look at that view," Phoebe shrieked with delight.

She wasn't wrong. The city of Madrid lay beneath us, lit up in all its glory.

It was breathtaking.

"Come on, we need to get a closer look." She grabbed my hand and tugged me toward the decorative railing. "Wow," she breathed. "You know, it's times like these I have to pinch myself and remember this is my life. Well, my life with Levi. Because let's face it, none of this would be happening to me if it wasn't for him."

She glanced back, eyes shining with love as she searched for Levi. He immediately looked up, the two of them like magnets, so in tune with one another.

"Listen, I know we haven't talked much, but I just wanted to say that I'm here if you need a shoulder. Before I joined the band on tour, I had some of my own stuff going on. I know what it's like to feel lost and alone."

"Thanks." It was a non-committal answer, but it was the best I had.

"I know you didn't want to come tonight, but we're celebrating and you're a part of us now."

"Phoebe, I..."

"I mean it. And not just because Hudson and you have a weird vibe going on. You're Eva's best friend, and in case you haven't noticed we all kind of love her. Which makes you one of us too." She laced her arm through mine. "So what do you say we leave all the crap at the door tonight and focus on the here and now? Because our guys just went platinum, baby, and we're in Madrid. Freaking Madrid."

Her excitement was infectious, and it was hard not to be swept away in it. Even if my smile felt a little forced and the constant stone in my stomach refused to shrink, I could do this.

For one night, I could leave it all at the door and soak up the here and now.

"Okay," I said. "Let's do it."

"Atta girl." Phoebe's laughter wrapped around me like a giant hug. "I'm thinking cocktails. Lots and lots of cocktails."

———

I FELT the lightest I had since showing up outside The Riff Bar in Atlanta almost three weeks ago. The drinks flowed freely, but I took my time, not wanting to make a fool out of myself. It would have been so easy to drown my sorrows with the many variations of cocktails from sugary sweet to bitter and tart. Even the guys had tried some of them much to Alistair's amusement, who had stuck to bottled beer.

"Okay, lovers." Levi stood, clinking a stirrer against his glass. "I'd like to make a toast."

"Isn't that supposed to be my job?" Alistair asked, earning him a round of boos and 'wait your turns.'

"If it wasn't for my bandmates: my brothers, my best friends, none of this would be possible. You make going to work every day a fucking dream. And I don't know about you all, but I count my blessings every day that we get to do this. Live this life, doing what we love, together. First platinum album in the bag, but the first of many. To us."

"Hear fucking hear." Hudson thrust his beer in the air. "Now can we get this party started? I want to dance."

"Ooh dancing." Phoebe leaped up, almost falling over Levi's legs.

"Seriously, babe. If you want to get on your knees for me—"

"Levi!" Alistair rolled his eyes. "The last thing we need is another public sex scandal."

"Jesus, Ali Boy, I can keep it in my pants... for now." Levi groped a handful of Phoebe's butt as she tried to get to Hudson.

"Eva, Letty, Mol, let's go."

"Oh no, I think I'll sit this one out." I didn't want to dance. No way.

A pang went through me as I watched them make their way to the small section of the terrace that had slowly become a dance floor. A few people pointed at Hudson, either recognizing him as the Black Hearts drummer or pointing out his ridiculous hotness. Either way, I didn't like watching a bunch of beautiful women look at him like he was a piece of meat.

Even if I'd been that girl once.

Jesus, Molly. Get out of your damn head. But it seemed all I was good for lately. Over-analyzing everything. Dwelling on what was and what could have been.

What would never be again.

God, I needed to stop this.

I snatched up a new drink and slurped it down.

"Whoa there, Molly," Rafe said. "You should probably—"

"Take it easy. Yeah, I know."

"Give the girl a break," Damon added. "There's enough of us to look out for her."

"You'd... do that for me?"

His words caught me off guard.

"Eva would have our balls if we didn't." He smiled, and strangely, I found myself smiling back.

"Can you believe the state of him?" He nodded over to where Levi was trying to sexy dance with Phoebe, oblivious to the stares they were getting. I spotted our security in position around the edge of the terrace, blending in with their background. Ready to strike at a second's notice. But the bar had promised to keep the crowd reserved for VIPs only. Letty had pointed out at least two glamor models earlier and a world-famous DJ I'd never heard of. We were in good company, and it was obvious to everyone how much the guys appreciated being able to kick back without fear of being hounded.

"You should go dance with them," Damon suggested.

"I... I can't."

"Go on. It's good for the soul. Some might say it's even better than those cocktails you keep necking."

I was about to tell him Strawberry Daiquiris were plenty good enough for my soul, when I looked up and had the wind knocked from my lungs.

Because Hudson was no longer dancing with the girls. He was dancing with a leggy blonde.

A model.

I couldn't take my eyes off them. How good they looked together, how in sync they moved to the sultry beat. But there was one gleaming problem.

I couldn't stop watching them.

While they only had eyes for each other.

CHAPTER TWELVE

HUDSON

"I can't believe I'm dancing with the infamous Hudson Ryker. This is... wow."

Serena Devereux, daughter of oil tycoon Mandrake Devereux, and up and coming glamor model, slid her arms a little tighter around my neck, anchoring us together.

She was hot with a capital H. Long legs, slim waist, sun-kissed skin and a great rack. I should have been counting my lucky stars she was rubbing all up on me like a bitch in heat.

But the truth was, I felt... nothing.

Nothing but Molly's intense stare from across the terrace. I avoided her gaze, but that didn't mean I didn't feel it, burning a hole into the side of my face.

"So, are you staying nearby?" Serena trailed a manicured finger down my chest. "Because I was thinking we should get out of here and go have a little private party for two."

"I... uh, I can't, sorry."

Shit. There's something I never thought I'd say to someone as gorgeous as Serena.

"Can't?" Confusion clouded her eyes. "I don't understand."

Of course she didn't. If she hadn't already heard the stories about me, something told me a woman like Serena wasn't used to people telling her no.

"We're out celebrating together. It wouldn't be fair to abandon them. But thanks for the dance." I leaned in to kiss her cheek, slowly untangling her arms from my body. She pouted, letting out a little whimper of disapproval. I assumed it was supposed to be sexy, but it wasn't working for her in the least.

"Thanks again," I said, slipping around her and making my way back to our table.

"Shit, Hud, was that who I think it was?" Damon asked.

"Serena Devereux in the flesh."

"She's gorgeous."

"Yeah," I murmured as my eyes flicked over to Molly. But she wasn't looking my way, suddenly finding her cell phone hella interesting.

Why did I feel like I'd done something wrong? We'd agreed on just being friends. I could dance with whoever the fuck I wanted.

Quit being an asshole, Ryker. She isn't even looking at you.

And maybe that was the problem. I wanted her eyes on me, watching me the way I couldn't seem to take my damn eyes off her.

Jesus, this was a special kind of torture.

But for so many reasons, I had to stay away.

I had to—

"Hud, I asked if you want another drink?"

"What? Uh, yeah, sure. A beer."

Or three.

After a couple more songs, the rest of the girls flounced over and got comfy on the huge sectional. Conversation flowed. The drinks kept coming. The good times kept rolling.

So what the fuck was wrong with me?

Why didn't I feel the usual buzz of anticipation, the high of walking into a room and having everyone's attention—especially, the women.

"Why so glum, Huddy bear?" Letty shuffled closer, and I frowned.

"Are you... drunk?"

"What? No. No, absolutely not." She leaned in closer and whispered. "Don't tell Ali, he won't approve."

"Your secret's safe with me," I said, grabbing another beer the second a fresh round appeared.

"And what about your secrets, Hudson Ryker?"

"What about them?" My brow lifted.

"You know, you could always go and talk to her." Her eyes moved over to where Molly was perched on a leather cube, still minding her own business.

"I think that ship has long sailed."

"So there was a ship, huh? Interesting."

"No, that's not... fuck, you're annoying when you're drunk."

"Don't flip the tables. We're talking about you and Molly." She grinned.

"No, we're talking about you and Alistair and what he'll do if he finds out you're wasted."

Letty poked her tongue out at me with an overdramatic roll of her eyes.

"Very mature," I said, taking another long pull on my beer.

"Are you looking forward to the photoshoot tomorrow?"

"Photoshoot? Do we have to?"

She slapped my chest, laughing. "You know we have to do the promotional stuff. And it's a big one, with Hola!"

"Yay." I grimaced, and she hit me again.

"I swear, you didn't used to be this miserable. I thought having Molly here—"

"Seriously, would you stop going on about her? It isn't helping anything."

"Looks like you missed your chance anyway." Letty grabbed my face and turned me, so I was following her pointed finger... right to where some guy was trying his luck with Molly.

"Motherfucker," I breathed.

She didn't look to be enjoying his advances, but she wasn't exactly walking away either.

"You deserve to be happy, Hud. Maybe she's your shot at that."

"Too much has happened..."

"To both of you. Too much has happened to *both* of you. But maybe together, all that stuff will seem a little less painful."

I flagged down the server and said, "I'm going to need another drink. Make it strong."

"Liquor never solved anything," Letty mused, swaying gently to the beat.

"Yeah, I know," I muttered.

But it was a damn sight better than sitting here sober.

———

"PLATINUM, PLATINUM, PLATINUM," we chanted as we entered the hotel, arms slung around each other. Phoebe and Letty were between us, laughing and giggling. They were drunk.

We all were.

Everyone except Eva, Molly, and Alistair.

He'd retired to the hotel sometime ago, leaving us to our 'wild ways.' The guy needed to learn to relax. Even Letty had found her inner party girl tonight, drinking shots with us like a pro as we celebrated our newfound status as a platinum selling band.

"Guys, maybe you should shush a little." Eva frowned, and Rafe broke away from our little group to go to his girl.

"Relax, Starshine. Nobody is listening."

"Nobody except the whole hotel." She beamed up at him, pressing her hand against his chest.

I didn't get that, the way they looked at each other like they were each other's oxygen. Couldn't ever imagine having that. Being so damn willing to give someone so much power over me.

"Hee-haw, Ryker." Letty jumped on my back and slapped my ass. "Ride 'em, cowboy."

"Oh my God," Eva said through a wide, slightly bemused smile. "I've never seen Letty so... so... well, this."

Never one to back down from a challenge, I galloped off toward the elevator doing a couple of loops, making Letty shriek as she clung onto me for dear life.

"Guys, come on, maybe we should—"

"Relax, Angel," Levi said to Eva. "It's called having fun. You should try it every once in a while." He winked, teasing her.

We all piled into the elevator and Letty hopped down off my back. "That was fun," she said. "Tonight was a good night."

"It was." Damon smiled, and they launched into a conversation. I only heard white noise though, my gaze snagged on Molly as she tried to press herself against the corner of the elevator.

Always on the periphery.

Such a contrast from the girl I'd met a year ago.

I liked both versions, but there was something about this version of Molly that called to me. I wanted to protect her, shield her from the world. From all the bullshit.

From whatever monsters lurked back home.

That particular thought sent a ripple of anger through me.

"What's up with you?" Damon asked me, and I shrugged, murmuring some half-hearted response.

Molly chose that moment to look at me. That moment to give me her dark brown eyes. Fuck, she was stunning. I'd spent the night surrounded by glamor models and socialites, women whose bodies cost more than the average person's salaries, yet I only saw her.

Molly fucking Steinberg.

I was drunk.

Ass over elbow drunk.

It was supposed to numb me, to make me forget about her. But apparently, it had the opposite effect because all I could think about, all I could see, was her.

"Dude, move it." Damon nudged me forward.

I hadn't even realized we'd reached our floor and the elevator doors had opened, most of our group already out in the hall.

"Jesus, you've got it bad." He clapped me on the back, chuckling as he moved ahead of me.

Running a hand down my face, I inhaled a sharp breath, trying to force air into my lungs. My chest felt a little tight and the air a little too thin.

But it wasn't the air or my lungs, it was her.

She was watching me. Standing down the hall, waiting and watching. At least, that's what my inebriated brain cells told me she was doing.

Until I got closer and realized she was frozen in terror, clutching her cell phone in one hand.

"Molly?" Her name echoed down the hall.

Her head snapped up and it was only then I saw the tears sliding down her cheeks.

"Hey, hey, what is it? What's wrong?"

"N-nothing, I should... I should go." She tried to go inside, but I gently grabbed her wrist, tugging her back to the wall.

"Talk to me. What's wrong?"

"It's nothing, I promise." She smiled, all forced and flat. Nothing like the smiles she'd worn naked in my bed. "I never got to say it earlier, but congratulations." Her smile grew but my eyes narrowed.

I was drunk. But not drunk enough to recognize she was purposefully deflecting my question.

"Thanks. It's been a good night. Are you sure you're okay?"

"Yeah." Her reply lacked any conviction and I wanted to push her for answers but started to leave. "I should probably go—"

"Wait." I gripped her arm again, only I tripped over my own fucking feet, careening into her.

We stumbled back against the wall. Molly managed to slam her palms into my chest to stop me from squishing her, but now her hands were on me, and my thoughts were running a mile a minute.

"I..." Molly glanced from her hands to my face and swallowed. "Sorry, I—"

"It's fine. No harm done." One of my hands came to her shoulder, squeezing gently.

Wrong fucking move.

A small whimper spilled from her lips, shocking the hell out of me.

"Molly?"

"I..."

The air crackled in the space between us as she gazed up at me, and I stared down at her.

"You are so fucking beautiful." Tracing my fingers up Molly's collarbone, I pushed her long waves off her shoulder, letting my hand linger against her soft skin. A shiver went through her, making her eyes flutter.

"This is a bad idea," I said, making no effort to pull away.

But the vibration of her cell phone ripped through the moment, and she used the distraction to slip away from me.

"Who is that?" I asked, trying to peer over her shoulder. "Is it him?"

Unfiltered rage poured into my veins.

Carson.

Her ex... whatever the hell he was.

The elephant in the room that no one had dared talk about since she turned up outside the club in Atlanta.

"N-no, it's not..." But she wouldn't look at me. She wouldn't let me see her eyes.

"Molly girl," I said quietly, gently tugging her shoulder. "Just tell me—"

"Is that what you really want, Hudson? For me to tell you all my dirty little secrets..." She scoffed as if the idea was ridiculous. And maybe it was. But she was here, standing in front of me with tears rolling down her cheeks. And I wasn't strong enough to resist.

Not tonight.

"Tell me," I breathed, lowering my head to hers and caging her against the wall. "Tell me what happened."

"I... I—"

"Yo, you two—"

I jerked away at the sudden appearance of Levi in the door. "Shit, I didn't mean... I'll just go."

I let out a frustrated breath. "Sorry about that."

"It's okay. We should go inside anyway." Molly made for the door.

"So that's it, huh? We share a moment and you're just going to run?"

What the fuck was I saying?

We'd decided to be friends. Friends only. But the words wouldn't stop coming and she made no attempt to stop me.

Before I could stop myself, I leaned in, plucking a stray curl between my fingers. "I know I already said it, but you are, you know. You are so fucking beautiful, Molly girl."

"Hud—"

"You're beautiful and strong and I hate seeing you like... like this." I inhaled a shaky breath, thinking about how much I missed her smile. The real one, the one you couldn't help but feel all the way down to your soul. "You never smile anymore, and when you do, it's all wrong. Like it doesn't reach your eyes.

"I think about it, you know, kissing you again. Getting lost in the feel of your body pressed up against mine." I ran my nose along the curve of her jaw, breathing her in. Molly was so still I wasn't sure she was breathing, but I couldn't stop myself.

Couldn't stop the words from pouring out.

"Yeah, I think about kissing you every second of every fucking day. But we can't... *we can't*, and it fucking kills me."

My lips hovered over hers, so close I could practically taste her, as I told her everything. As I tore my heart out of my chest and handed it to her on a silver fucking platter.

But when I was done, she looked at me with a sad smile and said, "You're drunk, Hudson. You don't know what you're saying," and then she walked away.

Like nothing I said mattered.

And me, I walked back into the suite, snagged a bottle of vodka from the mini bar, went straight into my room, and got shit-faced...

Until I couldn't remember her smile anymore.

CHAPTER THIRTEEN

MOLLY

THE SECOND we arrived at the studio for the photoshoot, the guys were swept away for hair and makeup.

"And you must be Miss Panem." A tall, dark-skinned man said, thrusting out his hand for me to shake.

"I... uh, I'm Miss Steinberg, her assistant."

"Pardon, my mistake." He studied me. "May I say you have very beautiful eyes."

"I..." What was I supposed to say to that?

Thankfully, Letty chose that moment to appear.

"Gerrard?"

"Ah, Miss Panem, so good to see you, darling." He air-kissed her cheeks, his big brown eyes fixating back on me. "I was just telling your assistant, Miss Steinberg, what an amazing look she has."

A faint smirk played on her lips. "Molly is very pretty."

"Indeed, indeed." He tilted his head as if considering

something. Until someone shouted, "Gerrard," and he snapped out of his weird trance.

"Ladies, I need to…"

"Go, we'll be here if you need anything." Letty waved him off.

"He's…"

"One of a kind. But he's one of the best, and this shoot is a big deal."

"It all looks very…" I didn't really know what to say about the photoshoot set. It was all very nineteen-seventies disco. From the psychedelic backdrop to the checkerboard floor tiles and glitter disco ball. It was like being in an Austin Powers movie.

"Do the guys know this is the theme?"

"They will soon." Letty chuckled.

"Mierda!"

We both glanced over to see Gerrard having a heated discussion with one of his team. Hands were flying and voices were getting louder.

"Come on." Letty motioned for me to follow her, and we approached the men. "Problem?" she asked.

"One of the models called in sick." Gerrard let out a dramatic sigh. "My vision is ruined."

"Isn't there another girl you can use?" I asked.

His eyes snapped to mine, and he appraised me from head to feet and back up again. "How tall are you?"

"Five seven, why?"

"I see it," the second guy said. "She has the perfect complexion and those eyes."

"W-what?" I glanced between them. "I'm not—"

"Perfecto. Miss Molly, you are exactly what we need."

"No. N-no. I'm not a model. Tell them, Letty, tell—"

"Nonsense, you are perfect." Gerrard looped his arm around my waist and started guiding me toward a door marked 'dressing room.'

"Letty?" I called over my shoulder, feeling blindsided by the turn of events.

She threw her hands up, shrugging. "If Gerrard thinks you are *perfecto*, who am I to disagree?"

"But... but..."

"Come, we must get you into makeup. Wait until you see your outfit." He talked a mile a minute, but I didn't hear a single word over the roar of blood in my ears.

Pulling me into the changing room, Gerrard guided me over to a chair. "Tia, this is Molly. She's going to be standing in for Monique."

"Wait, just wait a minute." I shucked out of his hold. "I can't do this. I'm sorry but I am not a model."

"Nonsense, you are beautiful. You have wonderful skin, those eyes, that smile... Tia will only enhance what God gifted you with. Come now, hurry." With a little shove, Gerrard maneuvered me into the chair.

These people clearly didn't take no for an answer and despite my protest, Tia began brushing and contouring, shadowing and rubbing. And before I knew it, the girl staring back at me barely resembled eighteen-year-old Molly Steinberg from Lyme, Tennessee.

I looked like the women from the bar last night. Glamorous. Perfectly put together. Sophisticated.

"Gerrard was right," Tia purred, fluffing my hair around my shoulders. "You look exceptional."

"But I can't do this... I'm not a model."

"You are for today." She winked. "Come, you need to change."

Sweet baby Jesus. Was this really happening?

She ushered me out of the chair and over to a clothes rail where another woman stood with a retro print dress with flared arms.

"Let's go," she said, then she thrust the dress to Tia and started stripping me from my own clothes. Pushing and pulling me like a rag doll until I was squished into a dress that barely skimmed my thighs.

"What size shoe?" she asked.

"Uh, me?"

"Yes, you."

"I'm a six."

"Okay, so a 37." Oh yeah, we were in Europe. She checked a shoe rack and pulled off some knee-high white go-go boots.

"Put these on."

I did as she asked.

This was crazy. I didn't want to go out there and model. Not with the band, and definitely not with Hudson. Not after the moment we'd shared last night.

The person I'd spent all morning trying to ignore.

But I also didn't want to be the girl who screwed up the photoshoot.

Oh God, what was I going to do?

"Wow," Gerrard reappeared, appraising me. "You look... perfección. Come, come, the band are just getting set up."

The band.

Hudson.

"Come now." He grabbed my arm and gently yanked me back toward the door.

My stomach churned and twisted.

This was a bad idea.

A really freaking bad idea.

"Gerrard, wait," I said, drawing to a stop.

He glanced back, frowning. "There is a problem?"

"I... I can't go out there. Not dressed like this."

"Nonsense. You look every bit the part. Now let's go. We don't have all day."

I pulled at the dress, trying to cover myself. It was too much. The dress. The makeup. The fact he wanted me to go out there and play model.

What the hell had I gotten myself into?

But before I could argue, the door swung open, and the entire shoot paused to watch me enter the room.

At least, that's what it felt like as I stuck closely behind Gerrard.

"Molly?" Eva's voice eased the giant knot in my stomach.

"Oh, Eva, babe. Thank God. Tell them I can't—"

"You look amazing." She clapped a hand over her mouth, tears brimming in her eyes.

Honest-to-God tears.

"Yeah, but I'm not a model, babe. I can't go out there."

"But you look so freakin' good. And I heard Letty talking to the shoot producer about paying you."

"Payin' me?" I whisper-shrieked.

"Well, you didn't think you'd be doin' it for free, did you?"

"I... I don't know what to think. This is insane. I'm not—"

Eva's expression dropped. "If you really don't want to do it, I can talk to the—"

"No, don't do that," fell from my lips without a second thought.

Maybe, after everything, a part of me needed this. Needed to reclaim some sense of feeling like myself. A beautiful young woman with the choice and power over what to do with her body.

"You want to do it, don't you?" Eva's smile returned.

"Is it weird if I say yes?"

"Not at all."

"I know... after everythin', that it might seem a little strange but it's like reclaiming that part of me or somethin'."

She reached for my hand and squeezed. "Molly, you don't have to justify it to me or anyone else. If you want to do it, do it, for you and nobody else."

"I'm going to. I'm going to do it."

"Thank the Lord," Gerrard sighed, obviously eavesdropping. "Now can we please hurry? We're on the clock."

"Yes, sorry." I brushed trembling hands down my dress and said, "Where do you want me?"

———

CLICK. *Flash. Click. Flash.*

It was hotter than Hades under all the lights as Gerrard directed us into pose after pose, shot after shot.

"Go here."

"Move there."

"Miss Molly, smile. Teeth, darling. We want to see teeth."

"More leg."

More teeth.

More smile.

More seduction.

More.

More.

More.

I was already flagging, wondering what I'd gotten myself into and when it was going to end.

The other models—five stunning young women in an array of psychedelic dresses and catsuits—took it in their stride, occasionally huffing under their breath at my inexperience.

Of course, Levi found the entire thing amusing. He'd done nothing but whisper playful taunts at me since we started the shoot almost an hour ago.

It was to be a double page spread for the summer special edition of Hola!

I was going to be in the Spanish edition of one of the biggest celebrity magazines in the world.

It was more than my small-town mind could comprehend.

"Okay, great. Great." Gerrard lowered his camera and moved toward us. "Now let's get one with the guys, each with a girl. Dancing, laughing, touching... It's a 1970s disco and love is in the air.

"Cherie, over here with Damon. Talia with Levi and

Rafe please, you lucky lucky girl. And let's see, for Mr. Ryker... ah yes, the beautiful Miss Molly."

My breath caught as my name rolled from Gerrard's lips.

Surely, this was a joke. Some sick, twisted joke. But when I found Hudson across the set, I knew it wasn't.

He looked as dumbfounded and uncomfortable as me.

"Vamos!" Gerrard clapped his hands, and everyone moved into position. Music poured into the room as the girls started dancing and swaying to the music. Rafe looked particularly uncomfortable as Talia wedged herself between him and Levi, smiling like the cat who got the cream.

A quick glance over at Eva told me she was just as unimpressed as Rafe was.

But this was business. Acting. Not real life.

"Molly?" Hudson was in front of me now, his eyes searching mine.

"I..."

"Yeah." He blew out a thin breath, rubbing the back of his neck. The click of the camera began going off again.

"Miss Molly don't look so afraid. He doesn't bite."

"Only if you ask nicely." Hudson smirked and his words seemed so ridiculous, so out of place given our strange predicament that I let out a bleat of laughter.

Taking my cue from the other models, I draped one arm over Hudson's shoulder and inched closer. Trying to angle my body into his as much as possible without actually touching him.

But he took control. Sliding his arm around my back

and pulling me closer, erasing the sliver of space between us until all of him was pressed up against all of me.

"Hudson," I breathed. A silent plea. For what, I didn't know. I was too lost in his eyes. Too transfixed by the wild beat of my heart in my chest.

The camera went off around us, Gerrard's words of encouragement brushing up against the bubble we'd found ourselves in.

"What?" I asked, blushing under Hudson's intense stare.

"You, Molly girl. You take my fucking breath away."

"I... okay."

"Okay?"

He smirked again. "Good to know I can still render you speechless." Heat blazed in his eyes.

"Hudson, I..."

"Shh. I know. I know." He tipped his chin slightly. "It's okay, I'm not asking you for anything you can't give. I'm not. But I couldn't let you leave here today without you knowing that you shine, Molly. You shine so fucking bright."

I couldn't have fought the smile tugging at my lips if I'd tried. Hudson brushed his thumb along my jaw and gently over my bottom lip. "There she is."

"Fantástico."

Suddenly, I was pulled back into the room. But when I realized everyone was watching us, I wished more than anything that we could have stayed in our little bubble for longer.

CHAPTER FOURTEEN

HUDSON

WHAT THE FUCK was I doing?

Molly's eyes went wide, her cheeks flushed with embarrassment as we broke away slightly, waiting for more direction from Gerrard.

When I'd overheard someone say Molly was going to fill in for one of the models, I'd thought it was a joke. A cruel, sick joke. But then she'd stepped out of the dressing room and my entire world had contracted, sucking the air clean from my lungs.

She. Looked. Stunning.

Molly was always gorgeous, but this was different. The neon floral print drew my eye to her curves, the short hem of the shirt giving me the perfect view of her long legs. Jesus. I had to stop myself from going to her and pulling her into my arms.

Especially after last night. There was unfinished business between us. I was a fool to try and deny that.

"Hudson, why don't you move around Miss Molly. Yes, perfecto, just like that," he said as I slipped around her and brought my hands to her hips. "Now look at each other and hold it."

"You good, Steinberg?" I asked, noticing how stunned she looked.

"I... this is all very... my heart is beating so fast."

"Ignore him. Ignore everyone and just focus on me. I got you, Molly girl."

Something flashed in her expression, but the *click click* of Gerrard's camera was an unwelcome distraction.

"Now slide your arm around her waist. Hold her like she's yours."

Mine.

Fuck.

Why did that do all kinds of weird shit to me?

The entire studio seemed to watch us. Watch this intimate moment between the two of us. It was staged, yeah, but it felt real.

Too fucking real.

My hand splayed on her stomach, and Molly's breath hitched. "You like my hands on you?" I whispered.

"Hudson..." She warned.

I was pushing her. Pushing us to a place neither of us was ready for. But it was like the dam had broken and I couldn't stop myself.

I did want her.

I'd wanted her for a while now. Maybe since the night I'd seen her standing there outside the club, crying on the sidewalk. A broken angel in the dark.

But things were complicated.

I was fucking complicated.

And I still wasn't sure I could be everything she needed. Everything she deserved.

Shit. This was dangerous, uncharted territory. I didn't get close. I didn't let people in, let people see past my cocky, bad boy persona.

But Molly was different.

She'd always been different.

"Closer," Gerrard barked. "Get closer. Perhaps let your mouth linger on her neck."

Heat curled in my stomach at just the thought of that.

"Fuck," I hissed under my breath, dropping my mouth to the curve of her neck, keeping my eyes right on the camera.

"Hudson." A shudder rolled through her, and I felt the heat from her body. The tether pulling us closer.

"Oh yes, yes," Gerrard cooed, snapping photo after photo. "You two are fire. Explosions. I think..." He pulled his camera away and glanced down at the screen. "We've got enough. Yes, yes. These are perfect."

"Thank fuck," Levi grumbled, stalking straight off set to find Phoebe. He didn't care that we had an audience as he pulled her into his arms and kissed her hard.

"I should probably go and get out of this outfit," Molly said, moving around me, avoiding making eye contact with me.

"Hey." I gently grasped her wrist, coaxing her to look at me. When I had her attention, I smiled. "I hope I didn't overstep... with the shoot, I mean."

"N-no, it was fine. You're fine." It came out in a rush of breath, her cheeks stained pink.

"I'm glad you think so." A smirk tugged at my mouth.

"Hudson!"

"What?" I asked, feigning innocence.

"Don't play with me, it's not fair."

I stepped into her, ignoring the people moving around us, deconstructing the set. "I'm not... that's not what I'm doing."

Her eyes narrowed. "So what are you doing?"

"Do we have to put a label on it?"

The air crackled between us as I waited for her to give me something.

Anything.

"Hudson, I—"

"Miss Molly, come..."

Molly visibly flinched at Gerrard's command, and I wanted nothing more than to tell the brash Spaniard to shut the fuck up. But before I could say a word, Molly gave me a weak smile and went after him.

Leaving me standing there like a fucking idiot.

———

"So..." Damon said when we got back to the tour bus.

We were rolling out of Madrid in the next twenty minutes, heading to Barcelona for tonight's show at the Olympic Stadium. Straight after that we had the long ass ride to Italy.

"That was intense."

I side-eyed him with annoyance. "I know what you're trying to do."

"Who, me? I'm not trying to do anything. It was just

an observation."

"Yeah, well keep your observations to yourself."

"I heard Levi invited the girls to ride with us tonight."

"He did, huh?"

"Yep." Damon smirked. "So guess that means Molly will be riding with us."

"Guess so."

"Okay then, I'll leave you to it. I need to wash the scent of those models off me." He sniffed himself. "I swear one of them had bathed herself in perfume."

My laughter was strained as Damon tapped the table and got up, heading down the hall toward the small bathroom.

The tour bus was as spacious as good tour buses came. Two bedrooms. Four bunks. A kitchenette and table with a curved banquette that doubled as our living area. It was a damn sight better than the old rusty van we'd toured local bars and clubs in at the beginning of our career, before Alistair found us and got us signed to Razorsharp Records.

No sooner had Damon disappeared into the bathroom, did Rafe and Levi appear, laughing and joking. Eva and Phoebe were close behind, not that I was surprised. The four of them were tight.

"Yo, Ryker. I told the girls we can play cards later, after tonight's show. You in?"

"Maybe."

"What do you mean maybe?" Levi frowned. "You have to play. I need to win some money back from you."

"Duke wants to leave soon." Letty stuck her head onto the bus. "You guys good to go?"

"As good as we'll ever be." Rafe sank down on the end of the bench, pulling Eva onto his lap. "Want to take a nap later?" He nuzzled her neck.

"Rafe." She tried to fight him off, but it was a half-hearted attempt if ever I saw one.

Letty and Molly joined us. She didn't look at me though, and it irked me.

Something had shifted between us at the photoshoot, I'd felt it. But we hadn't talked about it. After we'd left the studio and piled into the SUV, Levi had attempted to make a joke about the shoot and Eva had promptly shut him up. No one had said a thing since.

"I brought supplies," Letty said, emptying out a brown bag onto the table.

"Ooh, Twizzlers." Phoebe grabbed the candy and tore it open.

"You're worse than children," Letty said, watching as we all dug in. "So I was thinking, we should probably initiate Molly formally tonight."

"Oh no, no initiation required." Molly held up her hands.

"Nobody, not even you, escapes initiation, Steinberg." Levi jabbed a Twizzler at her, and smirked.

"Eva told me all about your initiation and I want no part of it."

"We can leave out the shots," Letty said. "But you have to play cards with us."

"I don't know, I think I'm getting a headache."

"Sounds like an excuse to me." Levi snorted.

"Levi, play nice."

"Relax, Angel. I'm only teasing. Molly knows she

doesn't have to do anything she doesn't want to. We can be teetotal together." He winked at her.

"Sorry, you guys. I know I haven't exactly been a lot of fun."

"No. Don't do that." Eva reached for her best friend. "We all get it. There's no pressure, okay?"

Molly's eyes glazed a little and I had the sudden urge to take her far away from here. But the engine rumbled to life, the entire bus vibrating beneath us.

"Fuck yeah." Levi banged the table. "Barcelona here we come and then it's onto Italy, baby."

"Is it me, or is he worse now than he ever was drunk or high?" I murmured.

"I am high. High on fucking love."

"Someone pass me the bucket. I think I just vomited in my mouth."

"Fuck you, Ryker." Levi flipped me off. "Fuck you."

"What'd I miss?" Damon joined us, in a fresh t-shirt and basketball shorts.

"Levi is high on love, I'm puking in my mouth, and Letty brought snacks."

"Ooh, snacks. Did you get any jerky?"

"Does a bear shit in the woods?"

"Nice, Let. Real fucking nice."

"So what's the plan?" he asked her.

"We're on the road for about six hours. Sound check, show, then we'll travel through the night and morning to Rome."

"Good times," Rafe said, and my eyes flickered to Molly.

I wasn't sure being cooped up on the tour bus with

Molly for the night was my idea of fun... or plain torture.

———

THE SHOW in Barcelona was a whirlwind. We'd hit traffic, arrived at the Estadi Olímpic with barely two hours to spare. It felt like I'd blinked, and it was over.

"I'm so fucking wired," Levi said as we made our way to the bus. The girls had gone on ahead instead of waiting for us to grab our gear.

We found them all sitting around the table. Letty already had the drinks, snacks, and playing cards ready.

"Ready to get this show on the road?" she asked.

"Fuck yeah." Levi practically dove for Phoebe, wrapping her into his arms. I only had eyes for Molly though.

We'd barely had a second to talk on the ride here thanks to Levi's insistence we rehearse, and then he wanted to talk and talk some more. I couldn't work out if he was high, over-excited, or just determined to cockblock at every fucking opportunity. In the end, I'd grabbed a hoodie, rolled it up and dozed to the sound of their incessant chatter.

I slid along the bench next to her. "Hi," I said.

"Hi." Her smile made my heart fucking squeeze as if she'd shoved her fist in my chest and wrapped her slender fingers around the damn thing.

"Your show was great."

"And now we're here." My brow lifted.

"I guess we are."

"Okay fuckers," Levi said. "Everyone grab a drink, and

I'll deal the cards."

Someone handed me a beer and I uncapped it, taking a long pull.

"Molly?" Eva whispered. "What's wrong?"

"I don't feel so good."

I looked over at her just in time to see her eyes flutter. "I think I'm going to—" She went down, slumping against Eva.

"Shit, is she okay?"

"She's passed out." Concern etched in Eva's expression. "Give her some room."

But there was no fucking room.

"Can we use your room?" I asked Rafe, knowing his and Eva's room was probably the better choice.

"Of course."

"Here, help me get her." I stood and tried to lift her into my arms. Eva and Rafe helped me. It was a struggle in the narrow passageway, but I made it work, carrying her down the hall to the bedroom at the front of the bus.

Inside, I lay her on the bed.

"H-Hudson?" It came out a cracked whisper.

"I'm right here. I'm going to get you some—"

"Water." Eva poked her head inside, offering me the bottle. "Hey, you. Are you okay?"

"I fainted?"

"Yeah."

"Oh God, how embarrassing."

"Do you feel nauseous? Hot?"

"No, I'm okay. Just a little woozy."

"Sip some water and see how you feel. If you feel unwell, we can always find a—"

"No, I'm fine. I promise. It's been an overwhelming day and I barely ate at lunch."

"I'll get you something to eat." Eva slipped out of the small room and closed the door behind her.

"I'm so sorry."

"Sorry? You have nothing to be sorry for."

"I didn't mean to faint on you."

"Molly girl, I already told you. You gotta stop falling at my feet."

"Does that line really work?" Her soft laughter eased some of the tension inside me.

"You tell me." I grinned, then smirked. I didn't know what the fuck it was. But I did know that this banter was so easy with Molly. It felt more than like some playful flirting.

It felt right.

"Hudson..."

"Yes, Molly?"

"Nothing."

"Nothing?" My brow went up.

"Nothing. Can I have some water?" She motioned to the bottle in my hand, and I approached the bed to give it to her, an entirely different set of images filling my head.

Get a grip, asshole.

"Thank you." Our fingers brushed, sending an electric current zipping down my arm.

What the fuck was that?

"I'll leave you to get some rest. If you need anything..."

"Stay." Her voice was barely a whisper, but the word clanged through me, making my chest tighten.

"Yeah?"

"Y-yeah. If you don't mind?"

Without thinking, I kicked off my shoes, pulled off my hoodie, and emptied out my pockets, leaving my cell phone and wallet on the small nightstand.

"Scooch over, Steinberg."

She wriggled back to give me space to lie down beside her.

"Hey," I said.

"Hey."

"I can't believe I fainted." She dropped her face, embarrassment rolling off her in waves.

"Hey, Molly girl, look at me." I slid my finger under her chin and tipped her face to mine. "There she is." The corners of my mouth lifted as I pushed the hair from her eyes.

"This morning... at the photoshoot..." Molly hesitated. "Why did you say those things to me, Hudson?"

I shrugged. "Because it felt right. I don't know. I'm not good at this, Molly. The serious stuff."

"You seem pretty good at it to me. But I'm still not sure I understand. I thought we both agreed—"

Leaning in, I touched my head to hers, my hand palming her cheek. "I know what we agreed, but I'm not sure I can do it. I'm not sure I can be around you twenty-four-seven and not be with you."

Her breath caught as she stared at me, eyes wide with wonder.

But then she said something that made my heart crack wide open.

"Hudson, I like you. I do... But I'm not the same girl I was before. I'm... I'm broken."

CHAPTER FIFTEEN

MOLLY

I saw the hurt flash in his eyes. Felt it swirling around us. Hudson thought I was rejecting him. But it wasn't that simple.

I wanted him.

I'd always wanted him.

But I wasn't sure I was ready to be with a guy again. Especially a guy like Hudson Ryker.

"Will you tell me what happened?"

And there it was.

The wall I'd erected between us. Between me and Eva, the guys, Letty, and Phoebe. They had given me space and time and left me to come to them, but it had been almost three weeks, and I still hadn't been able to breathe a word of it to anyone.

But everyone was right. Eventually, I needed to talk about it. I needed to tell someone.

And maybe Hudson was as good a person as any.

So why couldn't I get the words out?

Tears pooled in the corners of my eyes as emotion rose inside me like a tidal wave rushing to shore.

"Hey, hey, Molly girl." He brushed his thumb over my cheek. "I'm right here... I got you, babe. I got you."

"Carson was... he was the first guy after you I felt something for."

Hudson went deathly still.

"Sorry, you probably don't want to hear this."

"No, I need to." The words sounded pained. Forced. He swallowed roughly. "Tell me."

"At first, it was a game, I think. I liked you. Everyone knew it. But I also knew you weren't the kind of guy to make promises. So I agreed to go on a date with Carson.

"He was nice. Attentive. He made me feel good about myself. I've always been confident with guys, but I know it can be a lot. Guys don't tend to like a girl who has too much confidence. But Carson liked it. He liked me. It was nice, you know? Eva was off touring with the band, we were... we were never goin' to go anywhere, for all I knew you were with a different girl in every city. My life back home was so monotonous. I'd just graduated, the world was supposed to be my oyster. Instead, I was helping Mom with the twins, and workin' a dead-end job with no future in sight."

"Carson filled a void?"

"I guess. He made me feel special, Hudson. He made me feel important. I've never really had that before. My best friend is this big country star. My mom's life is her job and the boys. No one has ever put me first. No one. And I guess I was okay with that. I was. Because I want to see Eva shine, I want my mom to be able to progress in the career she's worked so hard for."

"Molly... What. Did. He. Do?"

I saw it then. Hudson's thin rope of control fraying.

"I didn't want to rush into anythin'. I guess part of me was still holding out hope that you might..." I dipped my eyes again, unwilling to splay my heart out before him like this. I could tell him, give him the words, but I didn't want to be completely vulnerable. In case this—whatever was zipping between us—wasn't real.

Hudson cared. I didn't doubt that. But I wasn't sure he cared enough. And I couldn't go back to how things used to be.

"On our third date, I noticed he was acting different. It was subtle but it was there. His touch was a little more forceful. His attention more intense. He asked me to go back to his place, but I made an excuse. I wasn't ready. Looking back, it was like my internal alarm was warning me not to go with him. But I played it down because he was Derek's nephew. Derek is my mom's boss. They're good friends. Derek vouched for Carson. Everyone in Lyme loves him."

"He didn't like you turning him down?" Hudson inhaled a thin breath.

I shook my head. "He didn't take me home. He pulled off down some quiet lane and cut the engine. It all happened so fast... I can't... oh God..." I pushed Hudson away, scrambling off the bed and falling to my knees.

The memories slammed into me with such force, I felt like I was splintering apart.

His weight on top of me, pinning me to the seat as he

clawed at my dress, my legs. I'd tried to fight him off, tried to scream, but it was no use.

No one was coming and Carson was determined to take what he wanted. What he thought he was owed.

"Hey, hey, it's okay. It's okay." Strong arms wrapped around me as Hudson pulled me into his chest. "He can't hurt you now. That fucker will never hurt you again, I swear it."

The tears came thick and fast, a torrent of ugly sobs that made it difficult to breathe.

I could feel him, his hot bitter breath, his teeth marking places he had no right to claim.

"You're safe now, you're safe."

But it didn't matter. Carson had broken something in me that night.

Something I wasn't sure I would ever get back.

I inhaled a shuddering breath, wiping my face with the backs of my hands. I was a mess. But it felt surprisingly good, to get it all off my chest.

I hadn't told a soul about that night. Not a single person.

"He drove me home like nothing had happened." The words poured out. "I think that's what hurt the most. He didn't care. He acted like... like *I* should be lucky he wanted *me*. He even kissed my cheek and whispered he couldn't wait to do it again.

"When I got inside the house, Mom was already asleep. I thought about waking her up and telling her, but then I found the note on the breakfast counter. 'Hope you and Carson had fun on your date. Mom.'"

"You didn't tell her?"

"I couldn't. Derek is her boss, Hudson, one of her oldest friends. It would have put her in an impossible situation."

"She's your mom, babe, she would have understood."

I glanced back to look at him and gave him a sad smile. "That's just it though. I'm not sure she would. For a second, I could imagine the fallout. Her asking me if I was sure we didn't just get carried away, if I didn't give him the wrong impression. And I'd hate her for it. Because the fact I even considered she might choose Carson and Derek's side means a part of me thinks she might."

"Shit, Molly... I... I don't know what to say."

"There isn't anything to say. The next morning, when I finally plucked up the courage to go downstairs, she was so excited about the date, she was practically picking out color schemes for our wedding. I told her I didn't feel the spark and that I wasn't sure I wanted to see him again and do you know what she said to me?" Bitter laughter spilled from my lips, the barbs of resentment coiled around my heart. "She looked me in the eye and said Molly Ann Steinberg, Carson Dutton could be your chance at somethin' good. He has a bright future, a good name, he's a good man. And the fact that he's looked twice in your direction is... well, it's a blessin', baby."

A blessing.

She'd called it a blessing. Like she believed the same as Carson. That I should have felt lucky to have caught his eye.

Hudson was quiet behind me. A silent tempest.

"I knew then I had to leave for a little while. I

withdrew all my savings, booked the first flight out to Atlanta, and left. You know the rest."

"Molly, look at me."

I twisted around, letting out a weary sigh. I felt lighter yet heavier all at the same time.

"You have to tell somebody. You know that, right?"

"I-I can't. Carson is... he's respected in Lyme. Everyone thinks the world of him. They... they wouldn't believe me."

Even if they did, Derek would find a way to bury it. He wouldn't want to ruin his reputation. To risk his business.

"Molly," Hudson asked, his voice barely a whisper. "You know I'm right."

"It's too late now. It's over... it happened."

"Fuck that." He went tense again. "He hurt you, Molly. He... he fucking raped you."

My eyes shuttered, the word fisting my heart and squeezing until I couldn't breathe.

Rape.

Carson had raped me.

And for the last three weeks, I'd tried so hard to forget about it. To pretend like it never happened.

I was in Barcelona. On a tour bus with one of the world's hottest rock bands heading for Italy. I was living a life most girls could only dream of.

But I was barely going through the motions.

Because I was the lucky girl who'd caught Carson Dutton's eye. The girl he'd wined and dined and lavished with flowers and compliments.

I was the girl he'd decided was his. Whether I wanted

to be or not.

The tears began again. I couldn't control them, purging my body of all the shame and hurt and embarrassment. I was barely aware of Hudson scooping me up in his arms again and laying me down on the bed. He'd managed to pull the sheets down and pulled them up over me.

For a second, I thought he might leave me. I didn't imagine Hudson Ryker had ever had a girl breakdown so epically on him before. I closed my eyes, trying to stem the tears, when the bed dipped behind me.

"Get some rest," he said, his lips brushing my shoulder. "I'll be right here."

MY EYES FLUTTERED OPEN, and confusion swam in my head for a second. Until reality seeped back in.

Fainting.

Hudson carrying me into the small bedroom on the tour bus.

My confession.

Breaking apart so badly that he had to put me into bed and hold me.

"Hudson?" I said, rolling over.

My stomach sank.

He was gone.

Flopping onto my back, I let out a weary sigh. He'd left.

Not that I blamed him.

A small knock at the door startled me.

"Hey." Eva poked her head inside. "Can I come in?"

"Uh, sure." Dread carved through my stomach.

"How are you feeling?" She perched on the edge of the bed. "Hudson said you were sleeping."

"He did?"

"Yeah."

"Oh." I dropped my gaze, feeling stupid.

"Molly?"

"It's nothing. I just thought..."

"Oh, oh. No, it isn't... crap, you think he left you. He didn't. Actually, he's been in here the whole time."

"He has?"

She nodded, smiling. "Texted Rafe to tell us not to disturb you and everything. He just came out about ten minutes ago to get a drink and go to the bathroom."

Relief slammed into me, and Eva chuckled.

"He didn't leave, Mol. He also didn't tell us anything beyond that you were a little upset and wanted some space. Want to talk about it?"

"I... will tell you one day, I promise. I just... I really need to process everythin' first. Is that okay?"

"Of course it is. Take all the time you need." She reached over and squeezed my hand.

The door opened and Hudson came back inside. "You're awake." He smiled.

You didn't leave, the words hovered on the tip of my tongue, but instead I said, "I am."

"Do you need anything? Something to drink, eat? Some headache pills?"

"Hudson." The soft laughter that spilled from my lips felt good. "I'm fine."

His expression said he didn't believe me, but he didn't argue. "I can give the two of you some privacy?"

"N-no," I rushed out. "Stay, please."

"Actually, it's gettin' really late." Eva stood. "Me and Rafe are going to take the bunks so you guys can sleep in here."

"No, you don't have to do—"

"Relax, Molly girl. It's all good." Hudson winked and a shiver ran down my spine.

Although we'd already shared a bed together—for the entire stay at Long Island—I didn't want him to think that because we were sharing a bed together tonight, here on the tour bus, that anything was going to happen. Because I wasn't ready. Not for that.

"Don't look so worried." A slight smirk played on his lips, and strangely, it settled some of the nerves bubbling in my stomach.

"Okay, then, if you're okay, I'm goin' to... go." Eva gave me a knowing look, and I flushed.

"We're not—"

"I know. But I'm glad Hudson is here to take care of you. Get some rest. I'll see you in the mornin' when we should be in Italy."

"Good night."

Eva left, taking the air with her. At least, that's how it felt. The tension so taut I was sure it would snap at any moment.

"What now?" I asked, immediately regretting how suggestive I sounded. "Crap, I didn't mean—"

"Relax, babe." Hudson chuckled, grabbing the hem of his t-shirt and tugging it over his body. "Now, we sleep."

CHAPTER SIXTEEN

HUDSON

MOLLY GAWKED AT ME, her eyes trying—and failing—to stay on my face. I didn't want her to think I was pushing her for anything. I wasn't. But this was the only way I knew how to lighten the mood.

"Do you want something to wear to bed?" I asked. "I got your bag."

"Thank you. I'd like to freshen up, I think."

"There's a bathroom back there." I motioned to the door in the corner of the room. "But it's really small."

"I'll make it work. I don't think I'm ready to face everyone yet."

"You know, they won't say anything. Not about you fainting or about..."

"This?"

"Yeah." I rubbed a hand down my face.

"Okay, well, I guess I should..." Molly climbed out of bed and grabbed her bag, making a dash for the bathroom. I toed off my sneakers, unbuttoned my jeans and slid them down my legs, then climbed into the bed.

My cell phone vibrated, and I grabbed it off the nightstand.

COUNTRY: Look after her. She's important to me.

I HAD to fight the urge to reply, 'She's important to me too,' instead sticking to something that required less explanation.

ME: I think I can handle it.

COUNTRY: I don't doubt you for a second. If you need anything, don't hesitate to shout... or text. Night Hudson. xo

ME: Night Country.

I SMILED. Eva had come a long way since the days of being a quiet uncertain girl afraid of her own shadow, not to mention her talent. Country was a nickname Levi had given her and it kind of stuck. She would forever be Rafe's Starshine. But to me, she would always be Country.

The bathroom door cracked open, and Molly slipped back into the bedroom.

"Hey," she said, tugging at the hem of her Black Hearts tour t-shirt. It was at least two sizes too big, swamping her delicate frame.

"Looks good on you," I said, earning me a faint smile. "Come on, get over here."

She slipped into the bed beside me, keeping a safe distance. We lay on our sides, facing each other. I leaned up and hit the light switch, plunging the room into darkness.

"This is... cozy."

"You didn't seem to mind earlier," I said.

"Hud..."

"In case you hadn't noticed, humor is my favorite coping mechanism."

"Will you tell me about her... your mom?"

"Oof, Molly girl. Going straight for the jugular."

"It feels only fair we trade secrets, after earlier."

"About that." My muscles tensed. "We're not done talking about it. It doesn't have to be tonight or tomorrow or the day after that, but we are talking about it."

When she had confessed what had happened with that piece of shit, I'd wanted to hurt something. Preferably that motherfucker's face. But I had to shelve my anger and put Molly's needs first.

I still couldn't believe she thought her mom would choose Carson and his uncle over her own daughter. I knew a thing or two about a shitty parent, but still, I couldn't get my head around it. I wanted to talk to Eva and get her opinion, but I knew Molly hadn't told her yet. And I refused to break her trust, not when it had taken so much for her to tell me.

"Will you tell me about your mom now?" she asked again.

"What do you want to know?" A trickle of unease slid down my spine, making my blood turn cold. I didn't like talking about her, ever. But maybe it would help.

Maybe Molly would understand.

"Everythin'," she whispered, and there was something so honest about it, so real, that I found myself wanting to spill all my secrets.

"My mom is sick. She's been sick for as long as I can remember."

"I'm sorry."

"It is what it is." I shrugged. "Can't miss something you never had, right? My dad abandoned us when I was just a kid, but I didn't just lose my dad that day, I lost my mom too.

"She was devastated. Cried all the freaking time. Started self-medicating. A few Vicodin, Xanax, Percocet, anything she could legally get a hold of. The first-time child services visited, she was so high they took me into emergency care."

"Oh my God, Hudson." Molly threaded her fingers through mine and squeezed. "I'm so sorry."

"Oh, it gets worse."

"Three more times they sent me back to her. She'd clean herself up, get sober, and make all kinds of promises. But we always ended up right back where we started. I was a reminder of the husband she'd lost. A burden, not a reason to want to do better.

"Anyway, the last time the social worker visited, I was eleven. I'd barely been in school, and I was practically starving. They arrested her, and she was locked up for nine months. I went into the care system and stayed there until I was granted emancipation at seventeen."

The only good thing to come out of that time of my life was meeting Levi at the local community center. We were both in a music program for poor school attenders and hit it off. We formed Black Hearts in that program, found our sound and our salvation, and I didn't doubt for a second that music had saved us.

"You still talk to her."

It wasn't a question and I wondered just how much Eva and the guys had told her.

"Yeah. She's like the bad habit I can't kick. But nothing ever changes, you know?"

"Is she better now?"

"She'll never be better. My piece of shit father broke her heart and she never recovered. And one day, it'll kill her."

That was the worst thing. The waiting. Knowing that one day when my phone rang, it would be somebody telling me she was gone. I hated that the most.

"Has she tried rehab?"

Bitter laughter crawled up my throat. "More times than I can count. But they can't fix a broken heart. Only she can do that. And no matter how much she tells me she's sorry, or that she misses me, or that she wants to fix things, the truth is, I'll never be my dad." And thank fuck for that. "I'll never be able to give her back that part of her he took."

"That's... horrible."

"And now you know."

Molly stared at me, a hundred things flickering across her expression. She reached out and traced the tattoo over my chest. "That's why you keep people... girls, at arm's length, isn't it?"

"I don't ever want to be responsible for breaking somebody like that."

"You can't be held responsible for another person's actions though, Hudson. We all make our own choices."

"It's easy to think that. But I've seen firsthand what love, what heartache, can do to a person. To a family."

Deep down, part of me knew my mom's reaction to my father leaving wasn't normal. But too much had happened. Too many disappointments and repeated behaviors. In the end, it changed you. Irrevocably shaped you.

"I'm sorry she couldn't be a better person for you."

"I have everything I need right here. The band, the guys, Eva, Letty..." *You.* I swallowed the word. "Family isn't always blood, it's the people you choose to surround yourself with. I just wish she could let me go. Then maybe it wouldn't hurt so much."

"Do you know what I think?"

"What's that?"

"You'd rather have this small scrap of her in your life than nothin'. She's your mom, Hudson. You only get one, even if she is a mess."

"I could say the same about you and your mom."

Her mouth twitched. "I guess I deserved that."

"It's not a competition."

"You're right." She smiled. "It isn't. But I'm sorry all the same. You deserved more, Hudson."

"And what about you, Molly Ann Steinberg? What do you deserve?"

Her smile dropped as she lowered her head, peeking up at me through thick lashes. "Honestly? I'm still tryin' to figure that out."

"Are you tired?" I asked.

"Not really. I feel surprisingly awake."

"A two-hour nap will do that to a girl."

"You're never going to let me live that down, are you?"

"Don't worry, babe," I said. "Your secret is safe with me."

WE TALKED FOR HOURS. About our childhoods, about our experiences of high school. I told Molly about the early days of the band. Playing in endless dive bars, trying to make ends meet while we practically lived out of our rusted old van. She told me about her twin brothers Silas and Timmy. I could tell how much she missed them from the sadness in her voice. But I also saw her determination, the fire in her eyes that fueled her to come to Atlanta, to join the tour and put herself first for once.

I still didn't quite know what to make of her mom.

I couldn't believe anyone who had given birth to and raised Molly could be a bad person. But the woman seriously had priority issues. Molly had virtually raised her brothers, sacrificed her own wants and needs for them so her mom could chase her career.

We didn't talk about Carson again, or my mom, shelving those topics for another day.

And then when she was heavy-lidded and sleepy, I'd pulled her into my arms, rested my chin on her head, and whispered, "Get some sleep."

It was morning now, and I was still holding her. Still soaking up the strange sense of comfort I felt at being so close to her.

"Hmm, mornin'." She stretched her long legs, our knees brushing.

Heat zipped down my spine at the contact, but I silently ordered my dick to stand the fuck down. The last thing I needed was to screw this up, make her think I couldn't even lie with her without getting turned on.

But then she looked up at me with hooded eyes, a faint blush to her cheeks, and I was hit with *her* desire.

Shit.

"I should probably get up," I said, trying to detangle our limbs. Molly had other ideas though, nestling closer, pressing the soft curves of her body right up against mine.

I inhaled a shaky breath forcing it out through my nose.

"Hud?"

"Yeah?"

"It's okay, you know."

"What's that?" I asked, the words rough against my throat.

"That you're... you know."

Nudging her away from my chest, I dipped my head and brought us eye to eye. "That I'm what, Molly girl?"

"You know." Her eyes twinkled with amusement while a hint of a smirk graced her mouth. Damn, if it wasn't a beautiful sight.

This is how she'd been before, when we'd hooked up. Playful. Sassy. Not afraid to call me on my shit.

"No, I don't think I do. You might have to spell it out for me." I smirked back.

"Hmm, well, either there's a pistol in your boxers or you're just happy to see me."

I almost choked on the breath caught in my throat. "Shit, babe. You can't say that to a guy when he's... trying to be on his best behavior."

"Maybe I don't want you to be on your best behavior... Maybe I want you to be bad."

I went as still as a post. "Molly, you don't mean that."

The blood drained from her face at the cold tone to my words. I didn't mean to sound like I was reprimanding or rejecting her, whatever the fuck I was doing, but she'd been hurt in the worst possible way. I wasn't about to jump headfirst into something physical with her. Not yet. Not until I knew she was okay.

"God, Hudson, don't look at me like that... like I'm damaged goods."

"Whoa, Molly, that is not how I'm looking at you. But you've been through something huge. You're vulnerable right now, and I won't take advantage of that."

She scoffed and tried to glance away from me, but I cupped her face, anchoring her in place.

"I like you, Molly. I've always liked you. And

something is changing between us. I feel it. But don't make me out to be the bad guy just because I'm trying to do the right thing."

Her expression softened. "You're right," she said. "I'm sorry. I don't know what came over me."

"Hey, don't do that. Don't apologize. I just don't want you to rush into something you're not ready for, okay?" I brushed my thumb along Molly's jaw, and she shuddered.

"Hud..." She wet her lips, a soft sigh escaping.

I couldn't resist leaning in and testing the waters, ghosting my mouth over hers.

She curved her hand over my shoulder and pulled me closer.

The kiss was slow, hesitant. But so fucking good. Our tongues tangled, and Molly rewarded me with a soft whimper. I could have spent the entire day just doing this, lying here, kissing her. Feeling her soft curves all up against my skin.

Until someone hammered on the door and shouted, "Rise and shine, lovebirds," reminding me exactly where we were.

And exactly what we shouldn't be doing.

CHAPTER SEVENTEEN

MOLLY

ITALY WAS BEAUTIFUL, just as I'd imagined it to be. From the ancient architecture to the narrow-cobbled streets, Rome was like nowhere I'd ever been.

"Wow," Eva said as we pressed our noses against the tinted glass.

"It's so pretty."

Something caught Eva's attention and I glanced around, suppressing a smile at the sight of Hudson wearing nothing but a towel. He used another one to dry his hair.

"Ladies." He smirked, and my stomach curled as I watched him disappear into the small bedroom we'd shared last night.

"Holy cow, Mol. That boy is..."

"Sin on a stick. Tell me about it."

"So... last night..."

"Eva..." Heat crept up my neck and into my cheeks.

But it wasn't last night making me blush, it was this morning. The sweet, sweet kisses Hudson had given me.

"What? All I'm sayin' is, you came out of that room looking happier than I've seen you since we found you outside the club in Atlanta, and I think a certain sexy drummer has somethin' to do with that."

"Shh, keep your voice down." It was bad enough that everyone knew we'd spent the night together. I wasn't sure I was ready for their constant taunts.

Levi had opened his mouth to start the second I'd stepped out of the bedroom earlier. Phoebe had grabbed him by the balls—literally—and told him to shut his mouth.

I was relieved to have the girls on my side. But I didn't want whatever this thing was between me and Hudson to be under the microscope any more than it had to be.

"More coffee?" I asked Eva, and she nodded.

"Thanks."

I made my way over to the kitchenette and turned on the coffee maker. Strong arms enveloped me and Hudson's gravelly voice said, "Good morning."

"Hudson," I scolded. "Everyone is—"

"Don't care. All I care about is you. Are you good with me hugging you? Because I can stop." He went to pull away, but I grabbed his arms, wrapping them tighter around me. "Didn't think so."

His laughter washed over me, filling some of the cracks inside me.

This was dangerous territory, trusting him with my already fragile, broken heart. Not to mention my body.

But he was right, something had changed between us. It had been changing ever since the night I arrived.

"Well, this is new," Levi said as he and Phoebe came out of their bedroom.

"Leave it alone, Hunter."

"Hey, man, didn't say a word." He grinned, waggling his brows as they squeezed past us to get to the table.

"Hey, Molly?" he said.

"Yes, Levi," I murmured.

"Ryker looks good on you."

Embarrassment flooded me, but Hudson refused to let me go. "Ignore him," he whispered right against the shell of my ear, sending little shocks zipping through me.

"Easy for you to say. I'm sure he's seen you the mornin' after the night before a hundred times."

I winced.

Crap. Why did I say that?

Hudson went still behind me.

I was about to apologize. To beg for forgiveness. But Hudson turned me in his arms and pinned me against the counter. I couldn't look at him. Hudson had never hidden who he was. Not from the world, and certainly not from me. He was the Black Hearts heartbreaker. The charmer. The love 'em and leave 'em drummer who had a different girl in every city.

It wasn't fair to condemn him for that.

I stared past him, hoping he wasn't about to make a giant scene.

"Molly, look at me." Sliding a finger under my chin, he lifted my face to his. "You don't get it, do you?" he whispered.

"Get what?"

"There have been girls. Lots of girls. More than I'm proud to admit. But there's never been another you, Steinberg."

"I-I..."

"Cat got your tongue?"

I nodded, my heart racing wildly in my chest. Sometimes he said something so beautiful I thought that maybe he should be the lyricist for the band instead of Levi and Rafe.

"Hudson, stop lookin' at me like that."

"Like what, Molly girl?" He leaned closer, nudging his nose against mine. "How am I looking at you?"

"You know." I pressed my lips together, trying to catch my breath, to force air into my lungs.

Because when Hudson looked at me the way he was right now, the world grew small and I forgot how to breathe.

Someone's cell phone chimed behind us, and Eva said, "Mol, it's yours."

"Move." I nudged Hudson playfully, slipping around him. "It's probably just my mom askin' again when I plan on coming home."

Snatching it up off the table, I opened the message, the ground going from under me. Because it wasn't my mom at all.

It was Carson.

And his messages were getting more and more insistent.

"I... uh, I need to call her, so I'll just..." I thumbed to the bedroom.

I couldn't look at Hudson as I disappeared down the hall.

But I felt his eyes on me the whole way.

———

OUR ARRIVAL in Rome was dramatic. Due to the narrow streets around the hotel, the plan was to take us to the Stadio Olimpico first where we would all pile into the SUVs and head back to the hotel.

But the fans got wind of our arrival and by the time we reached the stadium parking lot there was already a growing crowd, and they were rowdy.

"It's chaos out there," Letty said, peering through the blinds.

"The Italians are a passionate people."

"Didn't we say that about the French?" Damon snorted.

Letty's phone blared and she headed upfront to answer it. When she came back, she was pinching her temples. "That was Ali. Security isn't happy with the crowd. We've either got to sit tight until the Polizia di Stato arrive and disperse everyone, or we could turn this to our advantage and get some good optics."

"You want us to go out there?" Rafe asked.

"Don't look at me, this is Ali's call. But if it's the choice between staying on the bus or getting out of here..."

"Fine, let's do it." Levi stood up.

"I'm just waiting for Stalter to confirm they're happy.

We'll hand out merch and they can line up for an autograph or photo."

"We know the drill, Let. Relax."

"I'll relax when we're back at the hotel and there aren't two hundred wild fans screaming your names right outside the window."

"Phoebe, Molly, can you head over to the other bus and grab the two plastic containers of merch? I think there are some totes in there too. We can shove a couple of postcards and a poster in them and hand them out."

"Sure," Phoebe said, looking to me. "Let's go."

"Hold on a second," Hudson stepped forward. "I'm not sure Molly should go out there. Not after what happened last time."

"Hud," I said, touching his arm. "I'll be fine."

His eyes narrowed, the way they had when I came out of the bedroom earlier after lying to everyone about my mom calling.

He knew.

And I had no doubt he would have questions. But it wasn't the time or the place. Not when I had to work, and he had to play rock star.

"I'll be fine," I said.

"Yeah, okay." He stepped aside, clearly unhappy with the decision.

It was sweet he cared, but things were moving fast. One minute we were avoiding each other, pretending we were nothing to one another, and now he was getting worked up over me going to the other bus.

Men.

I followed Phoebe off the bus. We were greeted by

two of the security detail and the bellow of fangirls, shrieking and crying for their favorite Black Heart.

"Levi, Levi, ti voglio bene."

"Morirei per te."

"Hudson, Dio mio, Hudson. Voglio avere i tuoi bambini!"

"Your guy is the popular one." Phoebe winked at me. "I'm pretty sure she just offered to have his babies."

"He isn't my guy, Phoebe."

"We'll see." She shrugged and took off toward the second bus. They were parked perpendicular, so we slipped aboard without too much trouble. The flimsy barriers were keeping the fans at bay for now, but everyone knew it had the potential to spiral out of control.

"Does it bother you?" I asked.

"What, this?" Phoebe paused, the wail of young women filling the air. "A little, I guess. It's not the adoration, it's some of the skeezy things they shout. Like that's my boyfriend, bitch. It is totally not cool that you're offering to 'ride his dick like a champ.'"

Laughter peeled out of me. "I can imagine it gets tiresome."

"But it's part of their world and if you're going to stick around, you have to realize that the Hudson they get, the cocky playboy who will have you dropping your panties before you can blink... he's just a character. A fantasy."

I wasn't so sure of that. Hudson's escapades and playboy lifestyle were well documented in the press.

"You don't need to worry about this," she added. "I haven't seen Hudson so much as look at another girl since I started working with the band."

"You haven't?"

A knowing smile tugged at her lips. "In case you haven't noticed, he can't take his eyes off you."

We located the containers of merch and tote bags and started lugging them back to the other bus.

Before we reached the door to the Van Hool, she stopped and looked back at me. "Something is different this time, isn't it?"

"I think so," I admitted, warmth settling in my chest.

Hudson had been so patient with me all night. We'd talked and talked until I could barely keep my eyes open, when he'd pulled me into his arms and let me fall asleep on him. Then this morning, that kiss... it was hard not to get swept away in possibilities.

But there were still two glaring issues between us.

The fact Hudson was a world-famous rock star.

And Carson.

He was refusing to back down, texting me as if nothing had ever happened and I'd upped and disappeared leaving him and my family in despair.

It was sickening really, the way he had everyone wrapped around his little finger.

"Molly?" Phoebe touched my arm and I blinked. "Sorry."

"Hey, are you okay? You look like you've seen a ghost."

"I'm fine," I said, brushing it off.

But the truth was, I wasn't fine. I'd left my hometown, my brothers, my life in Lyme because I'd let some asshole chase me away.

A rush of emotion crashed over me, and I swallowed down the tears burning my throat.

"Ready for the crazy?" she asked me, and I nodded.

Because this was my life now.

And I was a world away from Tennessee.

———

IT WAS A GOOD PLAN. Once the fans knew the band were going to come out and greet them, they happily followed security's instructions to form two orderly lines on either side of the barricade. Phoebe and I worked our way down one line each, handing out tote bags stuffed with postcards and signed posters. A couple of girls became faint and had to be checked over by Johnson, who was our allotted first aider.

When all the merch was distributed, I stood with Phoebe, watching as Eva and the guys met the fans in small groups, posing for photos and signing autographs. Despite the language barrier, they smiled and laughed and made each girl, and the handful of guys in the crowd, feel important. It was a sight to behold. Especially when you saw so many reports of artists growing frustrated and tired with their fans.

But Black Hearts were still young in musiclandia. They knew their success was in part thanks to fans just like these ones.

"Oh shit, we've got a clinger," Phoebe said out of the corner of her mouth, and I watched in horror as a girl made a beeline for Hudson, practically throwing herself at him.

Ever the gentleman, he hugged her and tried to tuck

her into his side for a photo. But she wouldn't let go, tears streaming down her face as she gazed up at him.

Johnson started to move in on them, but Hudson held up his hand, halting him. He lowered his head, whispering something to the girl and she settled slightly, nodding up at him like he hung the moon.

Jealousy surged inside me. It was irrational; I knew that. This was his job, a huge part of his persona as Hudson Ryker, drummer of Black Hearts Still Beat. But all I could remember was him holding me like that, whispering soothing words in my ear.

It hit me then, that this was what life with a rock star would be like. Temptation was around every corner, in every city, every country, every venue. Girls were literally lined up ready to offer themselves up like candy in a sweet store.

Phoebe stepped closer to me, and I didn't understand at first but then Hudson tapped his cheek, grinning, and let the girl kiss him.

"Oh... *oh.*"

My heart sank.

Stop, it doesn't mean anything.

And it didn't.

She was just another fan in another city. After today, he would never see her again. Never think twice about her.

But jealousy was a poisonous monster and as I watched him give the girl one last hug, I couldn't help but think...

What happened when one of these girls caught his eye for real?

CHAPTER EIGHTEEN

HUDSON

"Where's Molly?" I asked Phoebe as we left the dispersing crowd and headed for the bus.

"She, uh... I think she already went inside." She flicked her head to the bus.

"Okay, cool, I'm just going to..." I moved around her, but she called after me.

"Hudson?"

"Yeah?" I glanced back.

"Just... go easy with her."

"What the fuck is that supposed to mean? Did she say something to you?"

"What? No! But we all know she's been through something big. You more than most, I suspect... Look, Hud, it's clear you both have this special bond, but she's new to this world. Perhaps you should ease her into it."

I stared at her, really not following. Things were good, weren't they?

This morning had been... well, it had been fucking amazing. Lying there with her, kissing her, just holding her. Something had clicked into place.

I'd never wanted to be with someone before. I had the starring role in so many girls' fantasies and I'd lapped it up—the fame, the attention, the freedom to do anything or anyone I wanted—but I'd never once wanted to be the center of someone else's world before.

Until Molly.

Now she was all I could think about, and Phoebe was telling me to go easy.

That was some fucked up bullshit right there.

Except, maybe she had a point. Maybe she had a unique perspective given she was with Levi and he was even more fucked up than me. The truth was, I didn't have any idea how to do this. All I knew was I wanted to be with Molly.

I wanted to be her person.

"Got it," I said.

Phoebe offered me a sympathetic smile. "I didn't mean to poke my nose in. Sorry if I upset you."

"Not a problem, Bee." Strangled laughter caught in my throat. "I'm clueless when it comes to this stuff. I should probably quit while I'm ahead."

"No, that's... that's not what I meant, Hud. I just don't want to see either of you get hurt. And when Molly goes home—"

"Home?" The word felt like ash on my tongue.

"Well, yeah. I mean, it's a temporary position. A favor. She won't be..." She blanched. "Shit, I'm making this worse. I should stop talking."

"You think she's going to leave?"

Because of all the baggage piled up between us, that was one thing I hadn't thought of.

"She has a life in Lyme, Hud. Her brothers, her mom... and we all know she's running from something. But eventually she'll have to go home and face things."

Shit. Phoebe was right.

Molly was only here because of what had happened with Carson. Otherwise, she would be back in Lyme, probably still dating that piece of shit, and I'd be here, going through the motions. Drinking and partying and sleeping my way through half the world.

Fuck.

I'd been so happy this morning and now everything felt... wrong. Tainted.

Finite.

It suddenly felt like we had an expiration date, which was ironic considering we'd barely even got started. But Molly would return to Lyme eventually and I would go wherever the band went. We wouldn't be together all the time like Rafe and Eva, and Levi and Phoebe.

"Hudson?"

Molly's voice startled me. I glanced up at her, a feeling of lead in my stomach. "Hey," I said.

Phoebe's glare burned into the side of my face, but I didn't look at her. I couldn't. I couldn't take my eyes off the girl who had stolen a piece of my fucking soul the first night I'd met her. Only I'd been too dumb back then to see it. Too adamant I didn't need anyone.

Too convinced that love made you weak, irrational, and powerless.

"What's going on?" Molly asked, glancing between me and Phoebe.

"Nothing. I'm just going to find Levi. But you two should make the most of the empty bus before anyone else comes back." She winked, leaving the two of us alone.

"You disappeared," I said, meeting Molly's cloudy expression.

"I got a headache."

"A headache?" My brow lifted, and embarrassment washed over her.

"Fine. I got jealous, okay?"

I shook my head with disbelief, and she added, "It's silly, I know. But watching that girl all over you... Just how often exactly does that happen?"

"Come on, Steinberg, let's raid the snack cupboard and we can talk."

Because fuck, there sure seemed like a lot we needed to say.

———

"YOU GUYS really know how to snack, huh?" Molly gave me a coy smile as she popped another Reese's cup into her mouth.

"Oh yeah, candy is a vital part of any successful tour."

"Right. Candy, success, got it."

"So... want to talk about the fact you were jealous earlier?"

"I'd prefer it if we didn't."

"You know all that out there is just for show, right?"

"Yeah, but one day it might not be." Molly lowered her gaze, plucking another Reese's cup out of the box.

"What is going on in that head of yours, Steinberg?"

"I..." A heavy sigh escaped her lips. "This is your world, Hudson. A year ago, I would have given anything to be a part of it. But now... now everything is different. I'm different."

"You're still the same old Molly to me." I nudged her shoulder with mine. "But you do have a point about us being from different worlds."

"I do?" Her brows knitted, and I hated that I'd put that glimmer of doubt in her eyes.

"Phoebe said some things and it got me thinking."

"Phoebe?" Realization dawned on her face. "I knew I'd walked in on somethin' earlier."

Her expression gutted me. We hadn't made it even twenty-four hours. But now Phoebe had planted the seed, I had to know—I had to ask her.

"Hudson?" she said, breaking the tension between us. "What is it?"

"How long do you plan on sticking around?" I blurted it out, hating how desperate the words sounded.

Her eyes widened. "Well, I guess I hadn't thought about it. I can't go home yet... I just can't."

"And you don't have to, you know that. But... and I can't believe I'm going to say this, maybe starting something between us isn't the best timing."

"You want to start somethin' between us?" Her lips parted with surprise.

"I thought I'd made it pretty obvious, Molly."

"I wasn't sure." She gave a half-hearted shrug. "We didn't exactly talk about things."

"Well, we're talking about things now... but—"

"No." Molly pressed her finger to my lips. "Don't. Don't say somethin' that will ruin things. Last night was..." She drew in a shaky breath. "Last night meant somethin' to me, Hudson."

Taking her hand in mine, I gently pulled her hand away. "It meant something to me too, but I don't want either of us to make any promises we can't keep."

"So, we don't," she said. "No promises. No labels. Maybe I don't know what is around the corner, and I know I must go home eventually, but right now, I need this. I need to be here. I want to be here." She took my hand and threaded our fingers together. "I want to be here with you."

"No promises?" I asked, not sure I liked the sound of that.

Because now I knew I might not get to have something with Molly, I wanted everything with her.

"Yeah, then neither of us have to get hurt."

"You want no promises, then I want something in return."

"Okay." She frowned.

"For the duration that we're making no promises to each other, I want exclusivity."

"Is that a joke?" Sarcasm coated her words. "Because I'm not the rock star sex god with girls lined up for me everywhere I go."

Dipping my head, I brushed my lips over her jaw,

letting my mouth linger there. "Did you just call me a... sex god?"

"I have a new rule." She held up a finger. "Hudson must try to rein in his cocky attitude."

"Molly must never speak about Hudson in the third person." I chuckled, kissing her again, sliding my lips down her throat.

Molly leaned back to give me better access, closing her fist around my t-shirt and pulling me with her. "I like this game, it's fun," she breathed.

"Hmm, where were we? No promises." I yanked down the neckline of her sweater and pressed a kiss there. "No handsy fangirls or cocky bartenders." Kiss. "I'll work on my stellar charm, and you'll work on your overuse of third person." Another kiss. "I think I have a final one to add."

Pulling away, I gazed at her. "Molly will give Hudson full and unrestricted access to her sweet kisses at all times."

"All times?" A smirk tugged at her lips.

I nodded around my own grin. "All the damn time, especially when we're half-naked in bed."

"Oh my God, you are such a goofball." She anchored her arms around my shoulders, pulling me closer. And this time when I kissed her, she kissed me back.

———

"So is anyone going to mention the Hudson and Molly shaped elephant in the room?" Levi asked as we all sat around in the hotel suite, waiting for pizza to arrive.

We'd gotten here an hour ago, but everyone had headed to their rooms to get freshened up. No one had noticed me pull Molly into my room, but they had noticed us come out.

Probably not my finest moment ever.

But after our talk earlier I couldn't keep my hands off her. Maybe it was foolish to believe we could do the whole no promises, no labels thing, but what the girl wanted, the girl got. Besides, I wanted it too. I wanted her anyway I could get her.

"Babe, leave them alone. I think it's cute."

"Yeah, but what is it?" Persistent fucker smiled at me, daring me to do it. To claim her in front of them all. "Ryker, care to fill us in?"

Molly ran her hand up my chest, burying her face in my shoulder. "Oh my God, make him stop, please," she whispered.

"What can I tell you, man. It's... us." I shrugged.

"Us... What the fuck is that supposed to mean?"

"It means we're going with the flow, right, Molly girl?" I nudged her out of her hiding place, and she glared up at me.

So fucking adorable.

"Uh, yeah... the flow."

"So you're not together."

"Levi," more than one person barked.

"What? I'm just saying I think we all deserve to know what's happening."

"Tough luck, Hunter." I dropped a kiss on Molly's head and got up. "Because I really need pizza."

The doorbell chimed and everyone laughed.

"It's like he can scent it," someone said as I went to collect the room service.

They all thought I was just hungry; what they didn't know was that I was already on the verge of breaking one of Molly's rules.

"Hmm, smells good." Rafe came up behind me to help with the boxes.

"Did Levi send you to get the insider info?"

"You'll talk to me when and if you're ready."

We went into the kitchen area and got plates and napkins.

"There's nothing to tell, man," I said. "We're taking it slow. Seeing where things go."

"Who are you and what the fuck have you done to Hudson Ryker?"

"I get it now." I ran a hand over my head and down the back of my neck. "I get how everything shifts when you realize you've found her."

"Whoa. I thought the two of you were sleeping together. I didn't think... it's that serious?"

I glanced over to where our friends were sitting, relieved that Levi seemed to have laid off his questions. "I want it to be," I admitted. "But it's complicated. I already got cold feet once today after Phoebe made me realize a few things."

"What things?" His brows pinched with concern, and I got it.

Molly was Eva's best friend. If things went sour between us, it would impact the entire group. But I wasn't sure I could stop, not now.

"That this has an expiration date," I said. "She'll go back to Lyme, and I'll follow you guys wherever you go."

"So..." He shrugged. "You do the long-distance thing."

I gave him a sideways glance and sighed. "We both know how that ends."

"Then you enjoy the moment... see what happens."

"Something like that."

He moved past me and grabbed my shoulder. "Just be careful, yeah? You both have a ton of unresolved shit to deal with. And I'd hate to see you get—"

"Hurt. Yeah, yeah, I got the memo." My teeth ground together.

"Hud, I didn't mean—"

"It's all good. We should go feed them before Levi turns violent."

I headed for the sectional, leaving my doubts and Rafe's warning behind me.

CHAPTER NINETEEN

MOLLY

"OH MY GOD, I love this one." Phoebe yelled over the beat. "Don't you just love this one?"

She bounced on the balls of her feet, clapping to the rhythm as Levi strutted across the stage, seducing the crowd in a way only he could.

"I take it you and Hudson smoothed things over?" she shouted.

"I guess you could say that." I kept my eyes on the stage.

"Keeping your cards close to your chest, I see."

Out of the corner of my eye, I saw her smirk. "You know, you're almost as bad as Levi."

"Girl, I'm offended." She chuckled.

"We're just goin' to enjoy it while it lasts."

No promises.

No labels.

God, why had I ever said those words?

But I knew exactly why.

Because those four little words were a way to protect my heart from the inevitable fallout.

I didn't want to waste a single second of my time with Hudson, and if we labeled it; if we made promises and said things we didn't have time to really mean, it would only hurt more.

"I give it two weeks. Two weeks and you'll be begging Letty to make your position permanent." Her brow lifted as if it was a forgone conclusion.

But my heart sank. "He's right... I can't stay."

Because Silas and Timmy needed me.

Guilt snaked through me, coiled around my heart. I'd been avoiding Mom's calls, texting her every day to make sure the twins were okay. I didn't know how to repair things between us. She thought I was selfish. She thought I'd up and left because of a break up. Because I was too weak to stay and deal with Carson.

But she didn't *know*.

And I couldn't tell her.

So where did that leave us?

"Hey, Molly, are you okay?"

I didn't even realize Phoebe had wrapped an arm around me. "You're crying." She pointed out.

"Crap, so I am." Quickly wiping my face with the back of my sleeve, I pasted on a bright smile. "I'm feelin' a tad hormonal. And they're just so damn good." I flicked my eyes back to the stage. Eva was about to go on, entering from the other side.

"You're in so much trouble." She hip-bumped me,

lacing her arm through mine and encouraging me to dance along with her.

I liked Phoebe. I liked her a lot. But as we stood there watching the band do their thing, I hated that she was right.

Hated that all the talk of no promises and no labels was bullshit. Because Hudson Ryker was trouble.

And I was in so deep, I couldn't see a way out that didn't end in devastation.

———

"HOLY SHIT, CAN YOU HEAR THAT?" Levi flew off the stage, straight into Phoebe's arms. I stood back, nibbling my thumb as Alistair and Letty all congratulated Eva and the band on another amazing performance.

Hudson was last off, his eyes searching me out. The minute they found me, my body went taut with tension, my stomach knotted as he moved around his bandmates and stalked toward me.

He didn't stop, simply grabbed my hand and pulled me down the darkly lit passage.

"Hudson, what are you—"

He yanked me behind a black curtain and pushed me up against the wall. "Been desperate to do this all night." He cupped my jaw, trailing the tip of his finger over my bottom lip.

Feeling bold, I caught it between my teeth and bit down gently. "You were amazin'." I looped my arms around his neck, my heart ratcheting in my chest.

"And you are in so much trouble for that."

"What, this?" Sucking his thumb into my mouth, I swirled my tongue around the tip, reveling in the way his eyes flared.

"Molly girl," he warned, the words rough against his throat.

I grinned, letting his thumb free with a *pop*. He leaned down, touching his head to mine, caging me against the wall.

"Kiss me," he rasped. "Kiss me like you mean it."

I gazed up at him, slightly unsteady on my feet thanks to the wild beat of my heart. Then I kissed him. And it wasn't gentle or sweet. It was hot and fiery and full of fire. It was every emotion I felt poured into a kiss.

Anger.

Sadness.

Pain.

Desire.

Need.

I let it fuel my kiss as I gripped him closer, erasing every sliver of space between us. Hudson grabbed one of my thighs, gently hitching my leg around his hip.

"Tell me to stop," he said.

"And if I don't want to?"

"Fuck." He hissed, grinding into me. "I don't want to hurt—"

"Shh, it's okay." I kissed away his worries, whispering against his mouth when I felt him hard and ready, grinding on me like he couldn't wait.

"I'm so fucking high on you right now," he whispered, peppering my face with kisses as we rocked together seeking more friction. "The whole time I was out there on stage, all I could think about was this. You."

His lips were everywhere: my jaw, the slope of my neck, while his other hand roamed my body, mapping my curves.

"We should probably sto—"

"Not yet. Just let me have this," he rasped.

Hudson seemed content kissing and dry humping with our clothes on, and there was something so innocent and refreshing about that, my heart swelled.

"Imagine me, Molly..." His tongue licked a path from my jaw to my ear, and he nipped my lobe. "My fingers on your hips, my tongue buried deep in your pussy."

Holy crap.

I arched into his body, desire pulsing through me.

"You taste so fucking sweet. I could eat you for days and never grow tired. Spearing my tongue inside your tight, wet heat."

"Hud." A violent shiver ran through me.

"And when you can't take it anymore, when you're screaming my name from the sensations I'm wreaking on your body, I'd slide my dick into you and make you forget your own goddamn name."

"Oh God," I cried.

I actually cried out, overcome with sheer lust.

"Do you want me to get you off?" he asked. "I won't touch, not really. But I'll make it feel good." My body stilled as he drew back to look at me. "We don't have—"

"Yes." I nodded. "Yeah."

"Thank fuck." The words formed on his lips as he

leaned back in, kissing me while his hand worked itself between our bodies.

True to his word, Hudson didn't touch me, not really. His hand stayed over my jeans as he rubbed and pressed, finding just the right amount of pressure to make it feel so freaking good.

"That's it, baby, ride my hand," he drawled, burying his face in my neck and grazing his teeth over my skin.

I was a riot of sensation, a tightly coiled spring waiting to snap. I hadn't thought I would feel this again... not so soon after what happened, but Hudson was healing me. He was eliminating every bruise and scar and replacing them with his touch and kiss.

"Oh God, Hud. I'm gonna..."

"Let go for me, Molly girl. Fly."

The spring snapped and I soared, burying my face in Hudson's shoulder as I came in deep, violent shudders.

"*Hudson*. Yo, Ryker. Where the fuck are you, man?" someone yelled, and I went rigid.

"Relax, babe." Hudson pressed another kiss to my neck. "They won't find us back here. We'll sneak out and join them in a second. I want you all to myself for a minute." He cupped my face again, brushing my cheek. "That was..."

"Unexpected," I whispered

"Inevitable." He smirked, but his expression fell. "I didn't... cross a line or anything?"

"Hudson," I said, fisting his t-shirt and dragging him closer. "It was perfect."

Almost too perfect.

"But we really should go before they figure out what

we're doin' back here."

"I'm pretty sure Levi figured it out the second I dragged you away from them." Hudson chuckled. "But he won't say anything. I promise."

"It's okay," I said. And weirdly, it was.

These were his friends—our friends. It was the one place we could be ourselves without fear of judgment. Levi's taunts notwithstanding.

"Yeah?" He looked at me, brows furrowed, and I nodded.

"Yeah."

As he pulled me out of our hiding place, I ignored the little voice telling me that my answer sounded awfully like a promise.

———

"What is this place again?" I whispered to Eva as we followed Letty and Phoebe down a narrow-cobbled street.

"It's a very exclusive club."

"Exclusive how?"

"You'll see." Letty snorted.

"And the guys are meeting us here?"

"Yeah, after they do the interview with Alistair."

"Right." I smoothed down my dress, the one Letty and Phoebe had insisted I wear. The shiny black material clung to my curves like a second skin, dipping low in the back and front. It was a beautiful outfit, something I would have once loved to wear. But I felt on display and wasn't sure I liked it.

The promise of Hudson's reaction though was enough

to put aside my fears.

Travis and Johnson directed us through a brick archway, and I gasped. "Wow."

It opened out into a small courtyard lit up with fairy lights. A line of women dressed in outfits much more revealing than mine, and men in tailored shirts and slacks stood along one side of the wall. Europe sure knew how to produce some beautiful people. High cheekbones, smooth olive skin, and dark features. The women were stunning, and suddenly I felt extremely underdressed.

"Relax," Eva said, taking it all in her stride. "You look just as gorgeous as any one of them."

"Mm-hmm," I murmured, hardly surprised when Travis led us to the front of the line. Letty stepped forward and did the talking, even throwing in a couple of Italian phrases. The girl had endless talent.

He opened the black door behind him and ushered us into the dark hallway. I gripped Eva's hand, straining to see the way. Eventually, the hallway opened out into a small reception room. There was a cloakroom built into the ornate brickwork and a velvet chaise pushed up against a mirrored wall.

"Fancy," I snickered, and Eva chuckled as we accepted a flute of champagne from the hostess, an olive-skinned beauty in a skintight catsuit, her hair pulled into a high slick ponytail.

"This way please," she said in a thick Italian accent. "Your table is ready."

Phoebe shot us an excited look as we followed the woman into what could only be described as a hedonistic paradise. Tropical plants crawled up the brickwork, blooming in pinks and oranges, a stark contrast to the high-backed black banquettes and chairs. Giant gilded cages hung from the ceiling occupied with dancers dressed in feathered costumes that left little to the imagination.

"Holy crap," Eva breathed, and I was inclined to agree.

I'd never seen anything like it.

"I trust this is satisfactory?" The hostess asked Letty, who nodded.

"I think it'll do." She gave us a knowing smirk.

"To drink?"

"A round of something sweet but strong please," Phoebe said.

"Our Paradiso cocktail is a club favorite."

"We'll take four," Letty said.

"Actually, make it eight." Phoebe grinned, sliding into the booth. It was a balmy night, but the curved leather banquette felt cool against my skin as I sat down.

"Don't look now," Eva said, her eyes wide as saucers. "But I'm pretty sure there's a couple having sex over there on that couch."

Of course Phoebe immediately glanced around to take a look, whisper-shrieking, "Holy crap, they are. But they're wearing the club uniform, so maybe they're actors."

Letty leaned back to look too. "That's some damn good acting."

The girls all chuckled but I was stiff as a post. What the hell was this place?

And more to the point when the hell were the guys going to get here?

CHAPTER TWENTY

HUDSON

"You sure take us to all the best places, Ali boy," Levi teased as we climbed into the SUV.

The interview at the radio station had been a bust. Alistair assured us it was legit, but I didn't know where he'd got his information from because the presenter was a total dick. So much so that when he'd asked me for the third time how I was finding the Italian women, I'd almost punched him.

Okay, so maybe I was feeling a little testy. But after the show—after dragging Molly behind that curtain and making her come apart by barely touching her—I hadn't wanted to leave her.

The girls had already headed to Club Paradiso. It was some exclusive place that had reached out to Letty asking us to show our faces. They wanted the free promotion; we wanted the free hospitality. It was a win.

Until the SUV rolled down some backstreet alley.

"Uh, Stalter, I think you took a wrong turn."

"GPS says otherwise," he grumbled, moving at a snail's pace down the cobbled street. "Okay, this is it."

We all stared at the brick alcove.

"Doesn't look like much," Damon said.

"Well, I don't know about anyone else, but after that shitshow, I need a drink," Alistair climbed out and loosened his collar.

It was unlike him to get things so wrong, but everyone screwed up now and again. Still, we enjoyed riding him about it.

Stalter and the rest of his team closed ranks around us as we moved down through the alcove and into an open-aired courtyard that looked like something out of *Mamma Mia!* the movie with Pierce Brosnan and his god-awful singing.

Alistair went ahead to deal with the door staff while we stood huddled together.

"Anyone feel like you're being lined up for an all you can eat buffet, and we're the only thing on the menu?" Damon chuckled, flicking his head to where a group of women were brazenly checking us out.

"Think they know who we are?"

They were older. Hot, sure. But a good few years older. Not that it mattered when you were famous. I'd had women pushing fifty hit on me more times than I could count.

"Too bad we're not here to play," Levi shrugged his shoulders.

"You don't mean that," Rafe said slightly aghast.

"Like fuck I do. Phoebe is worth ten of those cougars

any day. But you've gotta admit, bro, there are some stunners in Europe."

"You can take the rock star out of the dog… but you can't take the dog out of the rock star." Damon rolled his eyes. "Looks like we're good to go."

We all moved toward the door, but Levi turned back to us. "No one mention this to Bee, yeah? She'll cut off my balls if she knows I was—"

"Relax, man. Your secret is safe with us."

I glanced back at the group of women and one of them lifted her hand in a small wave, her eyes silently conveying her offer.

With a shake of my head, I ducked into the old building and exhaled a steady breath.

"This place is… holy fuck," someone breathed as we arrived in the main room. Girls in cages hung from the ceiling, their bodies writhing to the sultry beat.

Rafe elbowed me hard in the ribs and motioned to the back of the room where a black couch was currently occupied by a semi-naked couple going at it. Hard.

Fuck.

What was this place?

"Where are the girls?" Dread slithered along my spine. Molly wouldn't appreciate this. She wouldn't—

I found the four of them sitting in a large booth, sipping their cocktails like there wasn't a live sex show going on across the room. Their laughter floated over to us, and Levi snorted.

"Bee's drunk." He grinned. "Maybe she'll let me fuck her in the ass tonight."

"Dude, too much fucking information," Damon

muttered as Alistair stood there looking as white as a sheet.

"I'm going to... drink. I need a strong drink." He hurried off toward the bar, all kinds of flustered.

"He needs to get laid." Levi chuckled.

"Or perhaps try, I don't know, *not* talking about your sex habits with your girl in front of him."

"Us. In front of *us*," Rafe added. "I never need to hear those words again."

"Like you and Angel haven't—"

"Don't even go there, Levi. I swear to God."

"Relax, brother." Levi tapped Rafe's cheek. "I'm just busting your balls. Let's go see our women. Standing here watching that is making me all kinds of horny."

We made our way over to them and Bee welcomed Levi as eagerly as he did her, the two of them making out as if we weren't all sitting right there.

"Oh look, another live sex show," Damon drawled.

"You're just jealous, Donnelley." Levi flipped him off, barely coming up for air.

"So..." I shuffled closer to Molly, sliding my arm around her waist. "This place is interesting."

"It's fine if you keep your eyes ahead at all times." Her smile was tight, but amusement danced in her smoky eyes.

"Not a problem given I only see you anyway."

"Smooth, Mr. Ryker, very smooth." Her smile grew as she slurped her cocktail.

"Just how many of those have you had?"

"Enough to almost make me forget there are people havin' sex over there."

"I like your dress." I trailed a finger down her spine. "But most of it seems to be missing."

"The girls insisted."

"Remind me to thank them later."

Molly spun her straw in her glass, gazing up at me through hooded eyes. She looked so fucking gorgeous, I wanted to capture the moment on camera.

Digging my cell phone out, I opened the camera and held it up.

"Hud, what are you—"

"Say 'Hudson is the best.'"

She rolled her eyes. "How about, 'Hudson needs to learn the word humility?'"

"Okay, say 'Hudson has the biggest... hands.'"

"Oh my God."

"No?" I chuckled. "Okay, how about 'I really, really want Hudson to dance with me?'"

"You want to dance?" Her face did an adorable little scrunch, and I snapped a photo. "Hey, no fair." She tried to snatch the phone away from me. "I wasn't even ready."

"You looked beautiful, Molly." *So fucking beautiful it hurts.*

"Uh oh, looks like we've been found," Phoebe's groan pulled my attention, and I looked up in time to see three women approaching our table, including the blonde from outside. Shit.

"Ciao," she purred, raking her eyes over me despite the girl sitting beside me. "I'm Stefanie. This is Chiara, and Frida."

They both wiggled their fingers. Chiara only had eyes for Damon, but he barely glanced at her.

He was... a difficult guy to unravel sometimes. All work and no play made Damon Donnelley a dull guy. But I loved that serious fucker like a brother. He was family in all the ways that counted.

The redhead, Frida, nudged Stefanie, and she nodded. "We wondered, is it really you? The Black Hearts Still Beat."

"Nah," Levi said, tucking Phoebe closer into his side. "We get mistaken for them a lot though."

"I think you're lying," she said, arching a thin brow. "But don't worry, your secret is safe with us. You should come drink with us. Enjoy the... ambience." Her eyes wandered to the gilded cages, the girls dancing provocatively above us.

"We're sitting right here," Phoebe said.

"Of course, you're all welcome." The blonde's saccharine smile was full of bite, but Phoebe didn't back down.

It was strange to see Levi take a back seat and let his girl do the talking.

He was a changed man—all thanks to Phoebe and his expensive as fuck therapist—but it was a great thing.

"We're actually celebrating," Bee said. "But thanks for the offer." She dismissed the women with a flick of her hand, and Letty smothered a snort.

Chiara and Frida shrugged and walked off, but Stefanie lingered, her irritated gaze fixed on me. Molly stiffened beside me, but I slid my hand along her thigh, squeezing gently, letting her know I was right here with her.

"Enjoy your evening," she finally said before spinning on her heel and walking away.

"Well, that wasn't creepy at all," Eva said.

"Nah, Ryker has that effect on women. We call it the pussy spe—"

"Babe, it's called tact." Phoebe elbowed him in the ribs. "Use it."

"What was all that about?" Alistair joined us with not one but two drinks in hand. I guess he really wasn't joking earlier when he said he needed a strong drink. "Why are we here again?" he asked, visibly hot under the collar.

"They reached out to us. We scouted it and it all seemed kosher. Why?" Letty frowned.

"I'm scared they're going to make me drop my keys in a bowl or take me to the red room of pain."

"Wouldn't be such a bad thing." Levi smirked.

"I like the place," Letty protested. "It has…"

"Plenty of dick?" Damon tipped his head toward the couple getting ready for round two. The woman was currently on her knees, fisting his semi-hard dick.

"Okay," Phoebe drained her cocktail. "I don't know about anyone else, but I want to dance. Ladies, shall we?"

"Uh, I don't know," Molly said.

"Go on, it'll be fun. Besides, you can give me the full show." My eyes dropped to her dress again.

"Molly, come on." Eva and Letty were already on their feet.

Reluctantly, my girl got up and joined her friends.

Shit. *My girl.*

I sure liked the sound of that.

"We're lucky bastards." Levi leaned back against the leather seat and watched the girls move onto the dance floor.

"The cougars are circling."

"Bee will cut them down, she's feisty like that."

Sure enough, Phoebe was already glaring in the trio's direction, drawing a line in the sand.

"How is Molly?" Alistair asked. "Is she fitting in okay?"

"She's fine," I barked, and everyone looked at me. "What? She is." I shrugged.

"I wasn't sure about agreeing to her joining us, but if I've learned anything where the band is concerned, it's that I'm better off not to fight you on things."

"That's the spirit, Ali boy." Levi tipped his bottle toward our manager.

He slid his eyes to me. "But I have to ask, do I need to be concerned about the two of you?"

"Would you believe me if I say no?"

"Probably not."

"So don't ask."

"Hudson, I meant no disrespect."

"I know. But we're not putting ourselves under any pressure. I like her, she likes me. It's enough for us right now."

"Okay, okay." He held up his hands. "Message received loud and clear. It's a good thing I can count on Damon to keep his feet firmly on the ground."

"Yeah," he said with barely an iota of emotion. But it was more than that—he wouldn't look Alistair in the eye.

"I don't know about you fuckers." I slammed my beer down. "But I'm going to dance with the girls."

"You mean, you're going to mark your territory." Rafe chuckled.

"A guy's got to do what a guy's got to do."

"Good luck with that," he called after me. But I was already checked out.

Molly looked sensational, the dress showcasing her ample curves. It was downright sinful, falling low in the front, even lower in the back. It was a modest length, but still made her legs look incredible.

Fuck. I wasn't going to be able to keep my hands to myself.

And given we were in public, that was going to be a very big problem.

CHAPTER TWENTY-ONE

MOLLY

"Everyone's lookin'," I said, trying to squirm free as Hudson swayed us to the music.

"Let them look. The club assured Letty complete discretion. They have a very strict membership policy."

"Membership?"

"Yeah, this isn't the kind of club anyone can come to."

"Oh."

Laughter rumbled in Hudson's chest as he tightened his hold on me. Lots of people were dancing now, seemingly oblivious—or used to—the live sex acts taking place in various corners of the club.

At first, I'd been embarrassed, flushing from head to toe. But now I had a few drinks in me, I couldn't help but let my eyes wander over to one couple in particular.

"You like them, don't you?" Hudson asked, his lips brushing my neck, sending a chain reaction of shivers through me. "What is it you like about them?"

"He's gentle with her. He lets her stay in control."

"Would you like that, Molly girl?" Hudson brushed the hair off my shoulder and pressed a single kiss there. "Would you like me to let you take control?"

"I... I don't know. I've always been confident when it comes to sex. But now... I don't know." I looked at the floor, hardly surprised when he gently gripped my chin and tipped my face up.

"Whatever you want... always."

I nodded, too choked up to answer.

The song changed to something slower, sexier. Hudson spun me and pulled me back into his chest, gripping my hips as he encouraged me to move against him. *All* of him.

"She's still watchin' you," I said, spotting the blonde from earlier.

"Let her watch. I'll be leaving with you, not her." Hudson kissed the side of my neck.

It had been the same ever since he'd joined us on the dance floor a little over an hour ago. Some part of him was always touching some part of me. His hands on my hips, my waist; the tips of his fingers stroking down my spine. His mouth on my neck, his tongue tasting my skin.

He was a very tactile person, but surprisingly, I liked it.

I just didn't like feeling so on display. Especially given how much attention the guys were drawing.

Even if people didn't know them, they wanted to know them. It was fascinating to watch the way women vied for their attention. Even going so far as to completely ignore me and the other girls.

Of course, I'd enjoyed Phoebe tearing into the blonde earlier. She'd deserved it. Even if she didn't know me and Hudson were... well, whatever we were, she'd acted out of spite and arrogance.

I closed my eyes and tried to ignore her. The stares. The memories. The decisions I wasn't ready to make.

Hudson moved his body against mine, letting his hands roam up and down my waist. The liquor coursed through my veins, giving me a warm buzz. When I opened my eyes again, my breath caught. Hudson had moved us slightly, pulling us further into the shadows of the club. But now we had a front row seat to the couple I couldn't help but watch earlier.

I'd never considered myself an exhibitionist or a voyeur. I liked what I liked and that was that. But watching them, their bodies a slick tangle of limbs, sent a flash of desire through me.

The woman was straddling the guy, riding him, as he lounged back on the couch, ecstasy written all over his face.

"Watch them," Hudson whispered, his hand splayed across my stomach. "Watch how she takes him. So fucking hot."

My stomach curled, my core clenching. I was wet. So turned on, I was certain people could probably tell. But we weren't the only ones watching. Others were. Eyes dilated; cheeks flushed. Blood running hot. At least, mine was.

"Imagine it... babe. How good it would feel."

"Hudson..." His name got trapped in my throat.

He kissed my neck, licking his way up to my jaw and

nipping me there. "I can remember, you know. Remember how good your pussy feels clenched around me."

"Oh God..."

"Not God, babe. But I'll be anything you need me to be."

It wasn't a promise, not really.

But it speared my heart all the same.

Things were changing too fast between us. We'd gone from zero to sixty and I was powerless to stop it.

I wanted Hudson.

Wanted him in a way that terrified me.

But this—me being here—was temporary. A short-term fix.

Eventually, I had to go back.

I had to face things.

I'd always known Hudson Ryker had the power to ruin me. I just hadn't ever predicted it would be because he wanted my heart.

I turned in his arms, desperate to look at him, to see the guy who was slowly piecing me back together.

"What?" he asked.

"Thank you."

Confusion clouded his eyes, but then he dipped his head, bringing his mouth to my ear. "Don't thank me yet. Thank me later when you're screaming my name."

Humor was always his defense mechanism. His way of lightening the heavy mood.

I wrapped my arms around his neck and toyed with the hair at his nape. "Kiss me, Hudson," I whispered. Pleaded.

Kiss me and make me forget.

He ran his knuckles down my cheek, brushing his mouth over mine. Electricity crackled and pulsed between us. We'd always had a burning connection, ever since that first night in Atlanta, but this was... it was different. More.

And I knew then, it would be so easy to fall so completely and wholly for the Black Hearts' drummer.

He already held my fragile heart precariously in his hands. But whether he'd keep it safe was another question.

God, what was I doing?

This—us—it was almost certain to end in heartbreak. But it was too late now.

I couldn't stop myself even if I wanted to.

Carson broke me.

Hudson was healing me.

But I'd have to find a way to hold myself together when all of this was over.

————

WE STUMBLED out of the elevator, a tangle of limbs and laughter.

"Shh," Hudson pressed his finger to my lips.

"That was..."

"So fucking hot." He grinned, hooking his arm around my neck and dropping a kiss on my head.

Everyone had ridden ahead of us to the suite after Hudson pulled me into the stairwell and kissed me so thoroughly and deeply that I was breathless and practically begging him to touch me.

But I had a feeling that was exactly how he wanted me. Needy and so turned on I couldn't think straight. The drinks helped. The concoction of sugary sweet cocktails and strong liquor was a lethal poison in my veins, making me feel alive.

Making me want things I didn't think I'd ever want again. Not yet.

Johnson followed behind us but kept his distance, probably fed up of us groping each other like insatiable teenagers.

Hudson stopped before we reached the door to the suite and pulled me into his arms. "In case I haven't said it enough tonight, this dress looks incredible on you."

"You may have already told me once or twice." I batted my lashes, feeling brave. Bold and beautiful.

Nothing could touch me here. In the intensity of Hudson's gaze, the wonder in his voice.

"What do you want, Molly girl?" He ran his thumb over my jaw, staring at my mouth like it was his salvation.

"Everythin'. I want everythin'."

He swallowed, his Adam's apple bobbing against his throat. It was so damn sexy.

With a subtle nod, he grabbed my hand and tugged me toward the door, an urgency to his steps that wasn't there before. He didn't even stop to greet his bandmates, making a beeline for his room.

Our room.

I'd overheard him earlier telling Damon to find somewhere else to sleep tonight. A thrill had gone through me then, but it was nothing compared to the wild flutter of butterflies in my stomach now.

Hudson pushed the door open and motioned for me to go inside. He followed, sliding his hand around my waist and tugging me back into his chest as the door clicked shut behind him.

"Alone at last." He breathed the words against the hollow between my neck and collarbone. Shivers skittered down my spine despite the fact I was burning up on the inside.

Everything had been building to this moment.

Every touch, every glance and smile. Every slow slide of lips and tangle of tongues. We'd spent the night dancing, wrapped up in each other, watching that couple have sex. In the end though, I hadn't even noticed them. Too entranced by Hudson and the way he made me feel, the riot he caused inside of me.

"No promises," he whispered, as if he needed the reminder. As if he wanted me to take back the words.

I pressed my lips together, trapping the words there.

Promise me, I wanted to say. *Promise me this doesn't have an expiration date.*

Trailing his lips along my shoulder, Hudson gently pushed the thin straps of my dress down, sliding his hand inside.

"I've been dying to feel you." He gently cupped my breast, applying just the right amount of pressure to make me moan. "So soft," he said, peppering kisses on my skin. Nipping and licking and driving me wild. He was in no hurry though, taking his time.

"I want to unwrap you like a present and taste every inch of you."

"Yes," I whimpered.

God, yes.

Hudson spun me around and my dress slid down my body, pooling at my feet. He helped me step out of it, and without warning, picked me up and carried me over to the bed.

My soft laughter filled the dimly lit room as he dropped me down on the bed and loomed over me. "So fucking beautiful."

He slowly unbuttoned his shirt, revealing his lean torso and the grim reaper tattoo over his left pectoral. I wanted to reach out and touch him, trace the cuts and lines of his body. Learn every inch of him and then start all over again.

His hands went to his slacks, and he popped the button and then released the zipper. "We go at your pace, okay?"

I nodded, curling my fingers into the bedsheets in anticipation. I hadn't been with anyone since Hudson except Carson. But that wasn't anything like this. Carson had taken something from me that night—something I hadn't wanted to give. So the fact Hudson continually checked in with me was a huge turn on. He cared, and he wanted to make sure I was okay every step of the way.

For someone who always claimed not to care, it meant something.

Nervous energy tingled inside me at the sight of Hudson standing there in nothing but his tight black boxer briefs. His knees hit the mattress and he leaned over me, bracing his weight on his hands beside my head.

"Hi." He nudged my nose, pressing a soft kiss to my lips.

"Hi."

"Going to kiss you now, Molly girl," he whispered, flicking his tongue along the seam of my mouth.

A whimper crawled up my throat and I slid my hand over his broad shoulders.

This was how it was supposed to be. The butterflies and anticipation and tingles when you finally came together.

I'd just never expected to feel it so deeply with Hudson.

But now that I had, I didn't ever want it to end.

CHAPTER TWENTY-TWO

HUDSON

My heart was beating so hard as we kissed, I felt light-headed.

Molly's hand locked around my neck, anchoring us together. Not that I was complaining. Kissing her was my new favorite thing. I could still taste the lingering, sugary sweet syrup on her lips, her tongue as it tangled with mine.

I was rock hard. So fucking desperate for her. But I didn't want to rush. I didn't want to waste a single second of this moment.

All night things had been building to this, and now we were here, I wanted it to be perfect. Because to be here with me, like this, I realized Molly trusted me implicitly. After everything she had been through, I wasn't sure I deserved it, but I'd gladly take everything she was offering.

"You taste so fucking good," I licked the seam of her mouth, teasing her. Nipping her jaw.

"Touch me," she whispered, lifting her hips, seeking friction.

"Touch you?" I eased back slightly to look her in the eye. "I'm going to fucking devour you, babe."

She flushed and it was so fucking adorable. Nuzzling her neck, I gently sucked the skin there, leaving a slight mark. Molly didn't seem to mind. In fact, she didn't seem to care about anything except me touching her, kissing her, driving her wild.

I planted one more kiss on her lips before rocking back on my haunches and sliding a hand down her stomach to the edge of her panties. "These need to go," I said, hooking my fingers into the elastic and inching them down her hips.

Molly lifted her ass so I could work them off her legs. She was every guy's wet dream, laying there completely naked, her hair splayed out around her like a dark halo.

Nudging her legs apart, I cupped her pussy, sliding my thumb through her dark curls and over her clit.

"God, Hudson." The words caught in her throat as she bowed into my touch. "More..."

"Greedy girl." A smirk played on my lips as I took my time touching her, working her into a wanton mess. My thumb made lazy circles while I pressed two fingers inside her.

She was so tight, slick and warm.

"Is this okay?" I asked.

"Yes... God, yes." She fisted the bedsheets, arching off

the mattress as I worked her faster, rubbing a spot deep inside.

But it wasn't enough to watch her come like this. I wanted to taste her, to feel her explode on my tongue.

I shuffled back and dropped to my forearms.

"H-Hudson?" she choked out.

"Shh, Molly girl. I got you." Blowing a hot stream of air over her clit, I smirked at how responsive she was. The tiny whimpers and the way her body kicked up, silently demanding more.

There was nothing in the world hotter than this: witnessing her submission to me, to her desires.

I was a lucky bastard.

My tongue darted out, tasting her. Fuck. I could die a happy guy right here, buried between her silky-smooth legs. Sliding my hands under her thighs, I spread her open to me.

"Hudson..."

"What do you need, babe?"

"More... all of it..."

Pulling my fingers out of her, I replaced them with my tongue, spearing it inside her. Blood rushed to my dick, my heart slamming against my chest as I feasted on her like a man starved.

Molly grabbed my hair, scraping her nails over my scalp as I continued licking and sucking on her clit while I curled my fingers back inside her.

"Yes, oh God... yes..."

"You like that, babe? You like my mouth on you?"

"So good," she panted. "So, so good."

Her legs began to tremble as I upped the pace, going at her faster, deeper. "Hudson... I'm close... I'm—" Her cries filled the room, a deep sense of satisfaction settling in my chest.

"Oh. My. God," she breathed, tugging my hair for me to stop. I pressed a final kiss to her inner thigh and crawled up her body.

"Hi."

"Hi." She gave me a sated smile. "That was... I'd forgotten how good that can be."

"Well, get used to it, because I plan on doing it again real soon." I kissed her, soft and slow, letting her taste herself on my tongue.

Molly wrapped herself around me like a koala. It was nice to be held so tightly by her.

I'd never considered myself a hugger. Never considered myself a lot of things until her.

Pushing the hair from Molly's face, I ran my nose along hers. "Do you want to sleep?"

"Sleep." She frowned. "I thought..."

"You thought what?"

The little minx rubbed herself right over my dick. "I thought you were going to make me scream your name."

"Didn't I just do that?"

She swatted my chest. "You know what I mean."

"Are you sure? Because we can wait. I don't want—"

"Hudson." She gripped my jaw, narrowing her eyes at me. "I want you. I want you every single way I can get you."

"And you're sure that's not all the cocktails talking?" My brow quirked up.

"Do I need to go and find someone else to—"

I grabbed her wrists and pinned them on either side of her head. "Exclusivity, remember? You're mine, Molly girl. For however long this lasts."

Something flickered in her eyes, but as quickly as it was there, it was gone, replaced by burning desire. "I want to feel you, Hudson. All of you."

I pressed a kiss to her lips and climbed off the bed, grabbing a condom from my wallet. If we were doing this, we were doing it safely. At least until we could both get checked out.

Fuck, just the thought of going in bare had me tied up in knots. But I could wait.

Molly watched me quietly as I tore open the foil wrapper and rolled the latex over my hard length. "If you need to stop—"

"Hudson." She reached for me, curving her hand over my shoulder and pulling me down on top of her. My hips fell into the cradle of her thighs and we both moaned.

"I'm fine. Now are you goin' to keep me waiting all night or—"

I grasped myself and slowly pushed inside her. Molly gasped, a violent shiver going through her.

I stilled, searching her face for any sign of discomfort. "You good?"

"You feel... holy shiitake you feel good." My brows knitted and she burst into laughter. "I can't believe I just said that. I'm sorry, I'm nervous and you're... God, I'm sorry. Okay, shuttin' up now."

"Molly?" I caught her wild gaze and she instantly calmed.

"Yeah, Hudson?"

"I'm going to move now." Because if I didn't move soon, I would probably combust.

She felt *that* fucking good.

"Oh, okay." A pink streak ran up her neck and into her cheeks.

I leaned down, capturing her lips in a hungry kiss as I rocked forward, sliding all the way home. Molly whimpered but it was laced with pleasure. Grasping her thigh, I hitched her leg around my waist, allowing me to go deeper, but I kept it slow and steady. This wasn't about me; it was one hundred percent about her. About erasing what that piece of shit did to her and giving her back confidence in her body and the reassurance that she wasn't damaged or tainted or broken. She was fucking perfect.

Invisible scars and all.

"You feel so good, babe. So fucking good." I gazed down at her as I kept rocking my hips, building to a pace that had us both groaning.

"It's... God..."

She wasn't wrong.

There was something intense about it, the way our bodies moved together. The way our eyes held each other's, full of silent promises. Promises we'd promised not to make.

"Hudson, ah..." Molly pressed her lips together, breathless and moaning.

"Fuck, babe... you feel... *fuck*." It was impossible not to go faster... harder. Until our bodies crashed together.

Molly clung to me, meeting me thrust for thrust as my

fingers curled into her hips, needing her closer. Needing to be so fucking deep in her I didn't know where I ended, and she began.

Sex with Molly had always been off the charts, but this was a whole new level. Probably because I'd never let myself believe in a future beyond meaningless sex.

I'd never wanted it before.

Until she showed up in Atlanta and something had snapped into place.

Molly was mine, maybe she always had been, and it had just taken me a while to see it. And although part of me hated that it took Carson hurting her for me to realize what she meant to me, I wanted to be the one to protect her now.

To heal her.

To lift her up and show her what a fucking goddess she was.

"Oh God... God... I'm... *Hudson*," she cried, seeking my lips.

Our mouths collided as I reached between us and found her clit, circling it the way I knew she liked.

"Yes, yes... God, *yes*..."

She clenched around me, sending a bolt of pleasure shooting down my spine. She felt sensational gripping me, pulling me into her body.

"Come for me, babe. I need you to get there first." I dropped my head, flicking my tongue over her nipple, sucking it into my mouth.

Molly came hard, screaming loud enough that I kissed her hard to swallow the noise.

The sight of her flushed and panting was enough to

get me there, and I buried my face in her neck, latching onto her skin as I came.

"Fuck," I breathed, riding out the intense waves surging through me.

Molly stroked a hand up and down my spine, in no rush to move.

This was new. Basking in the aftermath. My usual MO was to get the fuck out of there or pass out. But now, I didn't ever want to leave. Her. This room. The giant fucking bed. We could spend our days talking and our nights with me buried deep inside her.

Sounded good to me.

"Hudson?" Her voice was a quiet whisper.

"Yeah?" I lifted my face to look at her.

"Thank you." Her smile was uncertain. Small and timid.

"You don't need to thank me, Molly girl." I brushed my knuckle down her cheek.

"Yes, I do. That was..." Tears pooled in the corners of her eyes.

"Shit, babe. Come here." I rolled off her and disposed of the condom before lying down and pulling her into my arms. "I can't promise I won't screw up, babe. I'm a guy, it's what we do. But I can promise I'll never—"

"Shh." She pressed a finger to my lips. "No promises, remember?"

I wanted to call bullshit.

What had just happened between us was a promise in itself. But if she needed more time—if she needed to tell herself that this, us, wasn't heading toward something more permanent, then I'd let her have that. For now.

But sometime soon, I would need more.
I'd need to hear her say it.
I'd need her to promise me that she was mine.
The way I was already hers.

CHAPTER TWENTY-THREE

MOLLY

"Hmm, mornin'." I snuggled closer to Hudson. His arm was slung around my neck, so that I was tucked into his side as he slept on his back.

His fingers slid into my hair, and he guided my face to his, kissing me.

"Morning." He smiled against my lips and my heart melted.

This was... it was everything.

Waking up with him like this. The way he'd loved my body in the night. Twice. Reaching for me while he was half-asleep, as if he couldn't bear to be apart from me for another second.

It was intense. Overwhelming in the best possible way. But despite my own rules, I couldn't help thinking about the future.

About what happened once the dust settled, and I finally went home.

Don't go there, not yet. Not while things are so good.

I deserved this. We deserved it.

Hudson pulled me half over him, gliding his hand down my spine, sending a delicious shiver through me.

"I like this," he whispered, gazing up at me. "Waking up with you, having you here."

"Hudson..."

"I know, Molly girl, I know. This caught me by fucking surprise." His hand moved to my nape again. "You caught me by surprise."

He leaned up, kissing me. A silent promise again to everything we were becoming. Everything we already were.

"We have time," I said, my stomach tightening.

"Yeah." Something flashed in his eyes. But then his easy smirk slid back into place. "I need a shower, a cold one."

"Or I could help you with that." My hand slipped under the bed sheet and glided down his lower stomach, until my fingers were mapping his happy trail.

"I can't believe I'm going to say this, but if we start something now, I'm not going to want to stop. And the others are up. I can hear them."

My head dropped to his chest, and I groaned. "Fine. Go."

He chuckled, brushing my hair from my face to look at me. "Later, tonight. And every night after that."

I pressed my lips together, nodding. Not trusting myself to answer. Hudson dropped another kiss on my head and lifted me off him to climb out of the bed. I drank in the sight of him. Tanned skin, inches upon inches of lean muscle. He was so freaking gorgeous. It wasn't any wonder he had half the female population lusting after him.

"What?" He glanced up at me as he pulled on some gray sweatpants.

"Just lookin'." I blushed.

He made a ridiculous show of getting dressed, but it felt good to be like this with him. Laughing. Goofing around.

"Keep looking at me like that, Molly girl, and you'll be getting me into all kinds of trouble with Alistair." He lingered, eyes fixed right on me, but then with a little shake of his head he disappeared into the bathroom.

My cell phone pinged and for a second, a bolt of dread went through me. But relief flooded me when I saw Eva's name and not Mom's or Carson's.

Eva: Are you awake?

Me: Yes.

Eva: Are you okay?

Me: I'm not sure... I think I'm in trouble, babe. So much trouble.

· · ·

EVA: So last night went well then?

ME: Holy shiitake babe, it was everything.

I FLOPPED BACK onto the mattress, unable to wipe the smile off my face.

EVA: I'm so happy for y'all. Rafe said he has never seen Hudson like this. You're changing him, babe.

"WHO IS THAT?" Hudson appeared in the door again, frowning.

"Just Eva." I smiled, grabbing the sheet and sitting up.

Suspicion lingered in his eyes though.

"It wasn't him," I said, hating that Carson had the power to ruin something so special.

"Okay." Hudson threw his bag on the end of the bed and started rooting around in it.

"Hudson." I sighed. "Look at me."

But he kept rummaging in his bag, refusing to meet my eyes.

"Hudson." Wrapping the sheet around my body, I shuffled on my knees toward him. "Stop."

He exhaled a long breath, finally meeting my gaze.

"It was Eva."

"And yesterday?"

"Hud…"

"He's texting you?"

I nodded. "But I'm not encouragin' him, I swear. He's just… he's actin' like nothing happened. Makin' out like I just up and left him and my mom and the boys."

"I don't like it, Molly."

"And you think I do?" Emotion clogged my throat. A sudden icy wall had slammed up between us and I didn't like it.

When he didn't answer, I dropped my gaze, shoulders slumping.

"Hey, hey, I'm sorry, okay." Hudson cupped my face, tilting it back to his. "I just think about what he did to you, and it makes me want to do something really fucking stupid like fly to Lyme and—"

He stopped himself, inhaling a sharp breath.

"Don't let him ruin this, Hudson, please." I ran my hand along his jaw. He curved his hand around the back of my neck and pulled me closer until his head touched mine.

"If I ever cross paths with that piece of shit, I can't promise I won't tear him to shreds with my bare hands." His voice quivered with sheer violence.

Looping my arms around his neck, I grazed my lips over his mouth. "I'm okay, I promise."

"I thought you said no promises." His eyes flared as he searched my eyes.

"Maybe I lied," I whispered.

———

ROME PASSED BY IN A BLUR. The band had back-to-back interviews and a promotional shoot for Masterpiece, as well as a special VIP meet for competition winners from a local contest.

I barely saw Hudson. But I was happy to watch him do his thing.

"Uh oh, you've got that look," Phoebe said, side-eyeing me.

"What look?" I played dumb.

"The puppy dog in love look. I remember it well."

"I hate to break it to you, babe, but you still wear that look often." I smirked, and she flipped me off.

"We're going to have to fight for the bedrooms on the tour bus though."

"No, nothin' needs to change." I didn't expect special treatment going forward, and there were enough hotel stays to make it bearable.

"I doubt Hudson is going to want to be apart from you."

"Do the bunks on this thing sleep two?"

"It's a tight squeeze but you can make it work with some careful positioning." Phoebe shot me a knowing wink.

"Please tell me you two haven't—"

"Girl, there isn't a single surface on the bus that me and Levi haven't christened one way or another."

"Oh my God..."

"What can I say? My man is insatiable. And he has an addictive personality, so what does anyone really expect?"

"That's... wow. I don't really know what to say to that."

"You'll see." She winked, and suddenly I had all kinds of images swimming in my mind. But they weren't of her and Levi. No, they were all of me and Hudson in various stages of undress, on various surfaces all over the tour bus.

My cheeks burned as I cleared my throat. "So... Budapest in two days, that's exciting."

"Don't think I missed what you just did there." Phoebe snickered. "What do you—"

My phone started vibrating in my pocket, but I ignored it.

"Shouldn't you get that?"

"It's fine." It stopped, and I breathed a sigh of relief.

But it started up again, and Phoebe gave me a pointed look. "She isn't going to go away."

"How'd you know it was my mom?"

"Because whenever it vibrates or pings, you get this look. I know it's none of my business, but you can't avoid her forever."

"I know."

Reluctantly, I got up and dug my cell out of my pocket. The guys weren't done with their sound check, and I didn't want to miss anything, but Phoebe was right, I couldn't keep avoiding her.

"I'm goin' to take this."

"Of course, go." She gave me an encouraging smile.

I waited until I was somewhere quieter to answer. "Hey, Mom."

"Molly, thank goodness. I've been tryin' to call you all day. It's Silas, he had an accident."

My heart dropped.

"He did? What happened?"

"I turned my back for a second, and the little scoundrel jumped off the swing set and broke his damn leg."

"Is he okay?"

"Fussin' like a baby but he'll live."

"Is he there? Can I talk to him?"

"He's sleepin'. The pain meds knocked him out good. Thank God because I'm not sure I could take any more of the cryin'."

"Poor Silas." I clutched my throat.

"When are you comin' home, Mol? With Silas laid up for six weeks, I need you more than ever. Mrs. Yates is a great help with the boys, but she isn't you, Molly. Your brothers need you home."

"Mom, I—"

"Now look, sweetheart. I know you think Carson isn't right for you, but I really think if you just gave him another chance, you'd see that he really is the best. He's been helpin' out with the boys and around the house—"

"H-he's what?"

"Oh, sweetheart, he's been such a help. I really don't know what I would have done without him since you... well, since you decided to run off to Atlanta and play rock star with Eva."

"That's not—" I stopped myself, forcing myself to take a deep breath. "I don't want Carson around the boys, Mom. Promise me you won't let him keep comin' around."

She scoffed. "I'll do no such thing. He's a godsend. Such a fine young man. He's waitin' on you, Molly. Says he'll give you another chance. You just have to come home, baby. And put all this… madness behind you."

Her words were like daggers to my heart.

I hadn't told her the truth, no, but surely she should have been able to see that me running to Atlanta—to Europe—was a cry for help.

But she'd never once asked me what had happened, just assumed that I somehow ruined my lucky shot with Carson Dutton.

It hurt more than I cared to admit.

"I'm sorry about Silas, Mom. I really am, but I'm not ready to come home."

Her silence was deafening.

"I see," she eventually said. "You know, Molly Ann, I really expected more from you now that you've graduated. Life isn't a wild adventure. It's hard and it requires sacrifice. You think I wouldn't like to be jet settin' around the world instead of working all the hours I can to provide for you and the boys."

"Mom, that's not fair and you know it. I've always helped out." Frustration bubbled inside of me. "I've sacrificed—"

"Don't talk to me about sacrifices, young lady, don't you—"

"I'm not doin' this with you, Mom. Tell Silas I'll call soon and see how he is. Give him and Timmy a big hug from me."

"Molly Ann Steinberg, don't you dare hang—"

I hit end call and a garbled sob spilled out of me as the tears burst free.

I don't know how long I stood there, crying tears of frustration and disappointment, but by the time Hudson found me, my eyes were sore, and my throat was dry.

"Come here." He pulled me into his arms and cupped the back of my neck. "I've got you, Molly. I've got you."

CHAPTER TWENTY-FOUR

HUDSON

SOMETHING CHANGED in Molly after that day. She hadn't said anything to me about sticking around long-term yet, but I'd heard her talking to the girls about it. Right after she'd told them the truth about what happened with Carson.

I was so fucking proud of her for that. I knew it couldn't have been easy, reliving that moment again. But she seemed lighter since confessing, and if anything, the four of them were closer than ever.

If Molly was scared of my thoughts about her staying on the tour, she didn't need to be. I loved having her around. I loved knowing she was waiting in the wings when I was playing. I loved stealing kisses from her at every given opportunity, sneaking off to the tour bus or to find a quiet room.

We were almost as bad as Levi and Phoebe, and that was saying something.

It had been four days since Rome, and we had performed another two shows. One in Milan and one in Budapest. We had a rare night off before starting the long journey to London tomorrow.

Originally, the label wanted us to fly, but we wanted to stay on the bus. So Duke was driving to Calais, France and we were crossing via Ferry. It was going to be a long twenty-four hours, but at least I'd get to do them with my girl by my side.

And she was mine.

We hadn't had the talk yet, but I felt it in every kiss, every time she laid her head on my shoulder and smiled up at me. Every time I buried myself deep inside her and watched her fall apart.

I was totally and utterly gone for her.

"Where's Molly?" Damon dropped down beside me on the couch. The hotel in Budapest was less fancy than the others we'd stayed in, but it meant I got to share a room with Molly, so I really didn't give a fuck.

"Sitting in on a conference call to Dusty and the label with Letty and Phoebe."

"Think she's going to ask to stay, officially, I mean?"

I shrugged. "We haven't talked about it."

"But you want her to?"

"Obviously. But I want it to be her decision. I know she's finding it hard being away from the twins."

She'd told me all about Silas and Timmy while showing me a bunch of photos of the two of them. They were cute kids, reminding me a lot of Molly with their big brown eyes and dark hair.

"Yeah, must be tough. At least we have a night off tonight. I'm looking forward to doing the tourist thing."

"I dunno, man. Underground caves don't really sound like my kind of thing."

"I think it'll be cool. They have catacombs down there too. I've been reading up on it."

"Of course you have," I murmured. "At least you won't have to worry about meeting a girl down there."

"Fuck you, Ryker. Fuck. You."

"Relax, I'm joking. What you do or don't do with your dick is none of my business."

"You're right," he said. "It isn't."

"Why are we talkin' about Damon's dick?" Letty and Molly appeared.

I reached for Molly, pulling her into my lap. "Missed you," I whispered against her lips.

"And that's my cue to leave." Damon got up. "What time are we heading out?"

"We need to leave at six."

"Got it." He gave us a two-fingered salute and disappeared into his room.

"I have a ton of work to catch up on before we leave, so I'll leave you two alone." Letty grabbed a bottle of water from the refrigerator and headed next door to her room.

"Alone at last." I nuzzled Molly's neck.

"Hmm, I like the sound of that." She laced her arms around my shoulders and brushed her lips over mine. Featherlight kisses that drove me wild. But when she sucked my tongue into her mouth, grazing the tip with her teeth, my dick strained painfully against my jeans.

"Bedroom, now." I tapped her thigh.

"We can't." Laughter bubbled out of her. "Everyone's around."

"Babe, you let me fuck you in the bunk two nights ago."

"Hudson!" Her cheeks flamed.

"Don't act like you didn't love every second." It had been as intense as fuck, trying to be quiet as our friends slept or did whatever the hell they did in their own rooms.

I'd rolled Molly onto her side and pushed into her from behind, rocking us gently while my fingers played with her clit. Fuck, just thinking about it got me all kinds of hard.

"It was... very nice."

"Very nice?" I scoffed. "Babe, if that's all you've got to say, I clearly wasn't doing it right. Maybe I should try again, just to be sure."

"Thirty minutes," she said.

"I only need ten."

I grabbed her hand and all but dragged her to our room. There wasn't time to strip her off, so I pushed her over the edge of the bed, yanked down her leggings, and pushed two fingers inside her.

"Sweet baby Jesus," she moaned.

"Ride my hand, babe. Need you nice and soaked for me."

"Hudson... *God*," she breathed.

I pumped her a couple more times while popping the button on my jeans and shoving them over my hips. Grasping my dick, I slid it through her wetness, letting the tip graze her clit. Molly cried out, pushing back against me.

"Greedy little thing." I chuckled, guiding my tip to her entrance and slamming inside. "Fuck," I groaned, anchoring my hand around her hip.

"Oh God, Hudson... it's... ahhh..."

"Yeah, babe, I know. Fuck, you're so tight."

I'd never felt so connected to anyone and not just on a physical level. It was emotional too. Molly had buried herself under my skin and coiled herself around my fucking heart, and every time I got inside her, the tether between us tied a little tighter.

Soon there would be no severing it.

And I didn't care.

I didn't care one fucking bit.

———

"EXCITED?" Letty asked us, corralling us into the SUV.

"It's a few underground caves, Let. Not sure what can possibly be exciting about it?" I grumbled.

I didn't want to visit the underground caves. I wanted to stay in bed with Molly. Naked. Maybe with some room service and liquor.

But it was group bonding time, and everyone had agreed to the trip to Szemlőhegyi Cave.

"Where the hell are Levi and Phoebe?" she asked, checking her watch. "We need to leave."

"They said they were right behind us," Molly said.

"If we don't—"

My cell started vibrating and I pulled it out. "I bet

that's them now." But when I saw the number, my body went rigid.

"Hudson?" Molly touched my arm. "What is it?"

"I-I need to take this." I stumbled out of the SUV and moved away from the car, aware of Johnson following me.

"Hello?" I answered the call.

"Hudson, that you, kid?" I winced at the sound of Kenny's gruff voice.

"Tell me..."

"It's not good, kid. Found her unconscious a couple of hours ago..."

I couldn't hear him over the roar of blood in my ears, latching onto the odd word.

Overdose...

Hospital...

Serious...

"Where?" I asked.

I felt empty. Hollow and numb.

I'd always known this day would come but I hadn't... fuck.

Fuck.

"Hudson?"

"Y-yeah, I'm here. I'll be on the first flight out. I have to make some arrangements, but I'll be there."

"Yeah, okay." Kenny hung up.

There wasn't anything else to say. It wasn't that I didn't like the guy, I didn't really know him. I didn't want to get to know my mom let alone her on/off boyfriend.

My mind was running a mile a minute, trying to process everything. I had to speak to Letty first, to get her to clear my absence with the label. The guys would understand. One of the backing musicians could cover a couple of shows if necessary. It wasn't ideal but it would work. People would understand, they would—

"Hudson?"

Fuck.

"Molly."

Molly.

Slowly, I turned, meeting her concerned gaze.

"What is it, what's wrong?" she asked.

"I need to go home." It came out cold. Detached. It didn't even sound like me.

"H-home? I don't understand, what do you mean? Did something happen?"

"It's my mom, she... she OD'd."

"Oh my God." Molly rushed toward me, taking my hand in hers. "That's awful. Is she okay?"

"It doesn't sound like it. So I need to go."

"Hudson, I'm sorry." She threw her arms around me, but I barely felt it. I was rigid. Numb.

So fucking numb.

I'd been waiting for this call for years.

And now it was here, and I was completely and utterly numb.

"What can I do?" Molly gazed up at me, her big brown eyes so full of pity. She waited, the silence stretching out before us.

What the fuck was she waiting for?

"I don't... what?" I ran a hand down my face.

"Do you want me to come with you?" She hesitated. "I'm sure Letty and the label would—"

"Come with me? Why the fuck would you do that?"

She reared back as if I'd slapped her. "Because... because I care about you. I-I thought... Hudson, what is happening right now?" She folded her arms around herself, holding herself together. But I couldn't reassure her. I couldn't give her anything.

It was strange. I'd always expected this day—wished for it so many times. But now it was here and I...

Fuck.

Fuck. Fuck. *Fuck!*

There was too much going on in my head and nothing at all at the same time. I was pretty sure I'd gone into shock.

"I need to speak with Letty," I said, moving around her.

"Hudson, wait. Please."

I stopped and let out a heavy sigh, glancing back at her.

"Don't do this, I'm begging you." Her expression guttered. "Don't shut me out."

"I have to speak to Letty." I walked away from her...

And I didn't look back.

———

"You've got everything?" Rafe stood in the door of the hotel room.

It had been almost two hours since I'd got the call from Kenny. Two hours of emergency conference calls with Dusty and the label execs. Letty had organized everything from my flight, my security detail, and my replacement for while I was gone.

"Think so." I zipped my bag and threw it over my shoulder.

"Have you talked to her?"

"No, she hasn't been up to the room."

"Can you blame her?" He gave me a pointed look.

"What the fuck is that supposed to mean?"

"You're shutting her out."

"Because this is my shit to deal with," I snapped. "No one else's. Least of all Molly's."

"But I thought you two were—"

"We all know it was temporary. She's going back to Lyme eventually, and I can't do the long-distance thing. It will never work out."

Someone gasped from behind Rafe. He turned around and I saw Molly standing there, hand clapped over her mouth, tears brimming in her eyes.

"Maybe I should give the two of you some priv—"

"It's fine." Molly squared her shoulders, her expression a mix of hurt and anger I didn't feel. "I think we've both said all we needed to say." She stared at me, waiting.

But nothing came out because I had nothing.

I was a fool to ever think we had a shot at something real. One way or another, it would only end in heartache. It always did.

Molly spun around and disappeared.

"I love you like a brother, Hud, you know that." Rafe let out a weary sigh. "But sometimes you really are a clueless fucking idiot." Disappointment flickered in his eyes as he approached me.

"I hope your mom is okay." He squeezed my shoulder. "And you get whatever closure you need."

CHAPTER TWENTY-FIVE

MOLLY

"Hey, you," Eva said, joining me on the observation deck. The sea breeze washed over me, and I breathed it in, hoping it might fix some of what was broken.

Hudson had been gone almost eighteen-hours, but it already felt like a lifetime. I wanted to call him or at least text him and ask him how he was. But I didn't.

He'd made it pretty clear where we stood.

I knew he was hurting. Knew that probably had something to do with the way he had treated me. But I also knew it was more than that. His mom overdosing had triggered something. Or reaffirmed something. Either way, I'd lost him.

I'd seen it the second he'd answered his cell phone and heard the news. The walls around his heart had slammed up, shutting me out completely.

"Hey," I said.

"I can't believe we're almost in England. It's surreal."

"Yeah."

We'd never made it to the underground caves in Budapest. Letty had gone into full crisis mode, making the necessary arrangements for Hudson to travel back to the US while dealing with the fallout of him potentially missing the next few shows.

And I'd just wilted into the background, staying out of everyone's way. Trying to reconcile what I knew in my heart to be true.

He wasn't just leaving the tour—he was leaving me.

"Hey, come on, Mol. I know things suck right now. But he'll figure it out, you'll see."

I didn't possess Eva's enthusiasm.

Walking in on Rafe and Hudson talking, hearing Hudson say we were never going to work out, had shattered all those precariously healed pieces of my heart.

"I think I'm going to go home," I said.

"What? Why? I thought—"

"That I was goin' to stay for him? I was." A sad smile tugged at my mouth. "But let's be honest, Eva. He'll come back eventually, and things will never be the same between us. People will side with Hudson even if they don't want to. And I get it. He's the rock star and I'm... I'm nobody. It's time for me to go home."

"Molly, that's not—"

"It's okay, babe. I'll be okay." I'd been fooling myself to think that I could stay and be a part of this tour.

A part of Hudson's life.

It was a fantasy.

And although it was exactly what I needed at the time, it was over now, and I needed to be okay with that.

"I'll kick his ass so hard for doin' this to you." Eva wrapped me into a hug. "I love you, Mol, and I think you're one of the bravest, most selfless people I know. But promise me you'll tell your mom the truth."

"I'll think about it."

I still hadn't figured out how to broach Carson with my mom. It would put serious pressure on her professional relationship with Derek, that was assuming she even believed me. But the girls were right. I needed to tell her. If not for her, then for myself.

"Gosh, I'm goin' to miss you." Eva hugged me tighter and tears started rolling down my cheeks. "I'll always love you, Molly Ann Steinberg. And if you can't stay there, you'll always have a place by my side. No matter what."

"Thanks, babe," I whispered.

It was a nice sentiment, even if we both knew I wouldn't come back, not once Hudson returned.

Which he would.

Because this was his home, the band were his family.

And there wasn't a place for me in that after all.

"Thank you, for everythin'." I hugged Letty, trying to keep the tears at bay.

We'd arrived in London about two hours ago. The band was heading straight for the stadium, but I was going to the airport. My flight was in three hours.

"Are you sure about this?" She held me at arm's length. "Hudson is hurting, and he's in self-protective mode. He wouldn't want you to leave, not before you've talked things over."

I nodded. "I have to go. I have to tell her."

And I couldn't be here when he got back, I just couldn't.

"Yeah... I know. And I'm so fucking sorry it went down like this. I really thought..."

"It's okay. You've been so good to me, Let." I hugged her again.

"Don't be a stranger, okay."

"Yeah, okay."

Letty released me, but I was pulled straight into Phoebe's arms. "Hudson Ryker is an asshole. He's always been an asshole... probably always will be. But that boy loves you, Molly. I've seen it. We all have. Please, *please* don't give up on him."

"Has anyone heard from him?" I asked, but the flash of hurt in her eyes gave me my answer.

Hudson had gone off the radar. Since he'd texted Rafe to say that he'd made it to Atlanta, no one had heard from him, and his cell was ringing out.

I knew because I'd called him too. Because I cared and I wanted to be there for him.

But it didn't matter. He'd made his decision.

"When he comes back... look out for him, okay?"

"You got it." She gave me another weak smile. "And you, who looks out for you?"

"I'll be okay..." I always was.

"Sometimes the hardest thing isn't walking away, it's coming back. Just remember that, Molly. You'll always, always have a place here."

It was useless trying to fight the tears, so I let them roll freely down my cheeks.

Rafe hugged me next, apologizing for his best friend's 'moment of insanity,' his words, not mine. "Take care of yourself," he said.

"You too. And look after Eva, she's kind of important to me."

Levi's hug was brief and a little uncomfortable. He hadn't known what to say to me since Hudson had left. And I got it. I was the outsider here. I'd turned up unannounced in Atlanta and ruined their plans.

"Good luck with the rest of the tour," I said with a small, forced smile.

He gave me a small nod and stepped back to wrap his arm around Phoebe.

Damon was last. The gentle, mild-mannered guitarist wrapped his arms around me and held me tight. "He's a fucking idiot. But he's our idiot. Don't give up on him just yet. He needs you, more than you know."

I wanted it to be true. More than anything I wanted to believe that my cell phone would start ringing at any second and it would be Hudson calling to apologize.

But I knew better.

Our time had always been finite.

Temporary.

And it had come to an end.

It was time to go home and face the music.

———

"Molly." Timmy grinned up at me. "Mom, Mom, Molly's home. Molly's home." He threw his little arms around me, and I hoisted him up.

"Hey, buddy. Did you miss me?"

"Hells yeah." He shrieked as I tickled his sides.

God, it felt good to see him.

"Okay, bud. Down you go. I need to love on Silas too. Where is he?"

"He's on the couch, being a lazy ass."

"Tim! You know Mom doesn't like you sayin'—"

"Molly?" Mom appeared at the end of the hall. "Oh, baby, thank goodness, I've been worried sick." She rushed over to me and wrapped me into her arms.

"Hi, Mom," I said.

"But what... I don't understand... I thought—" She sniffled, and it was then I realized she was crying.

"Mom, are you cryin'?"

"Now, now, baby." She batted my hands away, "Don't be ridiculous. Come on, Silas will be itchin' to see you. Silas, look who's back. Molly is—"

"Molly, yay, Molly is here." He flung his arms around in the air, fist pumping from his position laying on the couch.

"Look at you." Guilt slammed into me. "Oh, buddy, come here." I crouched down and wrapped him into a hug.

"I'm real glad you're home, Mol. We missed you."

"I missed you too, buddy. I missed you too."

Mom got the boys settled with a movie and snacks and motioned for me to follow her into the kitchen.

"Coffee?"

"Yes please."

She made our drinks in silence, tension stretching between us. I knew it would be hard coming home, so much had happened. But I also knew it was time to stop running.

"Mom," I said, and she looked over. "We need to talk... about Carson."

"Oh baby, that man is... he's a good egg, Molly. One of the most—"

"Stop, Mom. Just stop."

"Molly?"

Something about her expression changed, a tightness to her eyes that wasn't there before. I inhaled a shaky breath, curling my fingers into my thigh, grounding me.

"I didn't leave because Carson and I broke up, Mom." I hesitated, fear constricting my lungs making it impossible to breathe.

Breathe, Molly, just breathe. You can do this. Just tell her.

"We were...we were never together. At least, not from my side."

Her brows furrowed, confusion clouding her eyes. "But I don't understand, you said..."

"I know what I said, Mom. But I lied. I lied because I didn't know how to tell you the truth."

My heart crashed against my chest, like a storm battering the shore. I had to tell her. Even if she didn't believe me, even if she didn't take my side... I had to say the words.

I wasn't selfish, I didn't abandon her and my brothers. I ran.

I ran to protect myself, to avoid any further heartache.

"I really don't understand what you're sayin', Molly. Carson is a good—"

The words spilled out before I could stop them. "He raped me, Mom." I sucked in a painful breath and silently prayed she understood now. "Carson raped me."

———

THE SILENCE WAS ALMOST UNBEARABLE. Mom had tried and failed three times to respond to my confession. But each time, she snapped her mouth shut and shook her head, busying herself with something. The dirty pots. Making me another mug of coffee. Wiping the surfaces.

I let her do her thing, knowing she needed to process what I'd just said. But it had been almost ten minutes, and I was beginning to lose my patience.

"Mom, please, say somethin'," I finally said.

"I... I'm sorry, I just... Are you sure, sweetheart?"

Of all the things she could have said, those three little words were the most hurtful.

Was I sure?

As if there could ever be ambiguity around a man overpowering and assaulting you.

A bitter laughter bubbled up inside me as I rubbed my temples. "This is exactly why I didn't tell you."

"Molly, that's not fair."

"Not fair?" I seethed, slamming my palm down on the table. "I'll tell you what's not fair, Mom. It's that I had to leave my home. I had to leave the boys and my life here because I knew this would happen. I knew you wouldn't believe me."

She reared back like I'd slapped her. "Of course I believe you, sweetheart. I'm just... I'm confused. Carson is—"

"He's the devil in sheep's clothin', Mom."

"Sweetheart, talk to me." She finally sat down, taking my hands in hers. "Tell me what happened. Tell me everythin'."

So I did.

I told her about Carson's increasing frustration. The way his touch became a little too forced, a little too intense. Then I told her about that night, about how he refused to take no for an answer. About how he took something I never wanted to give him.

When I was done, we were both crying. But I felt lighter, like the burden—the poison living inside me—had been cut out of my chest, giving my lungs room to finally breathe.

"Come here." She pulled me into her arms. "My sweet, sweet girl. I failed you, baby. I failed you so freakin' bad. I'm sorry, Mol. I'm so, so sorry."

I knew then my worst fears had been just that... fears. But maybe I'd needed to run to make her see the truth. I guess I'd never know. It didn't matter now though.

All that mattered was that I was home, and one way or another, I would put it behind me.

CHAPTER TWENTY-SIX

HUDSON

MOM WAS GONE.

She'd died thirty-five minutes after I'd arrived at the hospital.

Anyone else might have seen it as a sign. That their loved one was holding on to give them a chance to say goodbye.

It just felt like the universe's way of shitting on me a little more.

At least she was at peace now. Me, on the other hand, I didn't know what the fuck I was supposed to feel. Relief she wouldn't be bothering me anymore. Anger that I'd never truly told her how I felt. Pain that I'd never get the chance now.

I was a fucking mess, holed up in some dive motel, trying to stay off the grid and drink my feelings away.

I wanted to call Molly, to hear her voice and have her

tell me everything was going to be okay. But I was too chicken shit—terrified she would tell me to fuck off.

It was the least I deserved after the way I'd left.

But I'd gone straight into self-protect mode. My mom—the woman who had given me life—had overdosed because she was broken. Because instead of choosing the life she was left with, she chose to mourn the life she had lost.

I wasn't enough for her back then, and I wasn't enough for her now.

It didn't matter now though, she was gone. And I thought I'd feel free when it finally happened. I thought it would unshackle me from the burden.

But all it did was confirm everything I've ever thought about love.

Love was messy.

Love was hard.

And in the end, love...

Well, it fucking destroyed you.

———

A LOUD BANG on my motel room door startled me. Empty bottles of whiskey littered the room, and I pushed up off the floor, trying to clamber to my feet.

Bang. Bang. Bang.

"Yeah, I'm com— fuck." My leg cracked off the side of the table, pain ricocheting through me.

Bang. Bang. Ba—

"What the fuck?" I growled at the person on the other side of the door.

Patton, my security detail, lifted a brow at me as he said, "He's alive," into his cell phone. "Barely."

"You can fuck off now," I said, ready to slam the door in his face. But he fisted my t-shirt and thrust his phone at me.

"Ryker," Rafe's voice came over the line. "I swear if you don't answer your fucking phone—"

"Yeah, yeah, Hunter. I'm a big disappointment. I'm letting the band down. I'm a selfish fucking—"

"Where the fuck have you been for the last three days? Hiding under a goddamn rock? It's Molly—"

"Molly?"

I staggered back into the door, her name like a physical blow to my chest.

"She left."

"Left... what do you mean she left?"

He let out an exasperated breath. "She went home, after you..."

Home.

She went home.

Back to that piece of shit.

Molly was in Lyme with the motherfucker who'd raped her.

My fist flew out, smashing against the wall. I barely felt the pain, only felt the warm trickle of blood down my hand. "You let her go home?" I snarled. "What the fuck were you thinking?"

Rafe clicked his tongue with disapproval. "We didn't *let* her do anything. She's an adult, asshole. And you left her. You just left, Hudson. Like she meant nothing. She was ready to follow you around the world and you just fucking left her. What did you think would happen?"

"I... I wasn't thinking. Kenny dropped the bomb about Mom, and I—"

"You panicked, yeah." He let out a heavy sigh. "I know. But you fucked up, man. Big time."

"Fuck... *Fuck*!" I went to punch the wall again but Patton grabbed my wrist, shooting me a bemused look. "Is Letty there? I need to talk to her."

"No, but I'll tell her to call you as soon as she's out of the meeting with PR."

"PR?" That got my attention. Letty only usually needed PR to fix something or to bury something. "What's going on?"

"That's the other reason I called."

"Rafe..." I warned, dread flooding my chest.

"There are some photos from that club in Italy. They hit the internet this morning."

"The sex club?" My blood turned to ice. "Tell me they didn't find out her name."

"Of course they did." Sympathy coated his words. "They always do."

Shit.

Shit!

"I need Letty to call me now." I stormed back into my room and started stuffing my things into my bag. "I need the first flight out to whatever airport is nearest Lyme... Wait, how long will it take to drive to Jamesboro County, Tennessee?" I asked.

"About four hours give or take traffic. You're going after her?" Rafe said.

"Of course I'm going after her. She's my..." Everything. She was fucking everything.

The words reverberated deep inside, a rightness settling over me.

Molly was mine.

Just as I was hers.

All the no promises bullshit was just that... bullshit.

I'd fucked up by leaving her, but I hadn't been thinking straight. I was thinking clearly now though, and she needed me. If she was going to survive the shitstorm about to rain down on her, she needed me.

I only hoped I wasn't too late.

"'Bout time, man. I was beginning to think you really were as dumb as you act sometimes."

"Asshole."

He chuckled.

"I need to go. I need to shower and get the fuck out of here."

"Yeah, okay. Call me when you're on the road. And Hudson?" he said.

"Yeah?"

"I'm sorry about your mom."

"Yeah," I breathed. "Me too."

———

BY THE TIME we found Lyme—after getting lost twice in the ass crack of nowhere—the vultures had descended.

"Fuck," I breathed, grabbing my cell and dialing Eva. "Have you spoken to her?" I barked the second she answered.

"No, she isn't answering. I texted… but so far, nothing. How bad is it?"

"Bad, Country. Really fucking bad."

"Oh God, poor Molly."

My teeth ground together. This was my fault.

All my fucking fault.

PR had tracked down the leak to someone inside Club Paradiso that night, but they needed to conduct their own investigation due to their strict membership policy and NDA.

"I bet it was that fucking blonde."

"Stefanie?" Eva gasped.

"Was that her name?" Jealous bitch. "She was watching us. Watching me and Molly dance. I openly rejected her and then I flaunted Molly right in her face. You know how these women are."

Crazy fucking bitches.

"Well, whoever it was, it doesn't change the fact that the photos are out there, and the world has dubbed Molly the latest victim to your immoral playboy ways."

"Eva, come on, that isn't fair…" I scrubbed my jaw.

"Yeah, I know, sorry. I'm just so mad, Hud. She doesn't deserve this. Not after everythin' she's been through."

"I know. I'll call you as soon as I'm there." I hung up, shame and guilt flooding through me.

It wasn't my fault that some jealous socialite had decided to make a quick buck. But I had coaxed Molly to dance with me that night, I had pushed her toward giving into her deepest darkest desires.

Fuck.

Opening the bookmarked browser, I stared at the

grainy images. My hands splayed over Molly's stomach, her head tipped back as my lips brushed her neck as we watched the couple go at it. It could have been worse—it could have been snorting coke off a naked body worse—but it was enough for some money-hungry journo to do some digging into the mystery girl I'd spent all night dancing with and kissing. There was even a shot of us leaving the club together, hand in hand, disappearing into one of the black SUVs.

"What do you want me to do?" Patton called from upfront. "Driving right up to the door might only make things worse."

"Yeah," I let out a frustrated breath. "I know. But I have a plan."

CHAPTER TWENTY-SEVEN

MOLLY

"Look at them, look at them." Timmy shouted through the window, "Hey, shitheads." He started banging on the glass. "Leave my sister alo—"

"Okay, buddy, that's enough window time for you." I scooped him up and carried him to the couch, dropping him down beside his brother. "Stay there, okay. We don't want to draw any more attention to ourselves."

God only knew I'd had enough of that pointed in my direction.

"Is it still as bad out there?" Mom came into the living room with drinks and snacks for the boys. She got them settled then went and peeked through the drapes. "Damn vultures."

"Mom." I sighed.

The day had been a total disaster. When I'd gone to bed last night, I'd felt hopeful. Like I could face whatever came next.

Mom had been great, much better than I ever could have imagined. She'd wanted to march straight over to Derek's house and tell him a few home truths about his so-called perfect nephew, but I'd talked her out of it.

I still wasn't sure what I wanted to do about Carson. If we told Derek and went to the police, it would be my word against his, and Derek was well connected. He could make an accusation like that disappear.

Part of me wanted to pretend it never happened and forget all about Carson Dutton. But I knew that wasn't going to happen given we lived in the same small town.

So I'd gone to sleep worrying over the what ifs and maybes only to wake up and discover that Carson was the least of my problems.

Photos of me and Hudson at that club in Italy had hit Entertainment News Online, and now my face was plastered all over the internet, dubbed the latest girl to be victim to Black Hearts heartbreaker Hudson Ryker's irresistible charm. They knew my name, where I lived—obviously—and everything from my waist size to my favorite class in high school.

Mom had tried to leave for work only to be met with a sea of paparazzi who had gathered overnight to all catch a glimpse of the girl from a small town in Tennessee who had dirty danced at an exclusive sex club with Hudson Ryker, world famous rock star.

It was surreal.

And a living, freaking nightmare.

I'd wanted to walk in his world, at his side, but I had never wanted this.

"I'm goin' to call Frank Jinks again down at the police

department. Surely, they can do somethin'." Mom patted my shoulder and left the room.

"Why does everyone wanna get your photo, Molly? What did ya do?" Timmy and Silas looked at me with their curious little expressions. "Is it 'cos you wents away with those, what did Mom call them, Si? Good for nothin' rock suns."

"It's rock stars, doofus." Silas groaned, rolling his eyes. "And she didn't go away for the rock stars. She went away because Carson wanted a 'elationship but Molly wasn't ready."

Sweet baby Jesus.

I smothered the laughter building inside me.

I couldn't help it; my brothers were too freaking adorable.

"It doesn't matter why I went away. What matters is, I'm back now. We'll figure out how to make those guys out front go away, and everything will be fine."

I hoped.

"Molly, can you come in here for a second please?" Mom called.

I got up and pinned my brothers with a firm look. "Stay away from the windows, okay? I'll be right back."

"What's up?" I asked Mom, the second I entered the kitchen. But she wasn't looking at me. She was staring at the back door.

"Mom?"

"I believe he's here to see you."

I glanced up and my world went sideways. "Hudson?" My eyes practically bugged out of my head. "But what are you—"

"Hey, Molly girl." He flashed me his trademark Hudson Ryker smile. "Can we talk?" His eyes flicked to my mom who was glaring at him like he was the devil incarnate.

"I think whatever you have to say to her, you can say in front of me. After all, it's your fault that circus is outside all waiting to get their inside scoop."

"Look Ms—Molly's mom. I'm sorry, really fucking sorry about this mess. Those photos shouldn't even exist, let alone have made it into the public domain. As soon as I found out, I came straight here. I didn't—"

"Save it." She silenced him with a single look. "I'm not the one you need to apologize to."

"You're right." His gaze slid to mine. "Molly, I—"

"Mom, please, just give us a minute. Go sit with the boys and make sure Timmy isn't causin' any more trouble. I'll be right in, okay?"

"I don't like it, Molly."

"I know, but Hudson came all this way. The least I can do is hear him out."

She narrowed her eyes at him. "You might be a world-famous rock star, but if you ever hurt my daughter or take advantage of her, I won't be held responsible for my actions."

Mom stormed out of the kitchen, slamming the door behind her. The crack of wood against wood went through me, making me flinch.

"You told her... about Carson?"

I nodded, still not quite able to believe my eyes. Hudson was here, in Lyme. Standing in my kitchen looking—

"What on earth are you wearin'?"

The sweatpants wasn't completely out of character, but the black oversized hoodie and ball cap was new.

"It was the only way I could make it here undetected." He whipped off the ball cap and dropped it on the counter. "Patton is currently stirring up a little distraction for our friends outside."

"I... I don't know what to say to that. You're here, in my kitchen."

"I'm here." He took a step forward, the air shifting around us. But I extended my arm, holding up a finger, stopping him.

"What are you doin' here, Hudson?"

"Isn't it obvious, babe? I came... for you."

"For me." Bitter laughter swerved inside me. "That's funny because four days ago when your world imploded and I tried to be there for you, you left me."

"Molly, I—"

"No, I need to say this. I was ready to jump in with both feet for you. The band, the tour, this crazy, crazy life you lead. I was goin' to turn my back on everything I've ever known... for you. Because I believed in us. I believed in you, Hudson. And the second things got tough you walked away. Do you have any idea how it felt hearin' you tell Rafe we were never going to work out? You pieced me back together and then you broke me, Hudson. You shattered me."

"I know and I'm sorry." He stormed toward me, cupping my face despite my best efforts to fight him off. "I'm so fucking sorry. But she's always been my Achilles' heel. I've spent years waiting for that call, years... and I thought... fuck, I don't know what I thought. But when he said the words, it was like every bit of armor I've ever built against her crumbled and I was numb. I was so fucking numb. Loving my piece of shit father did that to her, loving him *killed* her, Molly. I never want to be responsible for that. I can't—"

"She—she's gone?"

Something inside me broke for him and without thinking about what it meant, I pulled him into my arms. His hands anchored around my back, his face buried in the crook of my neck.

"I'm sorry, Hud. I'm so sorry."

"She's finally free," he whispered, shuddering against me as he gripped me tighter. "And I should be happy... relieved. But I... fuck, I don't know what I feel."

He pulled back to look me in the eye. "I locked myself in some shitty motel room with a ton of whiskey and drowned my feelings."

"Did it help?"

"It helped with the numbness."

"Hudson, why are you really here?"

"Rafe called Patton and made him make me take the call. When he told me you'd left to go home, it felt like he'd reached through the phone and slapped me. But then he told me about the photos, and it was like everything I thought mattered didn't matter anymore. The only thing I could think about was getting to you, Molly. I came as soon as I could.

"I'm sorry, babe. I am so fucking sorry."

A tidal wave of emotion crashed over me, and I

pounded my fists against his chest, sobbing uncontrollably.

It wasn't fair.

It wasn't fair that Carson had raped me, and that Hudson's mom had died. It wasn't fair that he was so damaged by her actions, her inability to love him, that he hadn't trusted me enough when he needed me most. It wasn't fair that someone had taken those photos of us on one of the best nights of my life. That the public now owned that piece of us, and we could never take it back.

None of it was fair.

He slipped his hand into the back of my hair, holding me close as I cried into his chest, letting it all out.

"I know I fucked up. I know I don't deserve your forgiveness, but I'm asking for it anyway. Because I'm in love with you, Molly girl."

"W-what?" I sniffled, drying my eyes with the back of my hand.

"You heard me, Steinberg. I'm elbow over ass in love with you, so you can't send me away because I'd have to camp out front with the paparazzi and it would be annoying, and I'd probably get into a ton of fights with them."

"You love me?" My heart spluttered.

"Yeah, seems I do." His thumb brushed my cheek.

"Okay," she breathed, "that changes things."

He loved me.

He was *in* love with me.

"Yeah?" He grinned. "I was hoping you might say that."

"I can't believe you came here. You should be with the band... the tour...'"

"Can wait." He stroked my jaw. "I'm right where I need to—"

"How dare you," Mom's voice echoed on the other side of the door.

"What's going on?" I pulled out of Hudson's arms and went to the door, cracking it open.

"Carson, I suggest—"

Carson.

The ground went from under me.

Carson was *here*?

"Molly, what—" Hudson started, but Mom's stern voice cut him off.

"You need to leave, now, Carson."

"Motherfucker," Hudson growled, storming past me.

"Hudson, wait." I tried to grab his arm, but he blew through the door into the hall.

"You," he spat. "I'll fucking kill you."

To my surprise—and I wasn't sure if it was because she didn't want to be on the receiving end of Hudson's wrath, or because she was team Hudson suddenly—Mom stepped aside and let him at Carson.

"So it's true then," Carson sneered, looking right past Hudson to me. "You really are messing around with this asshole."

Crack.

Hudson's fist smashed into Carson's face, and he staggered back, clutching his nose.

"You come anywhere near her again. If you even step foot near this house... I will end you; do you hear me?"

"Hudson, stop. Just stop." I grabbed his arm, trying to wrench him backward. "He isn't worth it. He isn't—"

"And to think I actually thought you were the type of girl I could—"

I moved around Hudson, pushing him behind me, and came face to face with Carson. "You're lucky I'm not calling the police after what you did. But if you want the entire town to know how you like to hurt women, then be my guest, please keep telling me how I am the one in the wrong here."

"We both know you wanted—"

Crack.

My palm stung where it landed against Carson's cheek. "I won't warn you again. I suggest you leave before I walk out of here and announce to the world what an absolute piece of shit Carson Dutton really is."

Hudson stepped up behind me and slid his arm around my waist, tugging me back into his chest. His presence made my heart settle a little.

"I think it's time for you to leave. Don't you even think 'bout comin' back here or anywhere near my daughter. Now, get the hell outta here."

Hearing my mom tell Carson off surprised me, but for once she's putting me first, knowing that there's a chance he'll go running to his uncle.

"You two are welcome to each other." Carson glared at us one last time before brushing off his sweater and taking off down the path, right through the media frenzy. Thankfully, they couldn't see enough of what had happened on the front porch to make me worry we were going to wake up to another slew of photos, but it was still disconcerting.

I closed the door and exhaled a thin breath.

"I'm proud of you." Hudson kissed my shoulder.

"I'm so sorry, sweetheart. I should have told him to stay away, but I didn't want to talk to him before you—"

"Mom, it's okay," I said, hugging her. Her eyes went over my shoulder, and I knew she had questions.

Reaching for Hudson's hand, I tugged him gently to my side and said, "Mom, this is Hudson. Hudson, this is my mom, Hattie."

"It's good to finally meet you, Ms. Steinberg."

"Oh, come here." She pulled him in for a hug. "Anyone who defends my Molly so vehemently has my blessin'. Just get rid of those vultures outside and I'll pretend I never saw those photos." Mom lifted a disapproving brow, but her eyes twinkled with amusement.

Hudson glanced back at me, smiling, and my heart fluttered.

"I'll see what I can do."

CHAPTER TWENTY-EIGHT

HUDSON

"You smell funny." Timmy crawled over my lap, sniffing my t-shirt. "What is that? Dog poop?"

"No, it's not dog poop, you little booger." I said, lifting the little shit off of me and dumping him on the couch. I grabbed my t-shirt and sniffed it, frowning.

"See, told you it smelled like dog poop. You got pooped on." He belly laughed. "By a dog."

"It's not dog sh— poop, kid. But you're right, this t-shirt doesn't smell too fresh."

"I probably have one you can borrow, although I don't know if it will fit you. You got all those muscles in your arms. Look at his muscles, Si."

"I see," the other kid said. "But they don't look that 'pressive to me."

Silas had definitely taken on the role as Molly's protector. For a six-year-old, the kid was kind of scary.

Those beady brown eyes followed me around the room, especially whenever Molly was close.

Which wasn't nearly enough for my liking.

"I have lemonade and some homemade cookies from Mrs. Yates." Molly and her mom appeared, and relief coursed through me.

I wanted to make a good impression, but I wasn't used to kids who wanted to know everything.

"So what did Letty say?" Molly said, perching on the arm of my chair.

I wanted to pull her onto my lap and hold her, but something told me Ms. Steinberg and the twins wouldn't appreciate that, so I settled on letting my hand dangle casually next to her leg; close enough to touch her, but discreet enough that it shouldn't get me in trouble.

"There isn't much they can do from their end except put out a statement. And word will get out I'm here eventually."

"So we wait it out?"

"Impossible." Her mom sighed. "I have work. Timmy has school. Poor Mrs. Yates was too terrified to even attempt coming over here. Maybe we should call the police?"

"You could but it's unlikely to help. So long as they're not trespassing on private property, which they're not, they're not breaking any laws."

"This is ridiculous. We can't hide out here forever."

"Which is why I have to go out there."

"What?" Molly shrieked. "No, you can't... no, Hudson."

"I'll go out there and give them a statement that my

mom passed and I'm spending some time here to grieve. I'll ask that they respect my privacy during this difficult time and that they let you and your family go about your business as usual. It won't completely stop them, but it should pacify them enough to move on to chasing a bigger story."

"Hudson." Molly took my hand in hers and gazed down at me. It felt good. It felt so fucking good to have her touch. "You shouldn't have to do that. What happened with your mom is private."

"It is, but I'll do it, for you," I said. "All of you."

I met Ms. Steinberg's gaze and she nodded.

"Thank you. If you think it would help, I would appreciate it very much."

"I'll come with ya, Huddy."

"Huddy?" I lifted a brow at Timmy, and Molly smothered a laugh, mouthing, 'I'm sorry.'

"Yeah, like Molly calls me Buddy, you can be Huddy," he said as if it was the simplest thing in the world.

"Right, got it. Huddy it is."

"Yes!" Timmy fist pumped the air. "Let's do it then. Let's go kick—"

"Okay, sweetheart," Ms. Steinberg said. "Why don't you come over here and let Molly and Hudson talk for a second."

"But I wants to help."

"I know, baby, and it's very kind of you, but Hudson should probably handle this himself."

"Yeah, I think I've got this one. But next time, okay?"

Timmy shrugged, climbing up on his mom's lap.

"Come on, we can talk in the kitchen." Molly stood,

offering me her hand. Our fingers tangled together, giving me hope for whatever came next.

She ushered me into the kitchen and closed the door behind us. "Sorry about Timmy and Silas."

"Don't be, they're cute kids."

"You're really goin' to go out there?"

"It's probably going to be the quickest and easiest way to get rid of them. Once they have their story, they'll move on. Hopefully."

"But what will you tell them when they ask about me, about why you're here?"

Closing the distance between us, I gazed down at her, pushing her silky hair behind her ear. "I guess that depends on you, Molly girl."

"I think..." She hesitated, her cheeks blushing. "I think I want to come out there with you."

"Babe, you don't have to do that. You don't——"

"They want a story, right?" Her lips curved. "Then let's give them one."

———

As we stepped out of Molly's house, the world exploded in a series of clicks and flashes. People yelled our names, bombarding us with question after question.

"Okay?" I glanced down at Molly, and she nodded. But I saw the hesitation in her eyes, the flicker of uncertainty.

Talk about throwing herself into the deep end.

"Hudson, is it true——"

"If you'll give me a second, I'd like to make a statement."

The crowd hushed, thrusting mics and recording devices into the air. I was used to it by now. The constant *click* of cameras, the blinding flashes, the din of questions being hollered across parking lots, sidewalks, and airport arrival lounges.

It was easy to deflect it all when it was stuff that didn't matter. Gossip sold tabloids and brought in ratings. But gossip didn't affect me.

Until now.

"As you're all aware, four days ago, I left the band in Budapest to return home to Atlanta to be with my mom. Sadly, she passed away."

Silence.

Utter silence.

Molly's fingers threaded through mine, and I inhaled a sharp breath, not realizing until that moment how much I needed her.

"As I'm sure you can understand, I'm taking some time to grieve, and ask that you give me the privacy and dignity to do so. The Steinbergs have been kind enough to open their home to me at this difficult time. I ask that you respect their right to privacy also. Thank you."

"Hudson, Hudson..." the questions started. "Why are you in Lyme? Is it true Miss Steinberg is the girl from the club in Italy? What can you tell us about—"

Molly stepped up to me and addressed the crowd. "For those of you who don't know me, I am Molly Steinberg. I live here with my mom and two brothers. We're just a normal family. My mom has to go to work, my brothers have to go to school. Please, don't make them part of this... this circus ring." She drew in a shaky breath.

"Hudson has asked for time and space to grieve. If you respect him at all, you will give that to him. Thank you."

"Miss Steinberg, why is Hudson staying here? Are the two of you an item?"

"H-Hudson is my..."

"Boyfriend. I'm her boyfriend." I glanced down at her and grinned. "That's it for questions. You have your story. Hudson Ryker is officially off the market."

They went wild at the tidbit of information, but I pulled Molly back into the house, slamming the door behind us.

When they realized we weren't going to answer any more questions, hopefully they would start dispersing, racing to get the story out there first.

"Holy shiitake," she breathed, "that was—"

"Amazing." I caged her against the wall. "You were amazing."

"I can't believe I said all of that. But they just made me so... so angry. How do you deal with that every day of your life?"

"You get used to it, I guess."

"I don't think I ever will."

"Does that mean you're not coming back on tour with me?"

"I... I can't. At least, not yet. Not until I know my brothers and my mom are okay."

My chest felt like it might cave in on itself, but I understood her hesitation. She'd been ready to give everything up for me once before and I walked away.

Leaning down, I touched my head to hers. "I love you, Molly Ann Steinberg. I love you in ways I never thought possible. And I want you to know, I'm yours. No matter how things play out, this"—I grabbed her hand and placed it over my heart—"belongs to you."

She palmed my cheek, curling her other hand into my t-shirt and pulled me down to meet her eager lips.

"Fuck, I missed this." I slid my hand into her hair and angled her mouth right where I wanted it, allowing me to lick her deeper.

"It's only been a few days."

"A few too many," I murmured, peppering open-mouthed kisses along her jaw. "I wish we were alone right—"

"Holy shiitake, my eyes. My eyes. *Mom*! Huddy is kissin' Molly... Jesus H. Christ, my eyes!"

"Oh my God." Molly buried her face into the crook of my neck, smothering her laughter.

"We might need to check into a motel, asap," I said, only half-joking. "Do you think it's safe to go in there?" I motioned to the living room door. "Or should I wear some body armor?"

"This is my life, hotshot rock star. You can take it or leave it."

"The twins are kind of intimidating. It's Silas I'm most worried about. The way he keeps watching me; it's some creepy child horror movie right there."

"Silas is harmless." She chuckled.

"Yeah, because he likes you. He probably knows I want to dirty up his sister and do very, very bad things to her."

"Hudson." She pinched my arm. "You need to behave."

"Which is exactly why we need to sneak out and find a

motel. Because I don't want to behave." I brought my lips to her ear. "I want to bury myself deep inside you and show you just how much I love you."

"I don't think I'll ever tire of hearin' you say that." She grinned.

"You know, you haven't said it back yet..."

Molly slipped out of my arms, beeped my nose, and said, "I know."

"Oh, it's like that, huh?"

"Yup." Her eyes twinkled with mischief as she walked away from me. But at the last second, she glanced back, "And Hudson?"

"Yeah, babe?"

"Timmy's right." She fought a grin. "You do smell."

BY THE TIME the boys went to bed, the crowd of paparazzi had finally begun to disperse. A handful lingered, hoping to get another photo or comment no doubt, but it was nothing Patton couldn't handle.

The media knew where I was. The label's PR team had put out an official statement confirming my situation, reiterating that I wanted time and space to grieve in private.

Though, the truth was, since arriving in Lyme, I didn't feel that hollowness I felt in Atlanta. Because Molly, she filled that void. She brought me to life in a way I hadn't even realized I needed. And it didn't matter how we'd gotten here, all that mattered was that we were here now.

"I think I'm goin' to call it a night," Molly's mom said.

"Hopefully, I'll be able to get out of the house tomorrow without any issue."

"There may be one or two journos hanging around, but Patton can escort you if necessary."

"I have lived in Lyme my entire life, Hudson, and never once have I let anyone intimidate me. I'm not about to start now. Good night, sweetheart. If you need anythin'—"

"I'm good, Mom."

"Yes, well, the guest room has everythin' Hudson should need. Including a very comfortable bed I expect him to sleep in, *alone*."

"Got it, Mom. Good night."

"Good night." She disappeared off down the hall.

I turned in toward Molly and whispered. "She terrifies me."

"She's harmless."

"Easy for you to say. Between her and Silas, I'm not sure it's safe for me to stay here tonight."

"You're bein' ridiculous."

"No, I'm being sensible. I can check in at a motel and—"

Molly shut me up with a kiss. "You were sayin'?" She smirked against my mouth.

"Do you think we can fool around down here? She never has to know." I cupped the back of her neck, brushing the skin there.

"She'll know." Molly snickered.

"Yeah, you're probably right." I sank back against the couch, letting out a heavy sigh.

"At least your statement worked."

"It buys me a couple of days at least."

"You mean you're stayin'?" Molly sat up straighter.

"Yeah, well, I mean, I only just got here. So if you wanted—"

"I want, I really want. But what about the band, the tour... I don't want to cause any trouble."

"Molly, my mom just died." The ache in my chest kicked up a notch, but it wasn't the same as it had been in that dingy motel room. Not now that I had Molly beside me. "And everything that happened between us... I think we deserve a couple of days to ourselves, don't you?"

I had already missed two shows. One more wouldn't hurt.

"Besides, we might never get this chance again."

Now we'd gone public, privacy would be a luxury we were rarely afforded.

"You know I can't go with you, right? Not yet, at least."

"I know." I barely managed to get the word out over the lump in my throat.

I didn't want to return to England without her, but it had to be her choice.

Still, I meant what I'd said. I would wait for her. Because Molly Steinberg wasn't only my salvation. She was my shot at something good.

And there was nothing I wouldn't do for her.

CHAPTER TWENTY-NINE

MOLLY

One month later...

The roar of the crowd was just as I remembered it. It was so loud, it made my breath catch, made every part of my skin tingle.

I wanted to be out there, in the wings, watching my best friend and the guys do their thing. But this was supposed to be a surprise, and I didn't want to ruin it.

Not when Letty had gone to so much trouble to coordinate everything.

"How are you holding up?" Phoebe appeared, giving me a thumbs up.

"I'll be better when they know. The anticipation is killin' me."

"You?" She gawked. "Try having this big secret you can't tell anyone else. I had to stop having sex with Levi because he uses sexy times to get me to spill all my deepest darkest secrets.

"I hope you appreciate that. No sex for almost ten days. I'm running out of excuses and all the distraction blow jobs are exhausting."

"Ten days? Try a month." I scoffed.

It had been a long month.

Hudson had been right. After the story broke about us, the interest in me and where I lived faded into oblivion. A couple of journos still hung around, hoping to catch me out and about I guessed. But overall, they left me alone.

The same couldn't be said for the residents of Lyme though. Suddenly, there was no greater source of interest than little ol' Molly Steinberg.

It was tiresome having to constantly put on a smile and act graciously. And I hated to admit it, but I had avoided going out around town for fear of being approached by people all looking to rub shoulders with Hudson Ryker's first and only girlfriend.

After that day, Derek contacted my mom and asked for a meeting between the three of us. I hadn't wanted to go, but she'd insisted. It was awkward to say the least, as he sat there and apologized profusely for his nephew's unseemly behavior and then offered me an envelope full of hush money.

Just as I'd suspected, Derek wanted to hide his nephew's indiscretion.

Mom had been livid, threatened to quit and everything. But I talked her out of it. Sometimes, the only way you won against people like Carson and Derek

Dutton was to show them that you weren't so easily broken.

I vowed to put what had happened behind me, but Mom needed to do the same.

It was a work-in-progress, but at least she was still going to work.

I'd gotten my own personal revenge on Carson when Cheri Dylan, the town's biggest gossip, deduced that I must have broken it off with him to go out with Hudson. It was the perfect slap in the face for someone who cared more about public persona and reputation than anything else.

"Molly." Phoebe nudged my shoulder and I blinked over at her.

"Sorry, what?"

"Jesus, I know you're nervous, but it's like talking to a brick wall. Are you going to be okay down here? If I'm gone for too long Levi will notice and get distracted, and that never ends well for anyone."

"Go, I'm fine."

"Okay. Well, see you soon. And just remember, he's a guy. They do stupid things when they're caught off guard."

Her words made my stomach churn. But what could Hudson possibly do?

One month.

It had been too long—maybe I was the one who would do something stupid, like try to jump his bones the second they got off stage.

Sometimes, I didn't know why I'd left it so long to visit him. But deep down, I knew.

After everything that had happened, I needed time to

just *be*. After Carson, I'd fallen so hard and fast for Hudson that it was hard to separate out what was lust and what was real.

So I'd stayed away. We'd talked and video called all the time... and sexted. Boy oh boy, could Hudson f'in Ryker sext. But every time he asked me to visit, I made an excuse.

The truth was, I was scared. I'd stood outside my house that day and declared myself Hudson's, but I wasn't ready to embrace everything that meant. Not yet.

Not until now.

Nervous anticipation vibrated in my stomach as I checked my cell phone for the time. God, I couldn't wait to see him. To see that cocky smile and feel his lips on mine.

I listened to the next couple of songs and started to make my way backstage. Letty had organized my pass. A couple of roadies gave me a second glance, but I kept walking; not stopping until I was in the wings, hanging back far enough that no one on stage would be able to see me. My heart raced, galloping like a band of wild horses in my chest as the notes of their final song filled the stadium, the thirty-five thousand strong audience a rising cacophony.

The sound of hearts breaking all over the world had been documented in great length after we announced our relationship. At first, I was constantly checking social media and online entertainment news to see what they were saying about me. But I soon stopped. Their opinions didn't define my worth. Just as their disappointment didn't affect the way Hudson loved me.

And he did.

Every day for a month, he'd made sure to tell me. Sometimes over the phone, sometimes via a text, or sometimes via a link to one of his favorite songs. It had become our thing—talking through music—and I lived for his next song just as I lived for our next text message or phone call.

There were no reports of him partying it up across Europe. No photos of him leaving clubs with a different girl every night. But even if there had been, I would have known they weren't true.

Hudson loved me.

He'd given his heart... *to me*. And I would make damn sure I protected it.

The song finished and the crowd broke into cries of 'more' and 'encore.' Of course, the guys gave them what they wanted.

They always did.

And then, the show was over. The roadies leaped into action, rushing past me to get on stage and start taking down the set. I saw Eva first, cuddled into Rafe's side. They were laughing and talking with Damon and Letty. No one noticed me, but I was happy to watch them for a second. To witness their joy as they congratulated each other on another amazing show.

Then it hit me. A trickle of awareness that ran under my skin, electrifying every inch of me. My breath caught, lodged in my throat as I spotted Hudson. He looked good enough to eat. His black shirt was unbuttoned, hanging open to reveal his ripped chest, the glint of his nipple piercing. He ran a hand through his damp hair and smiled at something Levi said, his eyes twinkling with pride.

Sweet baby Jesus, he was beautiful.

The second he found me in the shadows, everything stopped. The lingering din of the crowd. The crashes and bangs of the roadies dismantling the set. Our friends' laughter. It all drowned in the roar of blood in my ears, the furious clatter of my heart against my chest.

"Molly?" He blew toward me like a storm; strong, sure steps eating up the distance. Then he dropped to his knees in front of me, just like he had that night outside the club. Only this time, he threw his arms around me and pressed his cheek into my stomach. Laughter spilled out of me as I ran my hands over his head and hugged him closer.

"Holy shit, it's Molly," Levi said, his eyes widening. "Wait a second... Bee... tell me this isn't why you've been holding out on me all week. Ten fucking days. I knew you didn't have stomach cramps all this time."

"Babe, you know I give up all my secrets when you're inside me."

"I think I just puked in my mouth a little." Damon retched.

"You didn't tell me." Eva smiled but it didn't reach her eyes.

"I wanted it to be a surprise."

"Hud, man, you can get up now." Levi chuckled. "Fucking pussy."

"Hey." Phoebe elbowed him hard, and he grunted.

With purpose and an intensity I didn't think I'd ever felt from him, Hudson stood up, stared at me for a second then grabbed my hand and dragged me away from our friends.

"We'll see you later," Letty called over the sounds of our friends' laughter.

"Hudson, what—"

He didn't stop, winding us down the narrow passageway.

Déjà vu hit me when he pulled me behind a black curtain and pushed me up against the wall, caging me in with his arms. "You're here."

"I'm here." I smiled.

"I... but how?"

"There are these things called planes and they travel high up in the sky and—"

"Smartass." He nudged his nose up against mine, so we were sharing the same breath. "You're here..."

"I'm here." I wrapped my arms around his neck.

"But I thought we agreed we'd wait until Germany."

"I lied."

"Sneaky. I should probably punish you for that."

Heat curled in my stomach, igniting fire in my veins. How did he make it sound so dirty? So freaking delicious.

"Fuck, I've missed you." He touched my face almost reverently. As if he couldn't believe I was here. "I've missed your smile. Your eyes. Your sass. I don't think there's a single thing I haven't missed... and now you're here and I don't know what to do first."

"Kiss me," I breathed. "I think kissin' me would be a good place to start."

He swallowed, burying his hand in my hair and tilting my face up as he closed the distance. Our lips brushed, a wave of emotion crashing over me. This... this is what I needed.

Him.

This.

Us.

The spark hadn't flickered out in our month apart, it had only burned brighter.

"I love you," I whispered against his mouth. "I love you, Hudson Ryker."

He went deathly still, his breath hitching. "What did you just say?"

"I. Love. You. I'm sorry I made you wait to hear it, but I needed to know. I needed to know this was real."

"You love me, Molly girl?" He blinked. Once. Twice. A dumbfounded expression etched into the lines of his face. But then he was smiling. Grinning so wide.

"I do. I think I have since the moment you fell to your knees outside that club in Atlanta. You know, you really need to stop doin' that." A faint smirk traced my lips. "It'll start rumors."

"Don't give a fuck." He kissed me, plunging his tongue past my lips and claiming me. Devouring me. Our tongues tangled, slow then fast. Reacquainting with one another. His hands dropped to my waist, squeezing, mapping my curves as he let them wander around my back, up and down my spine and eventually resting on my ass.

"Fuck... I need you. I need you more than I have ever needed anything." He broke the kiss, chest heaving. "You're really here."

"I'm here, and I'm not goin' anywhere."

"What?"

"You heard me, rock star. I'm here to stay for a while. If you want me, that is."

"Want you...? Fuck, babe. I want to handcuff you to me so you can never leave me again." His eyes smoldered with intensity. "You're really staying?"

I nodded, fighting to hold back the tears. "Helped Mom find a nanny for the boys. They're totally in love with her, little traitors."

"I can't believe you... Shit. I didn't think—"

"What? That I'd choose you? Choose us? Me staying in Lyme wasn't a punishment, Hudson. It was just somethin' I needed to do."

"You're really staying?"

I kissed him, soft laughter rising inside me. "I'm stayin'."

MOLLY

"You all remember Ruby, my sister," Alistair said, smiling down at the petite redhead tucked into his side.

"Hey." She gave a small wave. "Alistair said the tour was amazing. Congrats. I don't mean to be rude, but there are some people I want to say hello to. Excuse me."

Alistair looked slightly dejected but let her go.

"Everything okay?" Rafe asked him.

"Yeah, just the regular family drama. But we're not here to discuss my life. We're here to celebrate your successful tour. You did it, guys. Almost six months. Twenty-four countries. Seventy-two shows. There were moments, I didn't think you'd do it. But you did. And I'm proud of you, so fucking proud." He lifted his beer in the air and grinned. "Congratulations."

"Couldn't have done it without you, man," Damon said.

"Ahem." Letty fake coughed, and everyone chuckled.

"You too, Let," Hudson said. "And Phoebe, and Molly." He hugged me tighter, kissing my hair. "You girls keep us sane."

"And drive us fucking nuts." Levi smirked, earning him an elbow to the ribs. "What the fuck was that for?"

Phoebe glowered at him, but then he ducked his head, claiming her lips.

"I won't miss that." Alistair sighed.

"Me neither," Rafe agreed.

Damon chuckled. "Me three."

Levi flipped everyone off, still kissing Phoebe. He dragged her away from us, into a dark corner of The Riff Bar but it was nothing we weren't all used to by now.

It felt like a lifetime ago I'd stood outside on the sidewalk, begging the doorman to let me inside. And in so many ways, it was.

I wasn't that broken lost girl anymore. I was happy. In love. Desperately in love. I'd seen the world and experienced things few people ever got to see and do. It had been a whirlwind, but I wouldn't change a single second of it.

"The champagne you ordered, Mr. Portman." A server appeared with a bottle of Bollinger and some glasses.

Letty passed them around and Alistair did the honors. "You know the label expects big things from your next album." He filled everyone's glasses.

"We'll be ready," Rafe said.

"I know. Enjoy your time off, you deserve it. But for the love of God, don't do anything stupid while you're gone."

His eyes lingered on me and Hudson, and Hudson balked. "What the fuck is that look for?"

"I'm just saying... stay out of trouble."

"Don't you know, Hud is a changed man now." Eva smiled. "Besides, Molly will keep him on the straight and narrow."

True.

I would.

Because Hudson was coming home to Lyme with me for the band's four-week break before they returned to the studio.

Four weeks staying with Mom and the boys was going to be interesting to say the least, but when I'd suggested we rent a place, he'd rejected the idea immediately.

Hudson wanted to stay with my family, and that meant more to me than he would ever know.

"I can't wait to get home," I said. "The boys have gotten so big."

The little terrors video-called me and Hudson as much as Mom would allow. Silas was still wary of my rock star boyfriend, but he had a lifelong fan in Timmy. So much so, he'd promised to teach him the drums when we got home.

"Babe," Hudson whispered in my ear. "I need you to come with me."

"W-What?" I blinked up at him.

"I need your help with something."

"My help?"

"Yeah, come on." He made our excuses and tugged me away from our friends.

A few people tried to intercept us as we weaved

through the crowd. Label execs, industry people, and friends of the band had all shown up tonight to celebrate a successful tour, but Hudson didn't stop for any of them.

He didn't stop until he'd pulled me into a dimly lit hallway.

"Hudson, what are you—"

"A-ha," he said after checking the second door.

Hudson pulled me inside, pushing me up against the wall. "Fuck, you look so fucking beautiful. I haven't been able to stop thinking about getting you alone."

Laughter bubbled inside me. "You will get me alone later, tonight, when we leave the party where everyone came to celebrate you and the band."

"Still so green, Steinberg. People didn't come to celebrate us; they came for the free food and drink." He snorted, pushing the door closed, shrouding us in darkness.

"Hud..." I breathed as he moved closer, caging me in with his strong arms.

We'd spent weeks enjoying each other. Loving each other in numerous cities across the world. But the spark hadn't dimmed. It only grew brighter, stronger. The second he put his hands on me all I could think about was kissing him, touching him... feeling him on me, in me, over me.

He caused a riot inside me every single time.

And I loved it.

I *lived* for it.

"God, I love how responsive you are, Molly girl." His hand slid up my stomach, squeezing my breast roughly through my black bodycon dress.

"I need you," I breathed, clenching my thighs together to try and ease the aching throb between my legs.

"I want to go slow, to savor you in this ridiculously hot dress..."

"Fuck me, now, Hudson."

"Well, when you ask so nicely." His lips curved, a slash of white teeth in the dark, as he leaned in and kissed me while grinding against me. I whimpered, pushing up on my tiptoes to better align our bodies and feel him where I needed him most.

His hands skated down my waist to my hips, as he pushed up my dress, letting it bunch around my midriff. With a quick snap of his belt, and a little help from me, Hudson pushed his jeans down his hips, lifted me up and pressed me into the wall.

"Hook your panties aside, babe. Let me in."

I did as he asked, a cry catching in my throat as he slammed into me.

"Fuck... *fuck!*" Hudson held still, staring at me intently. Searing me with his heated gaze. "Nothing, *nothing* will ever feel as good as this," he groaned, pulling out and sliding slowly back inside so I felt everything. Every ridge and bump.

Sweet baby Jesus, he was going to kill me.

Death by his long, thick, and super talented dick.

"I love you, Molly girl," he breathed the words against my lips, into my very soul. "I love you so fucking much."

I wrapped my arms around his neck and tightened my ankles around his ass and grinned. "I love you too, rock star, now show me."

A dark chuckle spilled from his lips as he rocked back into me, going deeper.

"It would be my pleasure."

———

AFTER HUDSON MADE me come twice, we finally broke apart and got cleaned up. I was wrecked. My hair was all over the place and my dress was crumpled, but I didn't care.

I was so freaking happy, I couldn't stop smiling.

Laughing, and still unable to keep our hands off each other despite our quickie in the storeroom, we slipped out of the room and down the hall. But movement up ahead stopped me.

Hudson slammed into me and grunted. "What the fuck— is that Damon?" He peered over my shoulder, his arms wrapping around me as we watched his bandmate arguing with someone.

Not just someone—

"Ruby," I whispered.

"*Ruby?*" Hudson said a little too loudly and I elbowed him in the ribs.

We both looked down the hall and I was sure I caught Damon muttering, 'Fuck,' as Ruby stood there, her face pale against the dim lighting.

"Maybe we should leave them," I suggested. But Hudson was already moving around me, dragging me toward them.

Damon said something to Ruby, but she shook her

head, glancing at us one last time before barging past him, and disappearing down the hall.

"What was all that about?" Hudson asked.

"Nothing." Damon was tight-lipped, but I saw the flicker of regret there.

"Is everything okay?" I reached for him, getting the sense that it wasn't.

"Fine." He shrugged me off, running a hand down his face. "Everything's... fine. We should probably get back out there."

"Seriously, bro, you good? Because you don't look—"

"Just leave it, okay." Shoulders slumped, he stalked off.

I glanced up at Hudson. "That was weird, right?"

"Yeah."

"Did you know he knew Alistair's sister?"

"No, no I did not." Something flashed in Hudson's eyes, and I chuckled.

"Down, boy. I'm sure there's a perfectly reasonable explanation."

But as I said the words, my stomach knotted. Because although I didn't know what we'd just walked in on, it was definitely... *something*.

They hadn't just looked like two people arguing; they'd looked like two people who knew each other well, arguing.

Damon was keeping secrets.

And we all knew that when secrets came out...

Things usually went to shit.

RAZE

A Molly and Hudson Bonus Story

CHAPTER ONE

"It's him!" I shrieked, my heart beating wildly in my chest. "It's Hudson Ryker."

Everyone stopped what they were doing, all heads turning to watch Hudson Ryker, drummer for one of the hottest bands of the moment—Black Hearts Still Beat—as he cut across the room.

He emanated darkness. It shrouded him like a black thundercloud, but when he stopped near our small group and smiled, his whole demeanor shifted.

"Sorry I'm late, y'all," he drawled, giving everyone a small nod. "I got... held up. You know how it is." His easy smile grew, and I grabbed Eva's arm, squeezing so tight she yelped quietly.

"Anyway," Hudson said, "I suppose I'd better get out there."

He was here to judge the talent contest I'd sneakily entered my best friend in. Eva loved music, she loved performing; well, she had before she got sick. Now she was better, I wanted to help her find her sparkle again.

"What, no words of encouragement for us?" Josiah Golden, one of the contestants called after him, stopping Hudson in his tracks. The Black Hearts drummer turned slowly, the light hitting his brow piercing, and smiled again. But this time it held an edge of annoyance.

"Good luck out there today," he said. "I'm excited to see what y'all have for us." And with that very short, very underwhelming proclamation, he disappeared through the thick curtain.

"Are you okay?" Eva asked me, as I kept on staring. "Molly?"

"I think I'm in love." I clutched my chest, feeling all hot and tingly inside.

"Love, really?" She teased. "If that's all it takes to win you over, I'm surprised you—"

"Oh, hush." I pouted. "You're ruinin' the moment."

"Moment? There was a moment just now?" Gentle laughter rumbled in her chest. "Because from where I was standin', it looked like—"

Colton Manner, the contests production manager yelled, "First up is Kelly Inkin, you're on in five. Evangeline Walker, get ready because you're up second."

"I don't think I can do this," She blurted.

I grabbed her hand, yanking her away from the group. "Eva, breathe."

Inhaling a deep breath, she shook her head. "It's not workin'." Panic danced in her eyes.

"Go to the restroom and splash some water on your face," I suggested. "You have time. I'll stay here and stall if necessary, okay?"

"I—"

"Eva," I narrowed my eyes at her, "you can do this. You *have* to do this."

She glanced toward where the restrooms were, and I saw the fear there. She wanted to run. My strong, brave friend wanted to flee.

"Eva—"

"I got it, I got it." The words spilled out, but her expression turned to one of determination, and I let out a small sigh of relief.

Eva could do this. I believed in her, so did her parents.

She just needed to believe in herself.

———

I WAITED with bated breath as Eva went in for her audition. Minutes after she disappeared behind the curtain, her soft musical voice filled the air, sending shivers skittering down my spine. She was so freakin' talented, always had been. But Eva lacked confidence and self-belief, even more so since the cancer.

Everything went quiet, the judges' comments muffled whispers.

The second I saw her appear through the heavy curtain, I rushed over to her. "Well?" I asked.

"I did it," she blinked. "I'm through, I got—"

Launching myself at Eva, I squeezed her tight. "I knew it. I knew you could do it." I finally let her up for air. "So what did they say? What did Hudson say? Tell me everythin'?" Looping my arm through hers, I led Eva back toward the holding area.

She was still stunned, it radiated off her in thick waves.

But I'd never doubted her for a second.

"So…" I prompted.

"Hudson was… not impressed." Her brows crinkled.

"Impossible," I scoffed. "I heard you, we all heard you. You killed it, babe."

"You heard me?"

I nodded. "I'm so damn proud of you." Guiding Eva over to a chair, we sat down. "How did it feel? Playin' again like that?"

"I… I don't really know. I kind of zoned out."

"You'd better call your parents," I suggested. "Your mom has been blowin' up my cell."

"In a minute. I need to let it sink in for a second." Eva screwed her eyes shut, inhaling a shuddering breath.

"You're smilin'," I said, and she peeked over at me.

"I am?"

I nodded again. "I always used to wonder what your mom meant when she said music is in your soul, but I get it now. Seeing you like this, hearin' you… music will heal you, Eva. If you give it a chance, I truly believe it can help you."

"H- help me?" Her face paled.

"Oh come on, you think I don't know you by now? Almost six months in remission, babe. Six months and you've barely stepped foot outside." She was hiding. At first, I'd got it. I'd understood. But as time went on, Eva only seemed to shrink more inside herself, and it broke my heart to see my best friend so lost.

"Molly, I go—"

"To the store with your mom. To the store with me. For dinner with your parents. To the coffee shop with me. That's not living, babe. It's barely survivin'. But what I can't quite figure out is if you're just scared the cancer will come back, or if it's somethin' else?"

She let out a weary sigh. "You're right. I'm just scared."

I studied her. "But the doctor said—"

"I know what the doctor said, Mol. But that doesn't mean it won't come back. It doesn't mean I'm home free."

"But you can't let fear shackle you. Not when you have so much to live for." Her talent was a gift. Unlike me, who couldn't string two notes together. Eva was the star in our friendship... and I was destined for a life working at The Lyme Grill and helping my mom raise the twins.

"You're startin' to sound like Pastor Branneth and Mom."

"I'm sorry," I chuckled, "I just worry about you. It's senior year. The year of big decisions and even bigger mistakes." My brows waggled.

"Oh no you don't." Her hands flew up. "I'll leave the mistake makin' to you, thank you very much."

I nudged my shoulder. "You mean you won't be my wing woman this year?" Because flirting with guys was about as exciting as my life got these days.

"Do I get a costume?" She grinned.

"Do you *want* a costume?" I grinned back.

We laughed and it felt good. It felt long overdue. I'd watched my best friend go through so much... it was time for her to start living again.

And I intended on being by her side every step of the way.

————

"THERE YOU ARE," I spotted Eva as she made her way backstage after the final round. "I've been lookin' everywhere for you."

"Do I even want to know how you got back here?" She frowned.

"As if they could stop me." I shot her a mischievous look. "How are you feelin'?"

"Like I'm on the Tilt-A-Whirl and it's getting faster by the second."

"You did so good. Like seriously, Eva, the crowd went wild. I thought your mom was going to pee her pants." I don't think I'd ever seen Mrs. Walker so excited over anything. It was cute.

"I hope for your sake she didn't."

We shared a smile.

"Where have you been anyway? I asked a couple of people after you, but they said they hadn't seen you since you came off stage."

"I needed a minute..." She let the words hang.

"Gosh, babe," I roped an arm around her shoulder and pulled her into me, "I can't even imagine how crazy this must all be for you. And overwhelmin'. But you've got this. There's no way the judges won't pick you after that performance. I had chills, Eva. Honest-to-God chills."

She had killed it.

Now all she needed was their vote to progress to the final show in Camdena in a couple weeks' time.

"Now I know you're just blowin' smoke."

I reared back. "I swear on Jesus. You know, I heard some of the other contestants talkin'. Apparently, there's always a party after—"

"No. No way." She blanched. "I signed up for the contest. I didn't agree to any parties."

I gave her my best puppy dog eyes. "Please, for me? We could blow off your mom and dad and hang out with the other contestants. I spied a couple of guys I wouldn't mind—"

"What happened to Hudson, huh?"

"A girl has to keep her options open. Besides, I can't imagine he'll want to party with us mere mortals."

"Will Josiah be there?" Her expression soured.

"I guess so." I shrugged. "But we can surround ourselves with much nicer, much *cuter* guys." He was kind of a slimeball.

"You're insufferable."

"But you love me."

Her resolve began to crack, until she was smiling. "Fine. Maybe we can check it out... *if* I make the final four."

"If you don't, and you will, a party might be exactly what you need. A little pick me up."

"Oh no, that won't work with me." She scowled. "If I don't get through, I'm headin' home to break out the ice cream and Blake Shelton albums."

"You really need to expand your musical repertoire."

"My repertoire, huh?" Her voice was teasing. "And what do you know about musical repertoire?"

"I know that you need to move on from the likes of Blake Shelton and listen to some rock for a new era."

"Let me guess, the kind of rock Black Hearts play?"

"Annnd she gets it." I fake cheered, barely able to contain my laughter.

"Go ahead, mock me, mock me all you—" Something caught her attention over my shoulder.

"Eva?"

"Y- yeah?"

I frowned as she met my gaze. "Is everythin' okay?"

"I just thought I saw someone."

"Who?"

"Hmm, no one. It doesn't matter." She smiled but it didn't quite reach her eyes.

Eva was hiding something.

And I couldn't help shake the feeling my best friend was lying to me.

CHAPTER TWO

"I'm not sure about this." Eva grabbed my hand, yanking me backward.

I turned around, rolling my eyes at her. "Eva, we are doing this. You need this. Hell, I need this." An exasperated sigh slipped from my lips. This was Eva's weekend, I knew that. But I'd been granted a rare weekend of freedom too. I wanted to make the most of it.

Besides, she'd done it. Eva had made it to the grand finale in Camdena.

"One night of normal," I said. "Of good ol' fashioned fun. Besides, your parents already left and your dad paid for the room upfront."

"I still can't believe he did that."

"Believe it." I smirked. "This is a good thing, babe. It means your mom is finally loosenin' the strings."

Like Eva, I was surprised that her parents had agreed we could stay. I was even more surprised when Mr. Walker checked us into the hotel where most of the contestants and judges were staying overnight; the same hotel where the party was happening.

But my surprise had quickly morphed into excitement. Unlike Eva, who looked ready to lock herself inside our room and never resurface.

"By the time we get home tomorrow," she went on, "I'm sure she'll have initiated divorce proceedings."

Eva was worried. It was more than her dad could afford, but I knew he only wanted to make Eva happy. She deserved it. She deserved it so much. Besides, Mr. Walker could handle her mom. He only wanted to see his daughter enjoy her life again.

And I intended on making her do just that.

"So we're stayin'?" I bounced up and down, grinning like a fool.

"Staying, yes." Eva smiled but it quickly fell. "The party though... I'm not sure, Mol."

"Please?" Lacing my fingers with hers, I pouted. "We'll just stay an hour. Two, tops. I won't leave your side, promise. I think it would be good for you to go, put yourself out there a little."

"I don't need a babysitter, Molly." Irritation coated her words.

"I know that, silly." I flicked my brown waves off my shoulder. "Ready?"

"As I'll ever be," She mumbled half-heartedly, letting me take the lead and pull her towards the tenth-floor suite.

The second we entered the room, Eva tensed up.

"Okay?" I asked her as she tried to take it all in.

I saw the fear in her eyes, the uncertainty. But it was just a party, and I didn't plan on leaving her side.

"I'll take one of those." I scooped up a glass of what I could only presume was champagne from a passing server. Eva's brow lifted and I gave her a shrug. "You didn't want one?" I asked and she glowered at me. Crap. I was an idiot. "Your meds—"

"It's fine." Eva was still on a cocktail of post-chemo drugs. She would be for some time yet. "You drink enough for both of us."

"I do not." I flashed her a knowing smile. So what if I liked to let loose occasionally? It wasn't like I got to do it a lot helping Mom with the twins. I was practically raising them... and going to high school... and helping with the chores. "Don't look now," I whispered. "But Scott Roscoe is comin'—"

"I was wonderin' if you'd show up," he said around a smirk. He was another contestant, and unlike Josiah he was charming and a total snack. His jeans hugged his thighs like a second skin and his flannel shirt molded to his muscles.

"Eva," he craned around me to greet her, "you killed it out there today."

"Likewise." She clipped out, but I saw the flash of regret.

I'd underestimated how hard this would be for her.

"Not much of a talker?" he asked, nothing but gentle curiosity in his gaze. "I dig that."

"Don't mind Eva," I intervened. "She's just..."

Eva tensed again, and my heart ached for her. Did she really think I'd reveal her secret?

"A little overwhelmed."

"Happens to the best of us." He smiled again. "But trust me when I say this is nothin' but a warm-up for the real party after the final show in Camdena. Colton might have a stick the size of Tennessee up his ass, but him and his team sure know how to throw a party."

"We look forward to it." I flashed Eva a wink, and she managed a weak smile.

"Well, I should probably..." He flickered his head over to a huddle of people. I recognized a handful of the other contestants.

"Isn't this a bit... unnecessary?" Eva said in a hushed voice.

"Babe," my brow shot up, "you really need to get out more. This is a taste of what it's like."

"What it's like?" She frowned.

"Yeah. Making it. Being someone in country musiclandia. You heard Josiah; he travels all over the state doin' these things."

"Yeah, but that's not what I want to do." Her expression darkened.

"But you looked so good out there."

"If I'm destined to have a career in performin', Mol, it'll happen when the time's right. But I'm not sure this is the path for me. One day maybe, but I'm not sure I want to regularly compete at these things."

I gave her a wistful smile.

"What?" she asked.

"It's just, I wish you could see what I see, babe. What everyone out there saw. You are born to be on the stage, Eva."

"It takes more than raw talent to make it these days." Josiah strutted up to us. "You need the whole package. You need to give the fans what they want."

"And what exactly is that?"

Darn, this guy was a real douchebag.

"You've got to let them in on the journey with you. Let them get to know you, your story." He downed the rest of his drink. "So, Walker, I have to ask, what exactly is your story? Because from what I'm hearin', you're a closed book."

"Who said that?" Eva pressed her lips together, glowering at him.

He shrugged. "Just idle backstage talk."

"You don't know anythin' about me or my story," She flushed. "I'd like to keep it that way."

Pride swelled inside me. Eva still had fight. That was good. She was going to need it if she was going to break into the industry one day. And I hoped she would. A talent like Eva's deserved to be in the spotlight. And God only knew, one of us had to make it out of the small town we called home.

"Oh, it's like that, huh?" His lips twisted into a smug smirk.

"It's like that, Goldenboy," I said, growing bored of his crap. "Now why don't you run along and annoy someone else?"

Thankfully, he took the hint. "Sweet baby Jesus, he's annoyin'." I screwed my nose up in disgust as we watched him melt into the sea of people. "Shall we mingle?"

Eva blanched but I wasn't about to let the likes of Josiah Golden intimidate her.

"I've got you, Eva," I laced my arm though hers and leaned in, "I've got you."

———

THE PARTY TURNED out to be a bust. After an hour of mind-numbing industry talk, we gave up and found a quiet seat away from the crowd.

"This is not how I saw the night goin'." I flopped down beside Eva on the loveseat.

"Aww, I'm sorry, Mol. I know how much you wanted to have fun."

"It's fine." I glanced at her. "At least you came. That's huge, Eva. Shall we call it a night? It's still pretty early so it doesn't have to be a complete washout. We can order room service and rent a movie?"

"You read my mind." Eva stood up and offered me her hand.

"I think Colton needs a lesson in party plannin'," I grumbled as we left the suite. It was only a little walk to the elevator, but we'd barely made it even a few steps, when I sensed someone behind us.

Half ready to tear Josiah a new one, I turned around, the air sucking clean from my lungs.

"Leaving already?" Hudson Ryker smirked.

"I, uh... excuse me?" Eva spluttered.

A slow grin teased his lips. "Do you always get this tongue-tied around people or is it just—"

"Hud," a deep voice said from behind him, and none other than Rafe Hunter, the bassist for the band, stepped outside from the shadows and smiled in Eva's direction.

"Hey."

"Holy cow," I breathed, my heart galloping like a band of wild horses in my chest. "You're..." I swallowed.

"The band," Eva sighed, "you're with the band."

Too many things were happening at once.

Hudson Ryker and Rafe Hunter—two halves of Black Hearts Still Beat—were here, talking to us.

And even more shockingly, Eva seemed to know Rafe.

He lowered his eyes, rubbing the back of his neck, and Hudson chuckled quietly. "I take it the two of you have already met?"

They shared a long look that made Eva sigh again.

"I'm sorry," she said quietly, "did you need something?"

"Actually, we wondered if you wanted to come and hang out?"

"You want us to *what?*" Her eyes bugged.

"Hang out, chill, kick back..." Hudson stared at Eva like she'd grown a second head, and I smothered a giggle.

This was... this was like all my freakin' dreams come true.

"Excuse us a minute," I grabbed Eva's hand, "me and my friend need to clear up some things." Pulling her away, I didn't stop until we were out of earshot of the guys.

"Hey," She protested, "is there any—"

"Do you have any idea who that is?" I gawked at her.

"He's with the band?"

"He's not just with the band Eva. He's *in* the band. That is Black Hearts' bassist Rafe Hunter."

"Rafe Hunter." His name rolled off her tongue as she glanced over to where he stood watching us.

"We have to go with them." What girl in their right

mind would pass up the opportunity to spend the night with Hudson Ryker and Rafe Hunter?

"What?" She whisper-shrieked. "No! Absolutely not. Hudson is an ass, and Rafe is..." She stopped herself but I saw the secrets in her eyes.

Interesting.

Just how well did Eva know Rafe?

Ignoring the sting of dejection I felt over the fact she hadn't confided in me about Rafe, I said, "Evangeline Star Walker, listen up and listen good." I leaned closer. "That is Hudson Ryker and Rafe Hunter, one half of Black Hearts Still Beat. Do you realize how many girls would kill to be in our shoes right now?"

"I guess," She grumbled. "But I'm not sure—"

I pressed my fingers against her lips. "I know, and I would never ask you to do anythin' you didn't want to. But this is Hudson Ryker and Rafe Hunter, babe. If we don't do this, we will regret it. For the rest of our lives."

I was going with them, with or without her.

Okay, I wasn't. I would never abandon Eva for a guy... but it wasn't just any guy. It was Hudson Ryker, a guy I had fantasized over since Black Hearts exploded onto the music scene a couple of years ago.

"Molly, I'm not sure..."

I turned on my best puppy dog eyes. I wouldn't abandon her, but I wasn't against giving her a gentle nudge of encouragement. Besides, I could see it in her eyes. She wanted to talk to Rafe again, even if she wouldn't admit it.

"They probably expect us to sleep with them." Her brow lifted.

"Please," I scoffed as if the idea was preposterous. "I'm not goin' to sleep with him. But I wouldn't say no to a heavy make-out session."

My stomach clenched just thinking about it. Me and Hudson f'in Ryker. It was the stuff dreams were made of.

"Molly!"

"Oh come on, babe. Like you wouldn't kiss Rafe. I saw the way you looked at him. What did Hudson mean, you two have already met? How did I not know about this?" A trace of hurt lingered in my words.

But Eva chose to ignore it, mumbling, "I can't believe I'm doin' this," under her breath.

I squealed with excitement, and before she could change her mind, I grabbed her hand again and pulled her toward the two hot-as-sin rock stars.

"So," I flashed Hudson a seductive smile, because this was really happening. We were going to hang out with Rafe Hunter and Hudson Ryker. Adrenaline coursed through my veins like wildfire.

"What did you have in mind?"

"We've got the penthouse suite. The view is pretty incredible. You want to come check it out?" Hudson swiped his thumb along his bottom lip, brazenly letting his eyes run down my body.

"It sounds amazin'." Heat coiled through me as I tried my best to play it cool.

"There's just one small catch."

"Go on..."

"You'll need to sign a non-disclosure agreement." Hudson flicked his eyes to Rafe who was silent and still beside him.

I gave them dismissive shrug. "It's no biggie for me." I'd sell my soul to spend the night with them. "Eva?"

"The show already made us—"

"This is different." Hudson cleared his throat. "This means you can't talk to anyone... about us."

"You think we're goin' to run back and tattle to our friends?" I frowned. It wasn't like I had a long list of people to tell.

"It wouldn't be the first time," he murmured. "But it's just the way it has to be."

"Fine, lead the way." I grinned, hardly able to believe this was happening.

Eva rolled her eyes, and Rafe snorted under his breath, lingering behind to walk with her. But I didn't let it faze me because I was about to hang out with Hudson Ryker...

And he was looking at me like he wanted to get to know me a helluva lot better.

CHAPTER THREE

"Eva, you have to see this," I said as we followed Hudson into the penthouse.

It was an open plan room with a long oatmeal sectional dividing the living area and the kitchen. Huge windows ran along the far wall, and the décor was warm but modern. Splashes of burned orange and browns complemented the dark varnished wood counters and coffee table. It was opulent and lavish and everything I wasn't.

"Eva, babe, get over here." I brushed off the unwelcomed self-doubt as I followed Hudson over to the floor-to-ceiling windows. I was trying to play it cool, but he wasn't making it easy, watching me like a hawk. "I've never seen anythin' like it."

"You get used to it," he murmured.

"I guess being a famous rock star has its perks." The words spilled from Eva's lips as she approached us, and Hudson's brow quirked up, his eyes narrowing on her as I watched on, horrified.

"What the hell?" I mouthed when she flicked her eyes to me.

"Different city, same view," Hudson added, his expression softening. "After a while, it all looks the same."

"I don't believe that for a second," Eva said, awed.

Rafe made his way over to us and handed Eva a bottle of water. "Thank you," she said.

"Guess I'll get our drinks," Hudson grumbled. "Molly, drink?"

"I'll take a beer."

"How old are you exactly?" He let his eyes lazily run down my body again.

"Old enough." I smirked.

"So long as you're legal it's all good." He shrugged, and my heart jackhammered beneath my ribcage.

Eva's eyes widened in my direction, but I was too busy smothering a nervous laugh. Rafe went after Hudson, leaving me alone with my best friend.

"What the hell are you doin'?" She hissed.

"Havin' fun. Relax, babe. Besides, he's only nineteen."

"But their lives aren't like ours, Mol. They're..." She glanced over at the guys who were deep in conversation. Rafe looked as concerned as Eva.

"Rock stars." I grinned. "It's like every girl's fantasy."

Her brows crinkled and she let out an exasperated breath. "Just promise me you won't do anythin' reckless."

"Only if you promise me, you'll try to enjoy yourself. Rafe seems... nice." My grin grew.

"Molly!" She warned.

"What? I'm just sayin' he's... oh, hey, Rafe. We were just—"

"Can I borrow Eva for a second?" he asked.

"Borrow away." I gave her a little push in his direction, and she stumbled into him. He caught her though, the two of them already lost in each other.

A pang of jealousy hit me. He was into her—like really into her. It was written all over his face as he stared down at her.

Suddenly, I felt like a third wheel to their intimate moment. But then Rafe led Eva to the other side of the room, and I was alone. Wrapping my arms around myself, I watched them. I was happy for her, I was... but—

"What are you doing?" Hudson's warm breath tickled my ear as I felt him step up behind me, his hard body brushing up against mine.

A shiver ran through me as his hand slipped down my waist. "I..." The words dried on the tip of my tongue.

Hudson Ryker was touching me.

Me.

Just a small-town girl with a heap of responsibilities.

"Come on, I want to show you something." He grabbed my hand and tugged me in the other direction.

And I went willingly, telling myself that when life handed you these rare opportunities you took them.

Consequences be damned.

———

THE CLICK of the bedroom door was like a gunshot to my heart, startling me.

"Relax," Hudson drawled. "I don't bite... much."

"I'm not going to have sex with you," I blurted out,

heat exploding in my cheeks as my pulse thundered in my chest.

His pierced brow quirked up. "It's like that, huh?"

"Yeah, it's like that," I sassed, inching backward.

The room was ridiculous. There was a huge bed pushed against one wall. It was drenched in luxury from the silk sheets to the gold-plated finishes. No expense was spared, but Hudson seemed completely unaffected by it all as he stalked toward me, his thumb pressing seductively against his bottom lip again.

Jesus, this boy. He knew exactly what he was doing. Knew exactly what buttons to press.

Because he does this all the time. I ignored the whispers of my conscience. I wasn't delusional, I knew guys like Hudson—world famous rock stars—had a new girl in every city they visited. But I was the lucky girl tonight, and I intended on making the most of it.

Nervous anticipation swam in my veins as he watched me.

"Come here, pretty girl." Hudson crooked his finger, calling me to him. I fell into his arms, my body a slave to his sultry voice.

Brushing the hair out of my face, he smirked down at me. "Ever been kissed by a rock star, Molly, girl?" My knees went weak as I shook my head. Hudson chuckled. "Brace yourself."

He was so freakin' arrogant, but it only made him hotter.

"I'm not having sex with you," I said again as his lips ghosted over mine.

"I can think of a hundred other ways to make you scream my name..."

Oh God... this boy.

This dirty mouthed, insanely hot, and talented boy.

"I'd like to see you try," I quipped back, feeling a lick of confidence shoot up my spine.

His eyes glittered with promise, but I saw the flash of surprise there. Then he was kissing me, plunging his tongue into my mouth, erasing every shred of rational thought from my mind.

My heart exploded, my body stirring to life. I'd been kissed before, but not like this.

Never like this.

Hudson lapped my mouth, tangling his tongue around mine, kissing me into complete submission.

"You're so fucking, hot, Molly, girl," he breathed the words against my lips, grinding his pelvis into me.

His was hard. So hard and big, my eyes widened with surprise.

"You like the feel of that?" He gripped my jaw in his big hand, licking and nipping my lips, as he ground against me again.

"Hudson," I whimpered.

"One." He chuckled, and I jerked back, confusion clouding my eyes. "You moaned my name. The first time of many."

"You did not just..." I gawked at him, but he dived back in, kissing me deeper. Harder.

Hudson kissed like he was a man starved. Hungry, desperate kisses.

I couldn't resist feeling him through his jeans, reveling

in his throaty moans as I palmed him. But when one of his hands trailed down my spine, squeezing my ass, before slipping around my hip to the waistband of my jean shorts, I froze.

"Whoa, there rock star." I slammed my hands into his chest, and he staggered back. "Slow down."

"What the hell?" His eyes narrowed. "You a cock tease, Molly, girl?" He hooked his hands into his t-shirt and yanked it over his head.

And I swear, I died and went to Heaven.

His body was all ink and muscle, lean yet defined. I wanted to lick him. To trace his obliques and abs with my tongue.

Sweet baby Jesus, he was fine.

And I was so far out of my depth I didn't know what to do next.

"See something you like?" he teased, throwing his t-shirt on the floor.

Hudson Ryker knew exactly what he was doing. He was used to turning on the charm and having girls fall at his feet.

But I wasn't most girls. And although I had no doubt he would leave his mark on me long after this weekend was over, I couldn't deny a little part of me wanted to leave a mark on him.

Scooping up his t-shirt, I arched a brow. "You want me?" Desire pulsed through me. I was drunk on him.

Completely and utterly lit on Hudson Ryker.

But I needed to catch my breath before I went any further.

He licked his lips hungrily, eyes hooded and blazing with lust.

"Come get me." I yanked open the door and dashed through it, giggling and gasping for breath.

"Molly, what the fuck?" He groaned.

"It's mine now, buddy," I shrieked, "I'm goin' to sell that shit on eBay, make myself a small fortune." Eva and Rafe watched on as I darted past them, Hudson hot on my heels.

Rafe mumbled something, right as Hudson snagged me round the waist, tackling me to the floor. "You're fucking crazy." He tried to wrestle his t-shirt off me.

"You haven't seen nothing yet." I grinned maniacally.

"Okay, you two." Rafe's hand slid around my waist as he hauled me to my feet.

"Give him back his t-shirt, Molly," Eva scolded.

"I was only jokin'." I smirked, hardly able to take my eyes off Hudson as he clambered to his feet. He eyed me carefully and I couldn't decipher whether he was terrified of me... or intrigued.

"We should go," Eva said, her words like a bucket of ice-cold water to the flames licking my insides.

"I'll walk you out," Rafe said to Eva, and the two of them disappeared down the hall.

"Here." I handed Hudson back his t-shirt. "I wasn't really going to steal it."

"I can't figure you out." His eyes drilled into mine, and it made me feel vulnerable.

"Is that a good thing or bad thing?"

"I don't know," he licked his lips again, "I haven't decided yet."

Yet...

He'd said yet.

"We'll be in Camdena," he added.

"You will?" My heart beat wildly in my chest.

"Yeah." Hudson closed the distance between us, plucking one of my curls in his fingers. "We should finish what we started tonight."

"Yeah," I croaked, feeling all tingly inside, "okay."

"Can I get your number?" he asked, handing me his phone. I stared at it for a second, before punching in my number.

A wicked smirk tugged at his lips as he took it from me. "Dream of me."

Rolling my eyes, I moved for the door, but Hudson grabbed me, cupping the back of my neck and kissing me hard.

"Hudson," I breathed when he broke away.

"Two." His smirk grew. "Now get out of here, before I do something we'll both regret." He smacked my ass.

And I left their suite with my heart in my mouth and feelings I had no right feeling blooming in my chest.

CHAPTER FOUR

Two weeks later...

Our room at The Camdena Royal was insane. An extravagant five-star hotel overlooking the Tennessee river, it reeked of money and privilege, and I freakin' loved it.

The hotel in Ploughton had been nice, but this was on another level. Eva set her guitar down while I took it all in.

"Is that Patsy Cline?" I moved beside Eva, leaning my head on her shoulder.

"It is."

"It's an omen." I clutched her hand. "What are the chances that we'd end up in a room with a portrait of one of your favorite singers of all time hangin' on the wall?"

She didn't reply, too lost in her thoughts, so I left her while I went to unpack.

"You do realize we're only here for two nights, right?"

She chuckled, eyeing the growing pile of clothes on my bed.

"A girl can never have too many outfits. Besides, if I want to seduce Hudson, I need to look my best."

"I don't want to be the one to burst your bubble, but the chances of Hudson textin' are—"

My cell started vibrating and my heart lurched into my throat at the sight of his name.

"That could be anyone," Eva grumbled.

"But, oh look," I smirked, "it's Hudson Ryker." I flashed her the screen. "He wants to know if we want to hang out with him and Rafe again later?"

"Are you sure I won't get into trouble?" Her lips pressed into a thin line. There are probably rules about that kind of thing."

"Rules smules," I snorted. "Besides, no one will know. The hotel is pretty much on lockdown for the show."

"I don't know..." She started protesting but I was already texting him back. "Molly," she cried. "What are you doin'?"

"Uh, tellin' him yes, obviously."

"But I thought... never mind."

"Jake will be down for us at eight." Sweet baby Jesus, Hudson wanted to see me again. I felt all giddy and light-headed.

"They're sending the bodyguard to fetch us, how romantic." Eva gawked but I wouldn't let her ruin my moment.

Hudson and I had unfinished business, and this time, I intended on not getting all weird on him.

"Don't be such a Debbie Downer," I said. "It's different here. Ploughton is like the ass crack of nowhere compared to Camdena. I bet they have to be a lot more careful here. You saw the fangirls outside with the banners and face paints."

She grimaced. "We could stay here, take advantage of room service?"

"And give up the opportunity to hang out with Hudson and Rafe?" I let out a frustrated sigh. "Not happenin'. You have less than two hours, babe. Get freshened up, choose an outfit, and get ready. Because tonight, Evangeline Walker, you are going to make out with a rock star."

———

JAKE WAS SEVEN MINUTES EARLY.

"Mr. Ryker has requested your presence," he said flatly. "Please follow me."

"So fancy," I mouthed at Eva as we filed out of our room. "So, Jake,"—Eva shot me a hard look but I continued—"Nice weather we're havin'."

The bodyguard suppressed a smile, humoring me. "The weather has been very good."

The elevator doors pinged open and we all stepped inside. Jake pressed the button for floor twenty, and as we rose higher, I could see Eva shrinking into herself.

I reached out and squeezed her hand. "Eeek, I'm so excited," I whispered.

Excited didn't really cut it, but I wanted to play it cool.

"We come together, we leave together," Eva said around a frown.

"Yes, Mom." I poked out my tongue. "I won't keep you out past midnight. I don't want you to turn into a pumpkin the night before your big show."

Jake was still and silent beside us, dressed sharply in a charcoal suit and white dress shirt. He fit in with the opulence of the hotel, but I couldn't imagine protecting Hudson and Rafe was an easy gig.

Finally, the elevator came to a stop and the doors sprung open. "This way please," Jake said, as if it was business as usual. But I didn't want to think about *that*.

"What?" I asked noticing Eva's hesitation.

"Are you sure about this?"

"Eva," I groaned before checking my reflection in the mirror as we followed our chaperone.

Clutching her hand in mine, I offered Eva a reassuring smile. "You have nothin' to worry about. Besides," I lowered her voice, "I know for a fact there is a certain bassist in there who can't wait to see you again."

"Oh yeah, and how do you know that?" She gave me a pointed look.

"I have my sources." I smirked. Hudson had told me as much earlier.

She didn't respond to that.

But I saw the flash of emotion in her eyes. Oh yeah, my best friend had it bad for the Black Hearts' bassist.

Jake pushed open the door and stepped aside, letting us pass. Eva hesitated again but I didn't, stepping inside.

"There she is," Hudson said, and I launched myself

into his arms. He caught me, laughter rumbling in my chest. "Hey, Molly, girl."

Checking myself, I stepped back, tucking some stray hairs behind my ear.

"Come on." Hudson grabbed my hand and pulled me over to the soft leather couch. Eva and Rafe joined us, sitting on the couch opposite.

"Do you guys always travel like this?" I asked, my eyes drinking in the lavish suite.

"What, in style?" Hudson smirked. "The production team are putting us up."

"And how come you're doin' the show but Rafe isn't?"

"Do you always ask so many questions?" His brows crinkled. "If I'd wanted to spend the night playing twenty questions, I would have invited my mom."

I blushed, and folded my hands into my lap, pressing my lips into a thin line.

I wasn't usually so eager around guys. But it was Hudson Ryker. He was this huge rock star, and I was no one. Just like that, he had reduced me to a bumbling idiot.

Way to go Molly.

"Hud, come on, man. Be nice," Rafe said, leveling him with a hard look. Hudson shuffled closer to me, running his hand up my thigh.

"Sorry, I'm feeling a little wound up. Forgive me?" His whispered words caressed the shell of my ear, sending shivers skittering down my spine.

I was vaguely aware of Rafe leading Eva away as Hudson's lips brushed my cheek. Shivers rippled through me as he tilted my face to his and kissed me.

"Fuck, you taste good."

My head swam with the taste of him. Mint and beer. A combination that shouldn't have worked but was suddenly my new favorite flavor.

I hadn't anticipated that we'd get straight to the kissing, but I wasn't complaining.

My hands curled around his neck as he moved over me, pressing me into the soft couch. "Eva—"

"Is distracted. Don't worry, Molly, girl, it's just you and me." Heat blazed in his eyes as he leaned forward and ran his tongue over the seam of my lips.

"God, Hudson." His name spilled off my lips and I felt his smirk.

"Not God, babe... Hudson Ryker, the best fucking sex you'll ever have." He pressed his brow to mine, staring at me with such intensity I felt winded. "Ready to cry my name over and over?"

I swallowed a whimper. His leg was pushed up against my core, the pressure almost too much.

"Are you wet for me, Molly? Are you going to come all over my fingers, like a good girl?"

Sweet baby Jesus, my heart drummed in my chest as he trailed his fingers down to my dress. Hudson found the soft flesh of my thighs, pushing higher and higher until his knuckles grazed my panties.

"I knew it." He smirked, and heat burst in my cheeks.

Hudson dived at me, attacking my mouth with hot wet kisses as his fingers dipped inside my panties, finding my center.

I couldn't stop him even if I wanted to, and I didn't. He felt too good. His kisses, his magic fingers making my body quiver and writhe.

"I can't wait to be inside you," he breathed the dirty words against my lips. "I want you riding my dick like a cowgirl." Hudson curled his fingers, rubbing me deeper.

It was too much. The intense waves of pleasure, his whispered words, and hungry kisses.

All it took was a simple glide of his thumb over my clit and I shattered around him.

"Hmm," he drawled, bringing his fingers to his lips and sucking them clean. My eyes popped and he smirked again. "You good?"

I nodded, trying to suck air into my lungs. I was breathless, boneless, and wrecked.

"I should go check on Eva," I said, needing a minute.

"Sure. I'm hungry... you want pizza?"

"I... uh, sure." Hudson let me up and I staggered to my feet, still dizzy from the lingering waves of pleasure.

Heading for the balcony, I burst through the sliding doors, grinding to a halt at the sight of my best friend looking almost as flustered as I was.

"There you two are." I waggled my brows suggestively. "We were just about to order room service. You two want anythin' or are you—"

"I could eat," Rafe said, moving away from Eva. "Is there pizza?" he asked.

"I'm sure for you two rock gods there's always pizza." I winked, my eyes sliding to Eva.

She shook her head discreetly, aware of Rafe watching our interaction.

"Come on, I'm starving," I said, lightening the heavy mood.

I didn't miss the way Rafe kept Eva's hand in his as he pulled her toward the door.

"Hudson sure works fast," I heard him mumble, but I chose to ignore it, tamping down the trace of regret I felt.

"Yo, Rafe, you want olives or not?" Hudson called as I curled up on the couch, trying not to watch my best friend and her rock star make out.

They moved like magnets. Watching them was intense so I couldn't imagine how it felt.

My stomach fell as realization sank into me. What they had wasn't fleeting. It wasn't a one night thing—it was real.

"Ordered." Hudson dropped down beside me, grinning. "You good?"

"Yeah, fine," I said, just as Eva and Rafe joined us. But even then, I couldn't help but notice the way Rafe kept her close, as if he needed her.

Unlike Hudson who was already on his cell phone, acting like he hadn't just had his fingers inside me.

———

"THAT WAS SO GOOD." I let out a contented sigh, sucking the grease off my fingers.

"Babe, keep that up and I might just have to..." Hudson leaned in, whispering, "Make you scream my name a sixth and seventh time tonight."

I batted him away, trying to rein in the desire swirling in my stomach.

Hudson had other plans though. He stood and grabbed my hand, tugging me up. "Come on, there's something I want to show you… on my iPad," he mumbled.

"On your iPad?" My brow quirked up.

"Yeah, band stuff." Mischief glittered in his eyes.

I could have said no. I could have clung to my final shreds of dignity and turned him down.

But I didn't.

Because I was weak. I weak and Hudson's attention, even if it was only for the weekend, made me feel special. It made me feel more than just a small-town girl with a bleak future.

Despite Eva's stare of disapproval, I said, "Lead the way."

Hudson practically yanked me into the bedroom. "Alone at last," he said.

The last time I'd been alone with him in a bedroom, I'd panicked. But not tonight; tonight I was determined to allow myself one night with a rock star.

A freakin' rock star.

I still couldn't believe it.

Hudson yanked off his t-shirt, blessing me with the beautiful sight of his body. I took a step forward and reached for him. But he snagged my wrist. "Patience, babe," he drawled. "This needs to go." His fingers dropped to the hem of my dress and he tugged it up my body.

I shivered at the gentle rush of cool air as he stripped me naked until I stood before him in my brand-new, black lacy underwear.

"Fuck," he choked out, letting his eyes drink me in.

"Cat got your tongue?" A smirk tugged at my lips as the heady feeling of power flowed through me.

Hudson Ryker was speechless... and all because of me.

"I'm going to enjoy this so fucking much." He brushed my long curls off my shoulders and leaned in to trace my collarbone with his tongue. My fingers went to his hair as he continued painting a trail of warm wet kisses up the column of my neck.

"Say it," he breathed against my lips. "Tell me you want me." Something flashed beneath his cool gaze.

"I want you." I didn't hesitate because this wasn't real life, not for girls like me. This was a fantasy. A moment in time you would never get to experience again but would never, ever forget.

Laughter reverberated in Hudson's chest as he slid his hands under my ass as he picked me up. I shrieked, winding my legs around his waist.

He carried me over to the bed, lying me down and crawling on top of me. His body felt divine pressed down on mine.

I'd had sex, gotten rid of my pesky V-card as soon as I'd turned seventeen. But it had been in the back of Kellan Denver's truck on chilly fall night. Totally underwhelming and over in minutes.

There was no heat, no passion or crackle of electricity between us.

"What's your name?" Hudson asked, gazing down at me with reverie.

"Molly." I frowned.

"No, your full name."

"Oh, Molly Steinberg."

"Steinberg, I like it. It suits you."

I didn't know what he meant, but all thoughts flew out of my head when he rolled his hips into mine.

"Hudson," I cried.

He gave me a crooked smile and said, "You ain't felt nothing yet."

AFTERWARDS, we lay for a few minutes before Hudson gave me some space to get dressed.

It had been... intense. Hudson was a generous lover, paying attention to my body the way he played the drums. But the second it was over, I felt his walls go up.

He wasn't rude and he didn't ask me to leave, but I felt the distance grow between us.

"I should probably go find Eva," I said to him over my shoulder. He'd climbed back into bed, the sheet draped over his sinful body as he checked his cell phone. He gave me a small nod.

With a little sigh, I left the bedroom and padded across the suite. But I came to a halt at the sight of Eva and Rafe on the balcony. He was holding her like she was the most precious thing in the world. It didn't look like two people riding the wave of one weekend together... it looked like something more.

They slipped back into the room and I shook off the strange sensation snaking through me. Folding my arms over my chest, I glanced between them. "Evangeline Star Walker, why do you look like you just—"

"*Molly!*" She hissed, her cheeks burning. Hudson

joined us and smirked, raising an eyebrow at Rafe who scratched his chin with his middle finger.

"We should, hmm, go. We should go," Eva rushed out, hurrying to my side. She grabbed my hand and yanked me toward the door.

THE SECOND we stepped into the elevator, I shrieked "You have some explainin' to do." My lips curved into a knowing smirk.

Eva rolled her lips together, refusing to answer.

"Please tell me what I think happened out on the balcony happened?"

Her eyes flew to mine, her cheeks burning with shame. I chuckled. "Eva, babe, it's written all over your face."

"I didn't have sex with him," she rushed out.

"Third base then?" I waggled her brows.

"Hmm, not exactly." Her cheeks flushed deeper.

"Okay, you're going to have to work with me here because from where I was standin' it sure looked a lot like the two of you were—"

"He made me... you know..."

"Come?" I asked, and she nodded, burying her face in her hands. "Babe, that is a good thing. A very good thing indeed. Did he...?"

"I think so. We were... we didn't actually touch each other."

My brow furrowed but then laughter spilled from my lips. "You dry-fucked."

"Molly, seriously." She blanched. "Do you have to be so crass?"

"It is what it is." My shoulders shook with a soft chuckle. "No wonder you looked like a deer caught in the headlights when you came back inside. That's very old-school. I dig it."

She buried her face again, but I pulled her fingers away. "You need to lighten up." She wouldn't look at me and I sighed. "Listen," I said. "Did you want it?"

Eva nodded.

"And did it feel good?"

Another nod as her eyes slowly lifted to mine.

"And did Rafe enjoy it?"

"I think so."

"So what's the problem? I should be commending you for not givin' it up to him." I instantly regretted saying the words when Eva's brow bunched with concern.

"Molly, tell me you didn't...?" I gave her a sad smile and she said, "Oh, Molly." She wrapped my arm around me. "You promised."

"I know, I know," I groaned. "But I'm a weak woman and he's... holy shiitake, Eva, does the guy know what he's doin'. It's okay though." I steeled myself, forcing out the next words, "I know this is all it is. One weekend with a rock star. A very hot, very talented rock star. And I plan on enjoyin' every damn second of it."

Eva didn't look convinced, staring off at nothing.

"Eva?" I brushed her arm, pulling her attention. "What is it?"

"Nothin'." She choked out the word, forcing a weak smile.

"Oh no... no, no, no. You weren't supposed to fall for him, babe."

"Fall? I'm not fall—" I gave her a pointed look, letting out an exasperated breath.

"I didn't mean to; it just happened," she admitted.

"One weekend, Eva. That's all this was supposed to be." But as I said the words, the knot in my stomach tightened.

It was one weekend, but I already knew it wouldn't be enough. Not know I knew how it felt to be the center of Hudson's world.

"I know." Her smile widened despite the sadness clinging to her words. "It's fine. I'm fine."

"Good because this life, their life... it's great and all, but we wouldn't last two minutes in their world. You know that, right?" I didn't know who I was trying to convince more... her, or myself.

"Rafe's different."

I smiled weakly. "He might be different now, here, away from the band and the spotlight. But did you know they're goin' on tour again soon?"

Eva averted her eyes, looking at the elevator buttons.

"Guys like them," I added, feeling dread snake through me, "guys with the entire world at their feet, don't want to be shackled to a girl." Especially not small-town girls carrying the weight of the world on their shoulders.

"Okay, I get it." She snapped. "It's doomed. I'll focus on the contest."

"Eva, come on." I went to her, pulling her into my arms. "I'm not saying don't enjoy it while it lasts. I'm just sayin' be careful. I'm so happy you're finally taking risks and livin' life, but I don't want you to get hurt. Not any more than you have been already."

She didn't reply and I hugged her tighter, refusing to let her go. Eventually, Eva managed to wriggle free.

"Do you hate me?" I blurted.

"I could never hate you, Mol. I just don't know what to say either."

"So don't say anythin'. It's the contest tomorrow, you need to focus on that right now. We can worry about the rest after."

It was just one weekend... we *both* needed to remember that.

———

THE NEXT DAY WAS CRAZY, but Eva was amazing. She hit every note, nailed every riff. I was so proud watching her, even if my thoughts had been on a certain Black Hearts drummer most of the day.

We'd had an amazing night together... one amazing night. Then this morning, I'd caught him flirting with two girls as if it never happened.

I didn't tell Eva, I didn't want to ruin her day. Besides, it wasn't like I had any right to be upset. He was Hudson Ryker, sex idol and playboy rock star. Still, I couldn't deny it had hurt to see him like that.

We were backstage now, waiting for the final announcements. Eva's cell phone vibrated, and I dug it out of her bag, handing it to her. "It's probably your mom." I smirked, waiting for her to read the message. Her eyes widened and a soft gasp escaped her.

"Molly," she gawked at me. "What did you do?"

"Hudson can be very persuasive." When he'd texted me earlier to ask for Eva's number, I'd wanted to tell him to go to hell. But I knew I couldn't interfere with whatever was growing between her and Rafe.

No matter how much it stung.

Just like I hadn't been able to tell him no when he'd asked if he would see me later.

"But I thought—"

"That I wasn't done cryin' over the fact after tomorrow I'll probably never see him again?" I shrugged. "Life's too short and Hudson Ryker is too damn good with his tongue." I played it off.

"Molly!"

"What?" I plastered on a grin. "Like you don't want to find out how good Rafe's lip piercin' feels pressed up against your—"

Eva clamped her hand down over my mouth, spinning us away from prying eyes and ears. "You're crazy."

"And you're so gettin' some tonight. Forget what I said before. Forget it all. If you don't do this, you will regret it. It's better to have loved and lost a rock star than to never have loved one at all, right?"

"And by loved you mean..."

"Do you really want me to spell it out for you?" I

chuckled. "Regardless of what happens in the final, tonight we make all our dreams come true."

I knew where this all ended, but I was too far gone to care.

"Well, don't just stand there," I leaned over her as she stared at Rafe's message, "text him back."

"Thank you?" I groaned as I watched her type the reply. "That's the best you can do? Give me the damn phone."

"Mol—"

I snatched it from her and began typing. When I was done, I handed it back to her, a sly grin tugging at my mouth.

Eva read my words. **"Were you listenin', Mr. Rock Star? I'm starting to think I might have a stalker**. Oh my—" Her cell vibrated with another incoming text. I peeked over her shoulder as she read it.

Unknown: Molly, is that you?

My brows drew together, and Eva exploded with laughter, only laughing harder when she saw my face. "Fine," I grumbled. "Have it your way."

I left her to her conversation with Rafe, checking my own cell. But there was nothing. I tried to tell myself it didn't matter.

"He's comin' to the party," Eva whispered, her face pale as she replied to him.

"Well, yeah. I figured Hudson would have to make an appearance since it's in his contract."

"But..."

"Don't look so worried." I offered her a reassuring smile, despite the sting of jealousy I felt. "Rafe Hunter likes you, Eva. Enjoy it, remember?"

I knew my change of heart had her confused, but I couldn't tell her the truth.

I couldn't tell her that I'd caught feelings for the playboy drummer who had promised me nothing more than a good time.

EVA CAME THIRD, winning the five-thousand-dollar prize check. She'd wanted to celebrate, just the two of us, but I insisted we show our faces at the wrap party. Especially since I hadn't heard from Hudson again. Besides, Rafe had asked to meet Eva there.

It was being held on the second floor of the hotel, in the Camdena Royal Suite, so we got ready and headed there. But the minute we stepped inside, I knew we'd gotten it all wrong.

"Well, this is... not quite what I had in mind." I glanced down at my dress. The sparkly black material clung to my curves, but I was overdressed given the amount of denim and flannel in the room. "Good thing, I stuck with my boots," I shrugged. "Come on, let's get a drink."

We weaved our way through the sea of people. A few stopped us to congratulate Eva. An industry guy, in his flashy suit, even gave her his card.

"I don't see them," I said, scanning the room, disappointment snaking through me.

"Maybe they got held up." Eva said.

"Yeah, maybe." I tried to keep my expression neutral, but I knew I'd failed when Eva said, "Hey, now, what happened to makin' our dreams come true tonight?"

She pressed her lips into a thin line, and I was about to tell her I was fine when Josiah strolled up to us.

"Walker," he stood that little bit taller and smugger. "Bad luck today."

"Go f' yourself, Goldenboy." I snapped, glowering at him. He'd been nothing but a thorn in Eva's side all weekend and having come second he was being even cockier.

"Easy, tiger," he chuckled, taking a long pull of his drink.

"Just go, Josiah," Eva sighed. "It's a party; you should celebrate."

He advanced toward Eva, and she sucked in a shaky breath. "We could celebrate, darlin'."

"Josiah, I really think you should go."

He crowded Eva into the wall, and she shot me a pleading look.

"Don't be such a spoilsport, we're just talking, havin' some fun."

"I'm not—"

"Relax, little lady." He reached out, snagging one of her curls and I glanced around ready to call for help. "I've been watching you. The way you've got them all wrapped around your finger. But you're not foolin' me, Angel," he drawled. "I know your game."

"I think she said leave." Hudson appeared out of nowhere, yanking him back sharply.

"What the hell, man?" Goldenboy sneered.

Hudson glared at him, a murderous expression on his face. And I swear, I swooned.

"Hey, hey, what's going on here?" Colton appeared, forcing himself between the two men, although Hudson was much younger than Josiah.

"You need to control your judges." Josiah rolled his shoulders.

"Hudson?" Colton said.

"It's not the first time I've caught him harassing Miss Walker."

"Harassin'?" Josiah balked. "Now let's not be hasty. It's nothin' but a little friendly—"

"Josiah, go wait over there. I'll deal with you later."

He shot Colton a look of disbelief but stalked away without argument.

"Evangeline?" The production manager looked at Eva. "Is what Hudson said true?"

"He... he makes me uncomfortable." She wrapped her arms around her waist, and I moved to her side, clutching her hand in reassurance. "But I didn't want to make trouble, so I tried to avoid him."

"I see." Colton tensed. "We don't tolerate any kind of harassment at Jamesboro County Productions. You should have come to me with this."

"I really didn't think—"

"The guy is a complete douche," Hudson grumbled.

"He's also the douche *you* put through to the final." Colton reminded him.

"Yeah, well, I'm beginning to realize what a huge fuck-up I made." Hudson's apologetic gaze slid to Eva's.

"I'll deal with Golden, if you promise to stay away from him. You're supposed to be making us look good, not dragging us through the mud."

Hudson tensed, anger rippling from him. "I fulfilled the terms of my contract." The tightness in his words mirrored his expression.

"I know, and we're grateful. But the show is effectively over, and I know how you guys like to... never mind." Colton pursed his lips.

An audience had formed around us, everyone trying to see what was happening between Hudson and the production manager.

It was Hudson who finally broke the thick tension. "You don't need to worry," he ground out, "I'm done." His whole demeanor had changed. Eyes narrowed and brows pinched, he looked cold and untouchable. A shiver ran through me.

"Hudson, come on, man, I didn't mean—"

"It's all good, Manners. I have somewhere to be anyway." His eyes moved over Colton and Eva and landed on me. But what I saw there made me shiver, and not in a good way.

"Thanks, for everything," Colton grumbled, as we all watched Hudson walk away.

And I finally released the breath I'd been holding.

CHAPTER SIX

"It's Hudson," I said, checking my cell. "He wants us to meet them."

After Hudson had stormed from the party, Josiah had also disappeared, and the rest of the night had been drama free. Boring, even. But we'd stayed. Part of me knew Eva was hoping Rafe would show, and I was hoping Hudson would text.

Despite being pissed with him earlier, I didn't want to leave Camdena regretting not having one more night with him.

"You want to go?" Eva asked incredulously.

"Don't you?" I pouted.

When she didn't answer, I conceded. "I'll tell him no." I stared at his text message. "We can go back to the room and order room service—"

"Tell him yes," Eva said with gentle resignation.

"Okay." I fluffed my hair unable to hide my smile. "Let's do this."

We left the party and I grabbed Eva's hand, pulling her down the hall. "I think it's this way."

"Boo," Hudson jumped out from around the corner, startling Eva. I rolled my eyes. Rafe lingered in the shadows, offering Eva a meek smile.

"Wondered if you'd come," Hudson said, letting his eyes rake over me. His easy smile was back in place, only adding to the serious case of whiplash I had from his hot and cold mood swings.

"So where are we going?" I ignored his blatant appraisal of me and took off down the hall. He thought he called all the shots, but I wasn't just going to roll over and take his bullshit. If he wanted me, he could at least work for it.

"Is she always this hard work?" I heard him ask Eva.

"Molly is—"

"Already bored of waitin'," I called, smirking to myself. "I thought you guys were supposed to know how to party?"

Hudson caught up to me and said, "Don't wish for things you can't handle."

"Hud, man," Rafe called after us, "maybe this isn't such a good idea."

Hudson slung his arm over my shoulder, glancing back at them. "Lighten up, Hunter. Besides, Molly and Eva are cool chicks, right? You can keep a little secret?"

A secret?

That had my interest piqued.

"Of course we can." I nodded at Hudson.

"Should we go?" Eva asked Rafe, hesitating as Hudson guided me toward the elevator.

We waited for them to join us.

"Aww look," Hudson shouted over, uncaring that we were in a hotel hall where anyone could see or hear. "They're almost holding hands."

"Fuck off," Rafe mouthed at him.

They had almost reached the elevator when Rafe grabbed Eva's hand, whispering something to her.

"What's going on?" I asked Hudson.

"You'll see," he said cryptically.

And I wondered what the hell we were getting ourselves into.

The second we arrived at Rafe and Levi's suite, I realized what the big secret was.

The room was crowded with people I didn't recognize, but people who looked like they belonged with the band. And there, holding court, was Levi freakin' Hunter, front man and vocalist of Black Hearts Still Beat.

Holy. Crap.

Hudson didn't give me time to freak out, grabbing my hand pulling me toward the kitchen counter.

"This is a... a band party," I choked out.

"No shit," he ran a hand over his head.

"But... this is—"

"Don't freak out on me now, Molly, girl." He grinned down at me, heat blazing in his eyes. "I have big plans for you later."

———

I'D PARTIED with Black Hearts Still Beat.

As Hudson led me to his bedroom, I still couldn't believe it.

We'd watched Damon Donnelly, the lead guitarist, and Eva play quarters. Then Eva had challenged Levi to a sing off. It had been the perfect distraction from a tense moment between Levi and Hudson, and the two of them had blown us away with their rendition of *Zombie* by The Cranberries. Levi and his entourage had left a few minutes ago, leaving me and Hudson, and Eva and Rafe.

They were out on the balcony, and Hudson had dragged me straight to his room. He hadn't been able to keep his hands off me all night, not caring that we were surrounded by his bandmates and their groupies.

Nervous energy tingled in my stomach, adrenaline coursing through my veins. I'd had every intention of making Hudson work for it, but he was standing there, looking at me like I was all his dreams come true, and my resolve crumbled.

"Fuck, you're sexy," he drawled, rubbing his bottom lip with the pad of his thumb. Which I found to be incredibly sexy.

"Come here." Hudson crooked his finger, and I closed the space between us. He ran a hand up my neck, gently squeezing as he leaned in and flicked his tongue over my lips.

"Tonight was amazing," I let out a dreamy sigh, staring up at him. "Is it always like this?"

"What?" His brows knitted.

"The parties? The groupies?"

"I, uh, yeah, I guess. But I didn't bring you in here to—"

"You're from Atlanta, right?" My hands slid up his chest. I wanted to know things about this boy. What made him tick; what he liked and disliked.

I wanted to know everything I could before our time was over.

The thought made my heart clench.

"Molly, girl." His lips dropped to my neck, brushing the skin there.

"Hud," I moaned softly. "We have all night. I want to—"

His mouth trailed hot kisses along my throat, peppering them up and over my jaw until his mouth found mine. "Less talking, more kissing."

A giggle spilled from my lips as my body melted into him.

"I want to take this slow," he whispered, "but feel what you do to me." He took my hand and pressed it against his hard length. "This is all for you, babe," he said, kissing me deeper.

Our clothes came off in a blur. His t-shirt went first, then my dress. I helped Hudson push his jeans off his hips, running my fingers down the deep V lines cut into the sides of his stomach.

"Fuck," he hissed as I grazed his dick. "Get on the bed."

A thrill shot through me at his order, and I lay down, waiting. Liquid lust swam in my veins.

Hudson dropped to his knees, taking my legs in his hands and holding them over his shoulders. He dipped his head, blowing a puff of warm air over my panties. My body quivered.

"Feel good?" His brow quirked up, and I nodded, stifling a moan. "What about this?" He flattened his tongue against me, over the lace, and licked.

God, it felt too good, the friction almost unbearable.

"Hudson," I breathed trying to grab his hair as he circled my clit again. He dipped a finger underneath, pushing it inside me all while he kept eating me through my panties.

"I hope you don't like these." He curled his fingers into the elastic and pulled. The rip of the material filled the room.

"What the he—"

The protests died on my tongue as he closed his mouth over me, licking furiously.

"Oh God…" I panted, barely able to catch my breath. The sounds he was making were so embarrassing, so dirty, but he didn't seem to care, spearing his tongue inside me.

"Oh yes…." I cried, fisting the bedsheets as intense waves of pleasure crashed over me.

As I slowly came down, Hudson stood and removed his boxers and got a condom out of his wallet. I watched through hooded eyes as he rolled it on and crawled over me.

He kissed me, tangling our hands together, as rocked into me with one smooth stroke.

"Fuck, Molly, you feel so fucking good." He stilled for a second, letting my body adjust around him. Then he started moving. Riding me hard and fast. His hands were everywhere: exploring the soft curves of my body as he kissed me, wrapping around my throat pinning me in place, in my hair, clamped around my thighs. There wasn't a piece of me Hudson didn't mark and brand, kiss or claim.

And when he flipped us over, letting me set the pace, I made sure I claimed him right back. I ran my fingers over his abs, rocking my hips in slow torturous circles, high on the way his body responded to mine. He watched me intently, breathing through his nose as he tried to maintain control. I tried to imprint him to memory, the image of him beneath me, the way he felt moving inside me.

Hudson's fingers dug into my hips as he guided me down on him, over and over, until sweat coated our bodies and my heart felt like it would beat right out of my chest.

"Harder," he gritted out, thrusting up to meet my every move.

"I'm close..." I said. "It's so..." My body splintered apart, clenching around him as waves of pleasure crashed over me.

Hudson pulled me down on him, burying his hand in my hair, bringing his lips to mine and forcing me to swallow his moans as he came.

We lay like that, our heads pressed together, our breathing ragged, while we floated down to Earth.

It was just sex.

Intense, amazing sex.

Yet, as Hudson kissed me again, cupping my face as if I was the most precious thing in the world, I couldn't shake the hope that maybe, just maybe, I'd marked him the way he'd marked me.

———

THE NEXT MORNING, I woke to an empty bed.

"Hud?"

Silence greeted me. Pushing the sheets off my achy body, I grabbed a robe and checked the bathroom.

He was gone.

No clothes strewn on the floor, no instruments laying around, no bags.

It was like he was never here in the first place.

A sinking feeling slowly spread through me. *Maybe they went out to get breakfast.*

"Eva?" I called, padding across the suite to Rafe's room. "Are you—"

"In here," she replied, and I slipped into the bedroom.

"Thank you, Jesus. I thought you'd been abducted by a very hot guitarist." I shot her a playful look, but it quickly melted away when I saw the sadness in her eyes. "They left, didn't they?" My stomach sank.

"Hudson didn't—"

"Leave me a note?" My eyes went to the paper in her hand, jealousy burning through me. "No." I tried to school my expression, but I knew I'd failed.

"I'm sorry."

Brushing her off, I said, "I knew exactly what I was gettin' myself into with Hudson. But what about you and Rafe?" I sat down on the loveseat. "Did you two..."

"We did." Her cheeks pinked.

"And?"

"It was perfect. Intense, sensual... it was everythin', Mol." She let out a dreamy sigh.

"I'm happy for you, truly." It came out tight because I was still stuck on the part where Hudson slipped out in the early hours of the morning without so much as a goodbye.

I thought I was worth more than that.

Tears pricked the corners of my eyes, but I swallowed them down.

"But...?" Eva frowned, tugging at the bedsheet.

"But I don't want to see you get hurt. You're my best friend and I love you."

"He said he'd call. He left a note."

"Then I'm sure he will." I forced out the words. Even though I didn't believe he would, because they were rock stars and we were lowly mortals. It still hurt that Rafe had left Eva with promises, and Hudson had left me with nothing.

He just left.

I knew it was only a fling, that I was just another girl in a different city. But I'd thought we'd shared something.

Something real.

God, I was an idiot.

I'd told myself I could do it... Convinced myself I could have my moment with a rock star and survive.

It was supposed to be fun, two weekends of impulsive reckless fun. But I had failed to realize one thing. Hudson Ryker wasn't just the hot drummer from Black Hearts Still Beat.

He was a storm.

In his wake, I had no doubt there was a trail of devastation across the country; a wreckage of razed hearts and broken girls who fell for the bad boy's charm and dirty words. And I was the latest casualty.

"He will," Eva said defiantly.

And I smiled. Because if he did call, if by some miracle Rafe called Eva and they pursued whatever had blossomed between them over the last few weeks, then I'd have to swallow my pride and be happy for her.

I *would* be happy for her.

No matter how much it would hurt knowing Eva was enough for someone like Rafe, and that I...

That I would never be enough for someone like Hudson f'in Ryker.

Anyone – Justin Bieber
Start A Riot – BANNERS
Everybody Wants You – Johnny Orlando
Fake – Lauv, Conan Gray
I'm Not Sorry – Gabriel Conte
Someone To You – BANNERS
18 – One Direction
Riot – Summer Walker
Wonder – Shawn Mendes
Fallin' (Adrenaline) – Why Don't We
Look Up At The Stars – Shawn Mendes
For Your Love – Gunnar Gehl

Angsty. Edgy. Addictive Romance

USA Today and *Wall Street Journal* bestselling author of over forty mature young adult and new adult novels, L A is happiest writing the kind of books she loves to read: addictive stories full of teenage angst, tension, twists and turns.

Home is a small town in the middle of England where she currently juggles being a full-time writer with being a mother/referee to two little people. In her spare time (and when she's not camped out in front of the laptop) you'll most likely find L A immersed in a book, escaping the chaos that is life.

L A loves connecting with readers.
The best places to find her are:
www.lacotton.com